Alternative Truths

Edited by

Phyllis Irene Radford

and

Bob Brown

B Cubed Press

Benton City, Washington

Interior Design (ebook): Vonda N. McIntyre
Interior Design (print): Bob Brown
Cover Design: Alexander James Adams

First Printing: 2017

First Electronic edition: 2017

Electronic ISBN: 978-0-9989634-0-2

Print ISBN: 978-0-9989634-1-9

Copyrights

Foreword

Rick Dunham

"Elections have consequences," Barack Obama told a riled up Republican critics three days after becoming U.S. president in 2009. "And at the end of the day, I won."

Yes, elections have consequences. Donald Trump's Electoral College victory in 2016 has had wide-ranging consequences that many Americans had never dreamed likely, from unraveling four decades of environmental regulation to promoting a "Great, Great Wall" along America's southwestern border. A small but telling consequence of Trump's triumph is that the Oxford English Dictionary's 2016 "word of the year" was "post-truth"–an adjective defined as "relating to or denoting circumstances in which objective facts are less influential in shaping public opinion than appeals to emotion and personal belief."

"This is the problem with the media," Trump lieutenant Corey Lewandowski told reporters and academics at a post-election seminar at Harvard University. "You guys took everything that Donald Trump said so literally. The American people didn't. They understood it."

For many journalists and writers, keepers of the flame of truth, the ascendancy of Trump has been a flickering journey to the first circle of Hell, sort of Kafka meets Dante by way of Orwell. It's not just that the former reality TV host has labeled journalists "enemies of the people" (a favorite phrase of Soviet dictator Joseph Stalin) or "dishonest" or "the lowest form of life." It's that the man who promises to "make America great again" has shown a great disdain for norms of civil discourse and factual decency. The Washington Post's *"Fact Checker"* column documented 394 cases of false or misleading claims by Trump during his first 84 days in office, an average of 4.69 presidential untruths each day. "Mendacity has become the norm," commented New Jersey Senator Cory Booker.

With facts in flux, it is not surprising that "post-truth" was only the beginning of a stream of new words used to describe our new reality. *Fake News. Alternative Truth. Alt-Right. Parallel media universes.*

Fake news was coined by media analysts to describe false reports planted on social media and the internet by allies of Russian leader Vladimir Putin. But it quickly was adopted by Trump to discredit any news report critical of the new American president. Alternative truth, a term invented by Trump counselor Kellyanne Conway, is an Orwellian concoction describing something that defies reality but that you insist is real. Alt-Right, an alternative to the Republican Right of the Reagan-Bush era, is a polite synonym for "white supremacists," or neo-Nazi nationalists. Parallel media universes refer to our fractured media world, where conservatives look to Fox News, Breitbart, and talk radio to tell them what to believe, and liberals seek information from the New York Times, National Public Radio, and MSNBC.

In a post-truth world, basic facts are subject to dispute, rather than simply to interpretation. Two-thirds of Trump's primary election backers believe that Barack Obama is a Muslim, according to a Public Policy Polling survey taken in May 2016, and 59 percent remain convinced he was born outside the United States, the phantasmagorical fiction of the "birther" movement. Neither is true. Esmond K.L. Quek, a business consultant and economist from Singapore, said during a discussion of the post-truth world in December 2016, "The philosopher in me says this is the decline of mankind and human decency."

Philosophers may be despairing, but fiction writers are not. After all, it's just one step from Kellyanne Conway's "alternative truth" to "alternative history," such as MacKinlay Kantor's 1961 novel, "If the South Had Won the Civil War," or Sinclair Lewis' 1935 warning of a fascist takeover of America, "It Can't Happen Here." Well, Donald Trump's election did happen here, and this anthology uses it as a jumping off point to give some of America's most creative science fiction writers an opportunity to conceive of their own alternative history scenarios.

As a journalist for 35 years and a journalism professor for four more, I feel that truth and fairness are our twin missions. Like many journalists, I feel uncomfortable being placed in a position of referee, writing that something a public figure has said is true or false. But in our "post-truth" world, it is my moral obligation to separate reality from "alternative truth." If I do anything less, I am becoming a propaganda tool of the prevaricators. "I hope those who want to devalue journalism, especially investigative journalism, get the message: a world without facts can't function," said Jim Asher, who won the 2017 Pulitzer Prize for his role in the Panama Papers project detailing the ways wealthy and powerful individuals around the world hide their assets.

There is some good news for truth-tellers. According to a March 2017 poll by Quinnipiac University, 89 percent of American voters say it is "very important" or "somewhat important" that the news media hold public officials accountable. The International Center for Journalists, with the support of the Craig Newmark Foundation, has created "TruthBuzz," a global fact-checking challenge to develop new methods for truth to reach the widest possible audience. And some major news outlets are demonstrating an aggressive commitment to speaking truth to the powerful. "Stand up for what you believe in," Martin Baron, editor of the Washington Post, said at Ohio University in September 2016. "Don't do it on impulse... You're not just entitled to do that, but you are obligated.

~oOo~

Rick Dunham is co-director of the Global Business Journalism program at Tsinghua University in Beijing. A veteran political journalist and one of America's foremost authorities on the use of social media for journalism, he is the creator of the popular blog "Texas on the Potomac."

He was Washington bureau chief of the Houston Chronicle from 2007-13 and also served as Hearst Newspapers Washington bureau chief from 2009 to 2012.

He is a past president of the National Press Club and the National Press Club Journalism Institute.

Editors' Foreword

Phyllis Irene Radford and Bob Brown

Editors, Alternative Truths

The *Alternate Truths* Anthology was formed, when on February 23, 2017 I, and many of my friends, asked what we could do to resist the taking of our country.

We were not rich, we were not famous, we didn't even have our own TV network. But we could write. So we did, we joined together in that noble tradition of Menken, Twain, and Swift to use our pens to poke the powerful.

So was born, B Cubed Press and our first anthology, *Alternative Truths*. We committed to an insane deadline to have this out to the public by Day 100, a designated date of assessment of any new President of the United States.

And we must give thanks, where thanks is due. Kellyanne Conway was not the first political operative to apply flexibility to truth, but she gave us strength and purpose when she coined the phrase, "Alternative Facts," in describing what George Orwell had, for all previous generations, labeled as *NewSpeak*.

Truth, like beauty, especially political truth, is in the eye of the beholder, and for years Americans have tolerated the common elements of exaggeration and rhetoric from their politicians. But not since the early days of the nation has such a mockery of truth been made in the name of politics. And in that vein we present to you, *Alternative Truths*.

Alternative Truths is a look at the post-election America that is, or will be, or could be. We attach no manacles to the word truth to bind it to our visions. Instead we free it to find its own way through the minds of the two dozen writers who have shared their vision of the future in either sensitively written allegorical tales such as *Relics* by Louise Marley, a woman who grew up bucking hay in Montana and moved on to a talented musical performer and successful novelist; or the raw humor of Adam Troy-Castro in his *Q & A*, which takes on the verbal veracity of Donald J. Trump.

Whomever or whatever you like, you will find here an absolute appreciation for the fact that we live in a great country where you can still publish a book like this. This is due in part to the continued efforts of the American Civil Liberties Union. To paraphrase Thomas Jefferson, the tree of liberty must be refreshed from time to time with the ink of patriots.

And patriots these writers are, for they speak truth to power, and do so in the public square. And they do so because of the Constitution of these United States, and the vigilance of groups like the ACLU. Because of this, we are treating the ACLU as a part of this work and a writer's share of the royalties will be donated to their unending quest for the freedom of the American People to express themselves. We hope you enjoy the read.

Dedication

In loving memory of Victoria E. Mitchell 1954-2017, a fabulous writer of science fiction and fantasy. She wrote a story for this anthology which we wanted to buy. Unfortunately she passed away before she could respond to the acceptance. We will miss her charm and her wit.

For more information about Vicki: http://www.v-e-mitchell.com/ or https://www.fantasticfiction.com/m/v-e-mitchell/

ACKNOWLEDGMENTS

Acknowledging the most wonderful group of writers that
have ever touched a keyboard.
They made this happen.

.

Table of Contents

Q & A

Adam-Troy Castro

Question: President Trump, do you have any comments on the recently discovered snuff footage of you strangling a small child to death with your bare hands?

Answer: Well, first of all, I thank you all for coming here.

I, really, coming off the greatest electoral college win of all time, there's never been a more popular President ever, children are good.

Absolutely!

Fabulous!

But the country is a big mess, a total disaster, murder in the streets, entire neighborhoods in flames, boroughs in New York being swallowed up by flaming cracks in the Earth.

Chicago, very bad!

Awful!

Obama didn't do a damn thing to stop it. This is why nobody, literally nobody anywhere, voted for Hillary.

Children: you have to ask who's paying the people who took the footage.

I have children, myself. Ivanka, look at her. I would have sex with her right now, on this podium, if I wasn't her father.

I think children, children, you know, with my success in business, a model for the things that make this country great, and people who say otherwise are a big joke, a bunch of losers.

Why don't you ask Rosie O'Donnell that? Another loser.

Next question...

END

THE TRUMPEROR AND THE NIGHTINGALE

Diana Hauer

Based on The Nightingale *by Hans Christian Andersen.*

Once upon a time, in the Northeast Kingdom, there was a
shining city of towers that touched the sky. The city had all
the tallest and oldest and most beautiful towers in the
world, built by men of vision and wealth. The greatest
among those men was Emperor Trump, the Trumperor. His
towers were the tallest and finest. The insides had all the
best furnishings, with cushions of velvet and plating of
gold. All envied him and his wealth.

The Trumperor wore the finest suits and bought all the
finest things. His hands only held pens and forks plated in
gold. Even his hair was golden, though it had a way of
refusing to be styled. Perhaps it reflected the personality of
the one whose head it rested upon. His skin held a tinge of
orange-gold that spoke to his royal heritage.

As the Trumperor's power grew, the common people clamored for a powerful leader. There was a grand debate; it took over a year to settle. More than twenty men and women vied for the affection and attention of the populace. In the end, while more people liked the wife of a former leader named Clinton, more provinces favored the Trumperor. And so it was that the Trumperor came to rule over many kingdoms. He was given a fine, white house, but most nights he stayed in one of his many beautiful towers so that he could properly look down upon all that he ruled.

One day in the spring, after a long afternoon of signing papers that boring people who talked too much lay in front of him, the Trumperor sat in front of his talking picture box to relax. The picture box showed him news from many foreign lands, and it showed him people to tell him how he should feel about the news. It also had shows to entertain, to excite, and inform. On one such show, the Trumperor heard of the nightingale. The nightingale was said to be the singer of the most beautiful songs in all the lands. The Trumperor was seized with a desire to hear the nightingale sing.

"Trumpress!" he yelled. "Attend me!"

A slender, brown-haired beauty, many years his junior rushed into the room. Her name was once Melania, but it had long ago been eclipsed by her role as the Trumperor's wife. The Trumperor bought her as a slave, raising her from a life of poverty to one of luxury as his concubine. She was his third wife by his choice and could be easily replaced. Never did he let her forget it.

She bowed her head and curtsied when she entered the room. "What is your wish?" she asked.

"Bring me this 'nightingale' that I heard about on the picture box," he said. "I want it to sing to me after dinner."

"I have never heard of the nightingale," said the Trumpress. "How am I supposed to find it?"

"I don't care," snapped the Trumperor. "It better be here tonight, or after dinner, you're fired!"

The Trumpress turned pale as a winter lily and retreated from the room, bowing and murmuring apologies.

In the corner, pale and silent, stood Little Baron. The youngest child of the Trumperor, and only child born of Trumpress Melania, he was the lowest of the royal children. His skin had barely a hint of the royal orange, though his hair was the same spun-gold as his father's. As he watched the scene unfold, he shrank further into the corner and hoped that he wouldn't be noticed.

He need not have worried. The Trumperor had eyes only for his magic picture box and the device that tweeted messages out to his adoring followers. Little else mattered to him when he was in such a mood.

~oOo~

The Trumpress had few friends of her own in the tower. In desperation, she turned to her husband's courtiers and sycophants for help.

"Nightingale? Never heard of it," said Conway Goldenhair, chief speaker for the Trumperor. "It sounds boring."

"Is that the name of a band of musicians?" asked Preice Reinbus, chief strategist for the Trumperor. "It would be a great name for a solo act."

"I can tell you," said Bannon the White, chief adviser to the Trumperor. "It will only cost you your soul." The Trumpress ran from the room without answering. Bannon's oily laughter followed her down the hallway.

The Trumpress wept in fear and desperation. Her husband had a fearsome temper, and if he turned her out, she would have nothing. And what would become of Little Baron without her? When she could cry no more, the Trumpress's hair and makeup were ruined from her tears and frantic running around. She summoned her stylist to put her face and hair aright. The stylist was one of many pretty, young women who served the royal family. She coaxed the story out of the Trumpress, either because she had a kind soul or with an eye to selling the story to the other courtiers.

"The nightingale?" asked the stylist, raising her perfectly plucked eyebrows so high that they vanished beneath her bangs. "I know her quite well. She sings in the central forest that I walk through to get home every night. If you give me a raise and a promotion, then I will happily lead you to her."

Gratefully, the Trumpress accepted the deal. She put on a nice walking dress, had the servants dress Little Baron in a suit and tie, and followed the stylist into the woods.

Naturally, half the court followed along. They were not about to pass up drama like this.

~oOo~

Little Baron held his mother's hand and stared about with wide eyes. He did not often get to leave the tower, let alone go anywhere as dirty and disorganized as the forest. The Trumpress had eyes only for the stylist and her goal. Off in the distance, a dog howled.

"There's the nightingale!" cried Conway Goldenhair. "How majestic and resonant."

The stylist rolled her eyes. "That's a dog, miss." Little Baron suppressed a giggle.

They walked over a bridge and onto a raised walkway that led through wetlands. Crickets chirped and frogs croaked.

"Which of those is the nightingale?" asked Preice Reinbus.

"Neither. Come on, we're almost there." The stylist urged the Trumpress and Little Baron along, doing her best to ignore the other courtiers. "You should hear her soon."

And then the nightingale began to sing. The assembled courtiers fell silent in awe, transfixed by the strength and beauty of the night bird's song. Silently, the stylist pointed to a branch high up in a maple tree, where a plain, brown bird sat and sang. A hint of red on her tail feathers was the bird's only embellishment.

"How plain and drab she is," murmured Bannon the White. "Perhaps seeing all these great and beautiful people frightened the colors off of her feathers. I could restore them, for a price."

"Nightingale," called the stylist, taking a large step away from Bannon. "Nightingale, the Trumperor wishes you to sing for him tonight. It is a great honor!"

"I shall sing with great pleasure," said the nightingale. "Which of you is the Trumperor?"

"He is not here," said the Trumpress, finding her voice as she wiped a tear from her eye. "My glorious husband is in his tallest tower. You are to sing in the dining room in the top floor, overlooking the city."

"I think he would enjoy it more out here," the nightingale said. "The song sounds best among the trees, under the night sky. But as you ask, I shall come."

Trumpress Melania bowed graciously and offered the nightingale a silken pillow, upon which to ride to the tower.

The nightingale giggled and said she preferred to fly. And so the courtiers returned to the Trumperor's tower, serenaded by the nightingale as she flitted from branch to branch alongside them. By the end of the journey, every courtier had tears in their eyes, and Little Baron had the barest hint of a smile on his face.

~oOo~

Every light in the tower was lit in anticipation of the nightingale's arrival. A huge, golden banner hung across the entryway. It said, "Welcome Nightingale, World Class Singer! Best Bird in the World!" The nightingale flew up to perch on its corner, cocking her head side to side as she examined the golden cloth. From a distance, she looked like a fleck of mud marring the banner's glossy shine.

After much bustling about, the court was assembled and dinner was served. The nightingale rested on a silken pillow set upon a golden table in the middle of the room and watched the proceedings. Courtiers who had not heard of the nightingale wondered why the small, dirty bird was sitting in a place of honor in the golden hall. Surely someone had made a mistake.

When dinner was finished and the nightingale began to sing, all the jewels and expensive clothes worn by the beautiful people were forgotten. All eyes turned to the drab bird with the transcendent song. The song transported them over field and stream, forest and mountain. It rose up into the starry heavens, bringing all the listeners with it. Tears rolled down the Trumperor's cheeks. He was so moved by the song that he offered the nightingale his golden ring to wear around her neck.

"I have already been richly rewarded," said the nightingale. "I have seen tears in the eyes of the Trumperor, and know that my song has moved his heart. What are gold and jewels compared to such as that?" And then she burst into song again.

All the ladies and gentlemen of the court gushed about the performance, each attempting to outdo the others with the most stupendous and overblown descriptions. Some even put water in their mouths and tried to mimic the nightingale's trills, as if to harness some of the birdsong's power. To a one, every dinner guest was both delighted and satisfied, which had never happened before in the history of the Trumperor's banquets.

~oOo~

The nightingale was a sensation throughout the Northeast Kingdom. People came to the city of towers from all over to hear the nightingale sing. For her part, the nightingale was given a palatial room in the tower and a dozen servants to attend her. Everything in the room, including the servants, was covered in gold, for this was how the Trumperor best knew how to show his affection. Guards kept the commoners, and even lower nobility, from disturbing the creature. She needed all her rest, it was said, so that she could perform her best for the Trumperor every night.

"She gives me more joy than I have ever known," said the Trumperor to speakers on the magic picture box. "I shall name my next tower 'Trump Nightingale Tower' in her honor." Not even the Trumperor's family had a tower named for them.

The common people grew to love the nightingale even more, though they could no longer hear her sing. Twelve named their sons "Gale" and eleven named their daughters "Gail" in the bird's honor. One clever courtier paid one hundred families one hundred dollars each to change their last names to "Nightingale."

One day, a crate was delivered to the Trumperor's favorite tower. Outside was stamped in large, black letters, "NIGHTINGALE."

"What could this be?" asked the Trumperor, when the box was brought before him. "Is it a painting, or perhaps a statue in honor of my beloved nightingale?" The Trumpress sat stiff and silent beside him as the package was brought forward, and Little Baron sat silent and pale beside her. Neither wished to disturb the Trumperor's good mood and earn his ire.

When the crate was torn open and the packing removed, an artificial nightingale on a golden pedestal stood in the center of the court. It was twice as large as the living nightingale. Its tail was studded with rubies, its wings with sapphires, and its eyes were glittering black diamonds. The pedestal was decorated with emerald leaves and ferns, as if it were a golden tree.

Under its wing was a note. "The Trumperor's nightingale is a sad, drab thing compared to our nightingale." It was signed by the owners of rival towers within the city.

When the golden bird was wound up, it sang one of the songs that the real nightingale sang. The gems glittered as it flapped its wings and bobbed its head in time with the music. All the court was enthused by the spectacle. The Trumperor ordered an appropriately snide thank-you note be sent to the nobles who sent this expensive, delightful gift.

The Trumperor listened to the artificial bird's song two more times, then bade the nightingale sing a duet with the metal bird. This did not go well, for the artificial bird's song was regular as clockwork, but the living bird's song was as free as its soul.

"They both sound nice, but only one delights the eyes as well as the ears," said Conway Goldenhair. "I favor the one that matches my hair."

"The one represents freedom, the other represents order," said Preice Reinbus smoothly. "Both have their place in the kingdom."

"But one should take precedence, if the kingdom, and the music, are to be properly governed," said Bannon the White. "The proper order must be maintained. And what is beauty if not order?"

As usual, the Trumpress and Little Baron said nothing. Trumpress Melania noted that no one had to wipe tears from their eyes when the artificial bird finished its song.

The court listened to the song twelve more times. "Now the other nightingale should sing," said the Trumperor. "Nightingale, sing for me! Delight and entertain me, as you have done these past weeks."

But the nightingale was nowhere to be seen. With all attention turned to the golden bird, it had flown out an open window and returned to its home in the central forest.

"What is the meaning of this?" roared the Trumperor. "Ungrateful bird! It is weak and disloyal. I hereby banish it from all my towers!"

All the courtiers nodded agreement.

"I have the best bird," crooned the Trumperor. "The greatest, most golden, most musical bird of all time."

And again, all the courtiers agreed. By the next day, all the papers that shared news and the people on the talking picture box agreed as well.

"But I liked the real nightingale," said Little Baron softly. The Trumpress hushed him before anyone important could hear.

~oOo~

For over a year, the artificial bird's song was played many times a day. It sang for the Trumperor in the morning when he woke, and in the evening it sang him to sleep. It played to greet guests and to accompany meals. There were even concerts held in the lobby of his wonderful towers with the bejeweled bird as the star performer. After a while, the courtiers knew every whir, every click, and every note of the golden bird's song.

Some of the commoners, those who had heard the nightingale sing in the forest, left the concert unsatisfied. "The Trumperor's bird is beautiful and sings prettily, but something is missing," they said. "I don't know what. It's as though I have eaten a meal, but I am still hungry."

One evening, as the Trumperor laid in bed listening to the artificial bird sing, something popped inside the bird's body. The music ground to a halt.

The Trumpress leaped out of bed and ran over to wind the bird again, but the key came off in her hand.

"What's the meaning of this?" roared the Trumperor. "Did you sabotage my beautiful bird? I will have you fired for this!"

"No, no, my love," cried the Trumpress, cringing in fear. "Let me go summon help for the bird."

"Yes, bring the best physicians! Musicians! Anyone who can fix my bird," ordered the Trumperor.

The Trumpress scurried away to do as he bid. After she called physicians and musicians, she also summoned the best clockmaker in town. Trumpress Melania was no fool.

The physicians came to examine the bird. "We cannot fix a patient of metal, your majesty." The Trumperor dismissed them with an impatient wave of his hand.

Musicians came and tapped on the bird, putting their ears up to it. "Nice resonance, but it's not working, your majesty." The Trumperor fired them on the spot (even though they were not technically employed by him).

Finally, the Trumpress presented the clockmaker. He opened the artificial bird's chest and examined the gears. "They're worn out, your majesty," said the clockmaker. "I can probably make new ones, but they'll be custom. Not cheap."

"How soon can you fix my beautiful bird?" asked the Trumperor.

"A few weeks," said the clockmaker, rubbing his chin. "Maybe a couple months. I'll have to disassemble the bird and take some of the parts with me to copy."

"Do it, and get out of my sight," grumbled the Trumperor, glaring at the silent, golden bird. "I want to hear it sing again as soon as possible."

~oOo~

After the clockmaker left, the Trumperor stomped around his royal apartments, seething with rage. He threw expensive sculptures at the wall. He kicked over mahogany end tables and chairs. He ranted and raved, shaking his fist at the sky. The courtiers hid behind doors and ran down hallways to avoid him. None dared gainsay him, and no one knew how to calm the Trumperor.

At the height of his rage, the Trumperor grew pale and collapsed. The Trumpress summoned the Trumperor's private physician, who shook his head. "I warned him to take it easy," said the doctor. "His body is tired, and so is his soul. There is nothing that can be done. He will not survive the night."

The courtiers shook their heads and went in search of the Trumperor's oldest son and heir. He would need advisers and sycophants to serve him.

"I can speak for the new emperor," said Conway Goldenhair. "His words are sure to be more intelligent than the old Trumperor's."

"I can help manage his schedule," said Preice Reinbus. "His actions are sure to be more mature than the old Trumperor's."

"I can tell him, er, help him decide what to do," said Bannon the White. "My services are always available, for a price." Under his breath, he added, "And a younger ruler should be easier to manage." He followed the others out to offer service to the new ruler.

Trumpress Melania looked at her husband, laying cold and pale on their golden bed. When he took his last breath, all of his wealth would pass to the eldest prince. Part of her wanted to sit with her husband in his final hours, but she knew that if she and Little Baron were to survive, then she must curry favor with the new emperor.

Besides, he was not aware of anything right now. He was barely breathing. It would not be long now. She opened a window to let the moonlight and fresh air in, then left to secure her future and protect her son.

~oOo~

The Trumperor could not move. He could not speak. He could barely breathe. A huge weight was crushing him. When he opened his eyes, he saw that Death was sitting upon his chest. Death looked just like him, he realized, but with a wicked, mischievous smile. He wore the Trumperor's golden crown on his head, the Trumperor's majestic red tie around his neck, and the Trumperor's golden ring on his hand. Death looked down at his dying twin.

"Let's see what's on, shall we?" Death picked up the control wand and turned on the Trumperor's talking picture box.

An old woman's face appeared. "Do you remember me? You foreclosed on my house. I died penniless, living in my son's basement," she yelled. "It's all because of you!"

"I never knew," whispered the Trumperor. Perspiration beaded on his forehead. Sweat dripped down his cheek, or maybe it was a tear.

"You never paid me," said a Hispanic man with a thick accent. "We had a contract, and you broke it! I lost my business because of you."

"No, no!" cried the Trumperor. "I never!"

One after another, Death showed the Trumperor his deeds, the good and the bad. And there were many, many bad. His past cruelties weighed heavily on him. With every recitation, every accusation, Death grew heavier. The Trumperor was being crushed under the weight of his deeds. He tried to lift his hands to cover his ears, but they were pinned under Death's enormous rump.

"Music," he gasped. "Play something for me, golden bird. Please, sing for me. Drown out these awful voices!"

The bird glittered in the moonlight and was silent. It had no heart to pity the Trumperor, only gears. No one was there to wind it, so it could not play a note. Death laughed and danced as the torrent of voices babbled on.

~o0o~

The Trumperor was sure that he was breathing his last when a trill of lovely song exploded from the windowsill. The nightingale had come. As she sang, the Trumperor turned his face toward the bird singing to him from the window. In the moonlight, the drab, brown little bird seemed to shine.

Her song drowned out the voices from the magic picture box, and the faces faded away. Death's weight sat less heavily upon the Trumperor. Death was transfixed by the nightingale's song. When she paused, he cried out, "Sing, sing, little bird!"

"Yes, if you give me the Trumperor's crown," said the nightingale. Death handed it over eagerly, and shifted some of his weight off the Trumperor's chest. In this fashion, the nightingale convinced Death to return each of the Trumperor's treasures. She sang songs of gardens and churchyards, fields and fen, and the joy of returning home after a long day's work. Her songs woke in Death a longing to return to his own home, with its lovely garden. Death flew out through the window, leaving the Trumperor in peace.

~o0o~

"You are saved," sang the nightingale. She flew to the Trumperor's bedside and perched atop the artificial bird. "I am glad that I got here in time. It must have been fate that I overheard courtiers walking in the wood talking about your illness. I came as quickly as I could."

"Yes," said the Trumperor. His voice was stronger. "Come closer, little bird."

The nightingale chirped happily and hopped up onto his bed, next to the Trumperor. With a great heave, the Trumperor rose and backhanded the bird. It flew sideways and hit the wall, then slid down to rest on the floor.

"You're disloyal and ugly," snarled the Trumperor. "If you hadn't left, I would never have gotten sick in the first place. You're fired!"

With that, he rose from the bed and headed toward his royal dressing room, calling for servants to bring one of his darkest suits. "I have some work to do. Everyone disloyal to me will suffer. I will pay Bannon the White's price, and he will fix my golden bird so that this never happens again."

The Trumperor noticed Little Baron in the doorway. The boy had heard the song of the nightingale and come to listen. He shrank and shivered under his father's gaze. "You," said the Trumperor, "clean that mess up, and be sure to wash your hands afterward. Wild animals are covered in germs."

When the Trumperor was gone, Little Baron crept hesitantly into his father's room. He found a towel and gently lifted the injured nightingale. Quickly and quietly, he ran back to his room. He found a shoe box and lined it with some of his silken underpants. By then, the nightingale was awake and looking around. Carefully, he helped her into the box. She held her wing at an awkward angle. "Is it broken?" asked Little Baron.

"I'm not sure," said the nightingale. "I don't think so, but it is hurt. I cannot fly right now." She cocked her head at him. "What do you plan to do with me? I warn you, I will not sing if you put me in a cage."

"Well," the boy swallowed hard. "Will you be my friend? It is scary and lonely in the castle. And my father, I mean, the Trumperor, is really mean sometimes."

The nightingale chirped to him. "I will, Little Baron. And I will sing to you of the wide world, and the people in it. The brave and the wise, the foolish and the weak. Some you can trust and love, others will look to you one day for protection. There are the deplorable ones who adore your father, and the desperate ones that hope he will save them. I see them all, and I know them. I can teach you much, child, if you want to learn."

Little Baron clasped his hands and looked at the nightingale hopefully. "Can you teach me to sing?"

The bird laughed. "Yes, Little Baron, young prince. I will teach you to sing. And perhaps in your song, people will find hope."

~oOo~

Many courtiers were fired, but Conway Goldenhair, Preice Reinbus, and Bannon the White survived the purge. Trumpress Melania's position was once again as secure as ever it was.

Three months later, the nightingale spread her wings and flew back to the central forest. Not for long, though. She returned to sing Little Baron to sleep almost every night, and on most nights, he sang along with her.

Over the next few years, the boy grew up. If he was silent, it was no longer from fear, but from thoughtful observation. When he spoke, his voice was soft, but powerful. The Trumperor soon realized that his youngest son possessed wisdom far beyond his years, and made the boy one of his main advisers. Little Baron was thrust deep into court intrigue, but he navigated it wisely and well with the help of the nightingale. The young prince was amazed by what a small bird can learn listening through an open window, and he learned to use the knowledge well.

Little Baron learned to read his father's moods, and he was able to blunt the Trumperor's sharpest impulses. Other courtiers grew jealous, but Little Baron charmed them with his sweet songs. Over time, the court grew to trust him and the people to love him.

Many years later, when the Trumperor died, the older princes squabbled over their father's holdings. Little Baron negotiated a truce between them, asking only for enough that he and his mother could live comfortably until the end of their days. The princes obliged and considered themselves lucky to be rid of the beautiful, golden-haired Little Baron (no longer so little), for he had grown into a charismatic young man.

When he came of age, Little Baron followed in his father's footsteps and convinced the many kingdoms to elect him as their ruler. Where his father had appealed to anger and rage, Little Baron appealed to compassion and love. He promised to care for all the frightened, the poor, and the unloved. The nightingale had told him stories of their suffering, and he had sworn long ago to do what he could for them. He kept his promise and became one of the most beloved emperors to ever grace the royal White House.

And of course, he made sure that everyone that wanted to learn, learned how to sing.

END

PRESIDENT TRUMP, GETTYSBURG, NOVEMBER 19, 1863

Jim Wright

Forty-seven years ago, our fathers, who were great people by the way, great people, like my father, who I learned a lot from, I have to say I'm very proud of him, proud, and fathers, who did a tremendous job of founding this great country, which is just incredible. But I have to say we're in trouble, trouble, Folks, because the Founding Fathers made deals that were, they weren't good, they were great people don't get me wrong, but, bad deals, Folks, bad deals which are catastrophic in terms of what is happening. People are saying we have made incredible progress, incredible progress, folks, on this continent, which as you know is the best continent. That's what people tell me, I don't know, but the liberty, people are conceiving in liberty, liberty babies, they come here and conceive the babies in the liberty and they're bad people, some of them, some of them are good people too, the best, just tremendous people, and babies, which are dedicated to the proposition, Folks, the proposition that all men are created, some people believe that, equal, and they have tremendous equality, just really good equality, optimism, which to some people used to mean "oh that's not good" but they're now saying is "Oh, that's good for jobs." Very different, Folks.

Now we are engaged in a great Civil War. Yes, a very great war. Everywhere I go people are telling me it's great, but the press won't tell you that, the failing *New York Times* won't tell you how great this Civil War is because, so dishonest. They have no respect for the Great American People who are so great, everywhere I go, the press, so dishonest. It's terrible. The level of dishonesty is out of control. We have to talk to find out what's going on, because the press honestly is out of control. The level of dishonesty, it's crazy, Folks. We are here on the great battlefield, it's great, really great, in that war, which is great. So tragic. People say that. And the jobs. Which they gave the lives for, to make America Great Again. Which is fitting, folks. Which the press won't tell you about, not all the time, and some of the media is fantastic, I have to say, they're honest and fantastic, but fitting. And proper. So we have to do this. Some of the things I'm doing probably aren't popular but they're necessary for security and for other reasons.

But in a larger sense, the greatest sense, which America is known for, we cannot consecrate, we cannot, folks, because ISIS—which is a mess I inherited—we cannot consecrate this hallowed ground, which so many men gave their lives for, bravely living men, so brave, and the dead, who struggled, Folks, they struggled, which is why we have to rebuild our military. Which is great. I love our military, tremendous respect, we have the greatest people, but it's so bad, Folks. It's depleted, it's depleted. And the equipment, which I used. I used it. We have to rebuild it. Had great support in the Senate. They say Trump had the highest electoral win ever. I don't know. That's what they say. And I think one of the reasons I'm standing here instead of other people is that frankly, I talked about we have to have a strong military. We can never forget what they did here, folks, so great. Very dedicated. It is for us the living, rather, to be dedicated to the unfinished work. The unfinished work, which is why I have ordered the construction of a Great Wall, which we have to start. We have to finish it, Folks, and mark my words the Confederates will pay for it. They'll pay for it. To the last full measure. I'm going to put that in the deal, it'll be a great deal, folks, I put it out before the American people, got 306 electoral college votes. I wasn't supposed to get 222. They said there's no way to get 222, 230's impossible. 270 which you need, that was laughable. We got 306 because people came out and voted like they've never seen before so I guess it was the biggest win since maybe James Buchanan. So we highly resolve, Folks, that these dead, which are great, the best dead, which didn't die in vain, that this nation, under God who gave birth to Freedom, God gave birth, Folks, to Freedom, so that government of the people, which has not been in contact with the Russians, who I've never spoken to, I have no business in Russia, and I said that very forcefully but most of the papers won't tell you that, but the people, the government people, of the people, which is why I've put the hiring freeze in place because too many people were being hired by the government. Crazy. It was just crazy, Folks, people, by the people and for the people, the worst people but some of them were good maybe, I don't know, that's what they tell me. We have great people. Who will not perish, Folks, they will not perish from the earth.

END

RELICS: A FABLE

Louise Marley

The banging of a sledge hammer woke Livvy from the heavy sleep of early morning. She opened her dry eyes gingerly, lifting the lids a tiny bit at a time, blinking to stir up some moisture. Gray dawn showed through the thin curtain of her single window. It was too early for birdsong. Not too early for the sledge hammers. Never too early for sledge hammers.

Livvy pulled her mother's handmade quilt over her head, and indulged in a few moments' longing for the old days, when Butch had been alive and they lived in a real house. It wasn't much of a house, being in the shade of the Wall, but it was far enough away so the racket of building and repairs didn't reach them. She longed for one night of uninterrupted sleep, but she knew better than to dwell on the past.

Some of the other relics, relegated to the shacks as Livvy now was, were deaf enough to sleep through the noise. Livvy's hearing was intact, though other parts of her weren't, and she slept uneasily since Butch died. She kept her single door locked, but it was only plywood. It wouldn't do a thing to stop the gangs if they came in search of food or blankets. There were guards here and there, of course, but they were meant for the Wall, not for protecting people who couldn't work anymore.

Livvy pushed back the quilt. "Get yourself up now, Olivia Sutton," she said aloud. Butch used to tease her about talking to herself, and her reply that she was talking to the cat, made him laugh. She wished Butch was still here to tease her. The cat was gone, too.

She smoothed her bed, and drew back the curtain gingerly, so the threadbare fabric wouldn't tear again. Her window faced the dirt lane separating the Wall and the dilapidated row of shacks from the houses of the village. The shacks were flimsy squares built from boards and metal pieces left over from construction of the Wall. Each was a single room with a toilet and a woodstove, built like a lean-to, attached to the massive bulk of the Wall itself. They were differentiated mostly by the colors and textures of whatever had been used to build them.

The shacks had been thrown together for Wall workers a long time ago. When the workers moved on to other sections, the Council pressed the shacks into use for people like Livvy, people who couldn't work anymore. It pleased the Council to call them "the Residences," but everyone else called them the shacks.

Sometimes, when the Wall shifted or settled, a shack would shatter, and tumble to pieces. If the inhabitants were lucky, they escaped with a few bruises. If they weren't lucky, they died.

Of course, the relics were close to death anyway, so no one cared much. Livvy suspected most of the relics didn't care much, either.

She used the toilet, changed into the shapeless dress she wore most days, and walked the five steps to the woodstove. She had a few grains of coffee left, brought to her by one of the church ladies, and a pitcher of water she had carried in yesterday. She could make one cup of coffee, probably her last. Coffee didn't grow on this side of the Wall. Coffee needed sunlight, and the Wall cast a long, deep shadow.

Soon there would be no coffee left except for the people who lived above the shade line, people with coins to pay the smugglers. It was illegal to buy from them, of course, but when it came to the people in the big houses, the law turned a blind eye. Even if Olivia Sutton had coins, she wouldn't dare buy from a smuggler.

Livvy heard that on the other side they had oranges, too. She loved oranges, the look of them, the weight of one in your hand, the wonderful scent that broke free as you peeled away the skin. Apples grew at the top of the hill, and she and the other relics were allowed to pick up the ones that fell to the ground, but Livvy longed for oranges. There had been a few in her girlhood, and later, in her working life, as an occasional bonus. Sometimes she craved their tart sweetness so much her belly ached in response.

She took care brewing the precious cup of coffee. When it was ready, she divided it in two. Porter, next door, had run out the day before. With both cups in her hands, she crossed the patch of dirt and gravel to his shack.

He hobbled out to meet her, leaning on a long, knobbled stick, moving as if every step caused him pain. "You look nice today, Mrs. Sutton," he panted.

She chuckled, and handed him the half cup of coffee. "You're an old sweet talker, Porter," she said. "I can guess how I look."

A rickety bench ran along the side of his shack, built from more Wall remnants. Livvy held Porter's arm as he struggled to settle onto it. It was cold in the shade of the Wall, and Livvy's skin prickled with goosebumps. The Wall grew higher every year, and every year its shade devoured more of the village. People complained their vegetables wouldn't grow, and their fruit trees were dying. Still the Wall rose higher. The complainers achieved nothing but warnings from the Council.

Livvy took a sip of coffee, and closed her eyes at the rich bitterness. "I'm going to miss this," she said.

"Kind of you to share," he said.

She opened her eyes and smiled at him. "Don't mention it."

Porter seemed to be fading before her eyes. His scalp showed through the few remaining white strands on his head. His eyes were clouded with cataracts, his hands bent and twisted by arthritis. There was a time, her mother had claimed, when there were remedies for arthritis, and cataracts could be taken out. Such things had disappeared before Livvy was born.

Her life, like her mother's, like Porter's, like Butch's, had been lived in the shadow of the Wall. Butch had died on it, putting a foot wrong when he was laying stones at the top, falling to an ugly death on the piled boulders at the foot. There was supposed to be a pension for his widow, but it never materialized.

Livvy had often tried to persuade Butch to find another line of work. He only shrugged. "What else can I do?" he said, every time. "They won't have me on the Council." He had laughed at the old joke, the way he laughed at everything. Livvy hadn't found it funny.

Now she shivered a little, and Porter said, "Let me get my blanket for you." He moved his stick, and tried to get to his feet.

"No, no," she said, as he fell back on the bench with a breathless groan. "I'm perfectly fine, Porter. Let's you and me enjoy this last bit of coffee, and then I'll see if I can't walk up the hill. Get some sunshine. Maybe see if there are some apples left."

"Wish I could escort you," he said. "These old legs won't hardly carry me no more."

"I'm real sorry about that, Porter."

His shrug reminded her, painfully, of Butch's. "Doesn't matter now," Porter said.

"Of course it matters!"

"Nah. Once a man can't work, that's pretty much it."

"A woman, too."

"Yeah, that's right, Mrs. Sutton. That's right. A woman, too."

The hill was steep and long, a single, mostly-paved road leading up to the big houses of the Council members. The shade didn't reach those houses. They rose proudly into the sunshine, their gardens full of flowers, their trees flourishing. Livvy had worked in one of those houses for years, cleaning and taking care of children, sometimes cooking. The housekeeper always called her Mrs. Sutton, and she let her take leftovers home to Butch. Sometimes she slipped packets of coffee and sugar into her apron pockets as little treats. Livvy's favorite days were spent minding the Councilman's children, taking them to the playground or reading to them.

When she couldn't get down on her knees anymore to scrub floors, the Councilman fired her. It was better than falling from the top of the Wall to break her neck, but not much. It was the end of good things in her life. She didn't bother asking if she could still come to read to the children. Truth was, if that Councilman met her on the street, he wouldn't know her, and he sure wouldn't care whether she wanted to see the little ones. The only good thing was that without a job, she could lend a hand to Porter, who had no one to see him through to his end.

Porter had never married. Livvy had never had a child who lived more than a few months. They made good neighbors.

He drained his cup, closing his eyes as she had done to savor the last drops. "That was good. Thanks."

She took his cup in her cold fingers, and rose. "You're welcome. You have something for breakfast?"

"Yeah. I have an egg."

She raised her brows. "Who brought you an egg?"

"Woman from the church."

"That was nice of her."

"Had to listen to her sermon, though."

Livvy chuckled, and the two cups clinked together. "Pretty bad, was it?"

"Yeah. Seems I ain't saved, at least not the right way. That really bothers her. Still let me have the egg, though."

"Do you want me to come over and cook it for you?"

"Naw, I can do it. You go try to get some sun."

~oOo~

Livvy's knees ached with the cold, but she managed, painfully, to climb the hill to the old school playground. She settled herself onto one of the children's swings that hung, empty and abandoned, from a rusting steel frame. The sun rose high enough above the Wall that the playground was bright by midday. She put her face up into the sunshine and waited for her aching joints to thaw in its warmth.

The school had closed decades before. There weren't many children about anymore, so the park was usually empty. She used to love pushing children on the swing, or waiting for them at the bottom of the slide. When she heard the mothers snap with impatience, she wanted to hush them, tell them how fortunate they were to have living children.

She never did it. As Butch said, better to keep your head down and mind your own business. You never knew if the Council was going to take after you. You could lose everything.

She lost everything anyway. First Butch, then her job, then her little house with its trio of tiny graves that never saw the sun.

Oh, and the cat disappeared. Thinking of the silly cat made her eyes sting.

Livvy muttered, "You gotta stop that, Olivia Sutton. Cat would be long dead by now." She blinked, and shaded her eyes against the glitter of sunlight.

From the playground, she could see miles of the Wall. She was curious to know how much higher it had grown in her lifetime. Butch used to say it was growing three inches a year. That seemed like too much to Livvy, but Butch was usually right about such things. She also had no idea how long it actually was. There had been a boy, when she was young, who swore he'd walked along it for two solid weeks and never reached the end.

Livvy had never been out of the village. She didn't dare leave, for fear the Council wouldn't allow her back in.

She pushed with her feet, and the swing rocked gently, forward and back. The Wall loomed below her, many yards thick at the bottom, growing narrower and narrower until it was only a foot or so across at the top. Butch said it used to be steel from top to bottom, one flat plane, but since there was no more steel—those factories had fallen to ruin long ago—now it was an ugly mountain of rocks and dirt and who knew what-all, patched together with cement.

It was protection, the Council said. To keep the people safe. Nobody could recall for sure what they were being protected from, but there were lots of rumors. Thieves. Murderers. Rape gangs. Kidnappers.

Livvy wasn't sure what to believe. Sometimes she imagined there were just people on the other side, people different from herself, but having their own hopes and dreams and sorrows. She didn't expect she'd ever find out.

She swung again, her knees and ankles beginning to feel warm at last. She was hungry, and thought of going to the soup kitchen in the church basement, but she was reluctant to leave the sunshine. The church basement smelled of cheap candles and old food, and echoed with hymns and lectures. She wished she could take a bowl of soup back to her shack, and eat it in peace, but they would never allow that. They liked the relics to behave themselves, and act properly grateful.

She was trying to decide whether to go home for a cold sandwich or subject herself to the church ladies when she heard a light step behind her. Stiffly, she twisted her body so she could see who had come into the park.

A little girl was climbing the stairs to the slide. She couldn't have been more than eight, with a thatch of fair curly hair and good leather shoes that looked as if they fit her well. One of the Councilmen's children, for sure. Livvy looked around for her minder, but didn't see anyone. Maybe the girl had escaped to seek a few moments in the sun, just as she had.

Livvy worked her body out of the swing seat, and limped to the foot of the slide. "I'll catch you," she told the child.

"Okay!" The girl put her legs over the edge of the rusty steel incline. She was wearing denim pants, and there were rough spots on the slide. "You might tear your pants," Livvy warned.

"I know," the girl said, and pushed off.

Now Livvy knew for sure she was the daughter of a Councilman. No one else could risk their clothes that way. The girl bumped down the slide, its surface no longer smooth enough for real sliding. At the bottom, Livvy put out her hands, though there was really no catching involved. It was nice, though, to touch a child's firm, warm body. She released her with a pang, remembering all the times she had caught children coming fast down the slide, shrieking with joy, flying into her waiting hands.

She folded her arms. "What's your name?"

"Pansy." The girl started for the stairs again.

"Where's your mama? Or your minder?"

"Mama's at home. She's feeling sick."

"Does she know you're here?"

Pansy had reached the top of the stairs. She swung her legs over again, but didn't push off. "No."

"Shall I walk you home?"

Pansy pushed herself off, and slowly bumped her way to the bottom of the slide. Livvy didn't try to catch her, or even put out her hands, though she would have liked to touch the child again, to feel youth and energy and warmth through her fingers.

Pansy said, "Did you used to go the school?"

"Yes, until it closed."

"Why did it close?" Pansy bounced on her toes as if standing still were impossible.

"Doesn't your mama tell you about that?"

"No."

"Well." Livvy turned to look at the faded school buildings, the windows boarded up, the old parking lot cracked and sprouting weeds. "Well, I guess people just lost interest in the school. They let it die."

"I wish I could go to school."

"Who's teaching you to read? To do your arithmetic?"

"Mama. But she doesn't read very well herself."

"Oh, I'm real sorry about that, Pansy. I do love reading books."

The little girl turned up her face, blue eyes sparking with interest. "Do you? Could you teach me?"

"I would, but I don't have books to use."

Pansy said, "I have books. I have three of them."

"That's nice. What are they called?"

"I don't know."

"Ah. You haven't learned to read at all, then."

"No." Pansy sighed, and looked around at the dilapidated play equipment. "Kids used to play here, I think."

"Yes, they did. I did."

"You were lucky."

"In some things." Livvy looked around, surprised no one had come looking for the child. "I think I should walk you home, Pansy."

"We could read one of my books!" The little girl bounced on her toes, and her curls shook with enthusiasm.

"If your mama says it's okay."

"Mama's lying down." Pansy seized Livvy's hand with her small, strong one. "Come on!" As they started out of the playground, Pansy asked, "What's your name?"

"Olivia Sutton, but you can call me Livvy."

Pansy swung Livvy's hand back and forth, and walked on her toes, as if regular walking didn't burn enough energy. "Are you old, Livvy? You look really old."

Livvy laughed, and it felt good. She hadn't laughed in a while. "I'm pretty old. It's what happens if you live a long time."

"Will I be old someday?"

Livvy squeezed the little girl's hand. "I hope so, Pansy. I do hope so."

It wasn't an easy climb, and she struggled to keep up with the child. She was out of breath by the time they reached Pansy's house, a solid sort of building with two floors and multiple windows, and an iron fence around everything. There was even a garage behind it, its door up, waiting for one of the few remaining automobiles to be parked there.

Pansy led her around to a side gate, and then in through a spacious kitchen with real cupboards and a stove with four burners. It made Livvy sigh with nostalgia. There was an electric coffeepot and an assortment of cups hanging on hooks above it. There was a counter with stools beside it, and a fruit bowl that held three apples and one single, perfect orange.

The sight of the orange made Livvy's mouth water. She averted her gaze.

Pansy dashed into another room, and came back with a little stack of three slender books. She held them out to Livvy. "Can we read now?"

Livvy cast an uneasy glance around her. "We should get permission from your mama first. She might think I—well, that I came for something else."

"What?"

Livvy didn't know how to explain to a child that she was at risk of being accused of theft, or abuse, or whatever offense might occur to someone. Pansy obviously didn't notice that she and Livvy were different colors. It had been interesting to Livvy that the little girl saw she was old, but not that she was dark. Pansy wouldn't understand the problem.

"Who are you?"

Livvy started, and whirled to see a young, very thin woman in a white bathrobe standing in the doorway to the kitchen. "Oh! Hello, ma'am," Livvy said hastily. "I just walked your little girl back from the playground. Didn't seem like she should be on her own that way."

The woman put a hand to her throat, holding the lapels of her robe close. She looked frail, and Livvy wondered just how ill she was. "Pansy," the woman said, in a thready voice. "You weren't supposed to go out of the yard!"

"Sorry, Mama," Pansy said, without sincerity. "This is Livvy, and she—"

"Olivia Sutton, ma'am. I used to work two houses down."

"Oh." The woman took an uncertain step to one side, as if she couldn't decide whether to go back upstairs or come into the room and face the situation. "Pansy isn't supposed to talk to strangers, but—"

"I told you, Mama!" Pansy cried. "This isn't a stranger. This is Livvy. Livvy's going to teach me to read."

~oOo~

It was the nicest afternoon Livvy had enjoyed in a very long time. Pansy's mother, called Sarah, was easily convinced that Livvy was no threat to her house or her child, and retreated to her bedroom. Pansy and Livvy made cheese sandwiches, and Livvy made Pansy carry one up to her mother before they ate. Afterward, she sat down with the little girl and read all three of her books. When she finished, she started again with the first, explaining how the letters worked. Once Pansy could read the title and the first sentence, she seized the book, and galloped up the stairs to show her mother.

Sarah came down once again, still barefoot, but dressed in a blouse and skirt. "Thank you, Olivia," she said. "Pansy has been longing to learn to read. Let me give you some money."

"Oh, no, ma'am, thank you, but I don't want to be paid. I enjoyed myself."

"Well," Sarah said, with a vague wave of her hand. "I should give you something. Pansy gets so lonely since I've been sick."

Livvy hesitated. She hadn't come to the house for anything except to read to Pansy, but the chance was too good to pass up. She hugged herself, and blurted, "Ma'am, if you have any extra coffee…?" At Sarah's surprised look, she said, "I'm down in the sh—the residences, see, and we don't get coffee too often."

"Oh!" Sarah said. "Oh, if you want coffee…" She pointed at the cupboard above the coffeepot. "Help yourself. As much as you like." Another wave. "There's some sugar, too, I think. Cheese. Anything you want, really. Just take it."

Ten minutes later, Livvy was on her way down the hill, her pockets bulging with things from Sarah's kitchen. She had a precious pound of coffee, and a half pound of good yellow cheese without a speck of mold. She had two eggs, and best of all, she had the orange from the fruit bowl. The walk took her a long time, downhill being worse than uphill for her knees, but she spent it planning the feast she would prepare for Porter in the morning.

She placed the orange in a saucer, and set it out in imitation of Sarah's fruit bowl. She hid the coffee behind her kettle, and set the cups ready for the morning. She went to bed early, and slept well, with a tummy full of cheese sandwiches, only waking when the sledgehammers began in the early dawn.

They sounded closer today. She supposed they had discovered another tunnel. The blows rattled her walls, and made the woodstove shimmy on the plank floor.

Muttering instructions to herself, she filled the woodstove and lighted it. She boiled water for coffee, and while it was steeping she peeled the orange into sections, savoring the smell of orange peel. She steamed the eggs in the rest of the water, and when everything was ready, she went across the patch of dirt to Porter's shack.

She had to wait while he hobbled to the door, and pulled it open. "Mornin', Porter," she said.

"Why, Mrs. Sutton," he said. His voice was rough with sleep. "What brings you here?"

"A feast," she told him.

It took a bit of persuading, but soon she had Porter in her shack, seated on her only chair, with a cup of fragrant coffee between his shaking hands. She worried he might drop the cup, but he didn't. He drank it slowly, smiling at her between sips. She sat on her bed as they each ate an egg, then carefully shared out the orange.

At the first taste, Livvy groaned with pleasure. "I haven't had me an orange in so long."

"Me neither, Mrs. Sutton. It's like this is my birthday or something."

They smiled at each other, two old relics enjoying a good meal. And coffee.

When she had helped Porter back to his shack, Livvy looked up the hill to the playground. She didn't see anyone there, and she was tired from her climb of the day before. She decided she would rest, though it wasn't easy with the banging and cracking going on.

The next day, when she had drunk a precious cup of coffee and taken one to Porter, she went out for water and saw someone was in the playground again. It was too far for her to be sure, but she thought it might be Pansy. She took a shawl this time against the cold, and clambered up the steep street.

Pansy ran to meet her. She had her first book with her, the one she had started reading in, and she had an orange in her pocket.

They fell into a routine, Pansy and Livvy, with Sarah's all-but-invisible support. When the weather was fine, Livvy and Pansy read at one of the picnic tables in the playground. When it was rainy, Livvy labored up the hill, and she and the little girl worked in the warm kitchen. Sarah found more books for her daughter, books she herself could barely read, and Pansy devoured them.

They went on that way for weeks, and it was almost like the old days. Livvy came away each time with cheese or eggs or oranges, sometimes coffee, often apples from beneath the tree in Pansy's yard. Pansy glowed with enthusiasm. Livvy's joints eased from being in the warm house so often. Porter flourished, too, in his modest way, with a bit of better food and a cup of coffee each morning.

Then, one afternoon, Livvy looked up from the book in Pansy's lap and saw a tall blond man staring at the two of them. "What are you doing in my house?" he demanded.

Livvy jumped to her feet, and Pansy did, too, the book falling to the floor. They hadn't heard the automobile come up the hill. "I'm Olivia Sutton, sir. I—I'm teaching Pansy to read."

"I'm reading, Papa," Pansy said in the smallest voice Livvy had heard her use.

"Your mother is teaching you to read," he said, in a flat voice that made Livvy's belly tighten, and Pansy shrink against her.

"Sir, Sarah—uh, Miss Sarah—she wasn't feeling well, and—"

"She's lazy," he snapped. "Nobody feels well if they lie in bed all day."

Livvy made no answer. There was no point. She bent to pick up the book, and laid it softly on the sofa where she and Pansy had been sitting.

Pansy's papa said, "Did she hire you? Without asking me?"

Livvy had no answer for that, either. She had no way of knowing what Sarah might have spoken to her husband about. She wasn't hired exactly. She didn't know what to say, but she could see this was the end.

She tried not to look longingly at the three oranges in the fruit bowl. She didn't go anywhere near the cupboard where the coffee was kept, or the electric refrigerator where there were always eggs and cheese. She said, "Pansy, I'm gonna have to go now."

Pansy's sweet little hand slipped into hers, and squeezed, but she didn't say a word. Livvy wanted to kiss her, but under her papa's glare, she didn't dare. She murmured, "You can read those books to your mama now, Pansy. You know all the words."

"Sarah can read them for herself," her father snapped. He

stood with his hands in his pockets, watching Livvy walk out the kitchen door as if he was afraid she was going to steal something on her way.

Empty-handed, heavy of heart, Livvy limped her way down the hill to her shack. She didn't mind so much not bringing back an orange or a couple of eggs. She minded leaving Pansy with a father she was obviously afraid of, and a mother who hadn't admitted to her husband that she couldn't teach their daughter to read because she couldn't read herself.

Porter came out as she crossed the lane. "Good day up the hill, Mrs. Sutton?"

She shook her head. "My little girl's daddy came home. Wasn't happy to see me."

"He didn't know about you."

"Guess not." She trudged toward her door. Her knees had begun to ache in earnest. "I didn't bring anything this time, Porter. I'm out of coffee, out of cheese—everything. I'm sorry."

"That don't matter. You've been so generous already. I think I have the fixings for some soup. Would you like some?"

"No, thanks. I'm going to have a lie-down, I think. This is making me sad. My poor little girl."

"You taught her a lot, I think."

"I don't know if it does any good." She opened her door, and stared into the dim, dusty interior. "It's not right, Porter. Those people up there with so much. Us down here with nothing."

"Always things in this world aren't right, Livvy."

"Yes. I oughta know that by now." She lifted her hand to him, and went into her shack.

~oOo~

Livvy went to bed without eating anything, though she still had a wedge of dried-out cheese and two slices of bread that weren't too moldy. She had no appetite. She kept seeing Pansy's desolate face, and her heart ached all over again. She didn't know where she would find comfort for this loss. At least when the babies died, she had Butch to hold her, cry with her.

When she finally fell asleep, it was the thick nightmare-ridden sleep of exhaustion. When the rumbling started, it seemed to be part of her dreams. Not until it got so loud she couldn't ignore it did she wake fully, sitting up in bed with her quilt clutched to her bosom.

The rumbling grew to a roar. Her shack began to vibrate, then to shake. Gray dust sifted from the ceiling to powder her quilt, her floor, her hair. She scrambled from bed, her painful knees almost giving way. Stiff-legged, she struggled across to her door.

It wouldn't open, though she shook it and banged on it. Through the dimness, she saw her side walls tilting, pulling loose from the Wall, jiggering her door so it wouldn't budge.

Rocks began to fall, battering her roof, bouncing against the off-kilter walls. One burst through the growing crack between the shack and the Wall, and rolled across the floor, just missing her bare feet. She thrust her feet into her shoes and began to kick at the door. The noise intensified into a mind-numbing cacophony of falling rocks and cracking wood. She found herself screaming against it, as if her voice could stop the obliteration of her home.

The door finally gave way beneath her kicks. It fell outward, taking the front wall of the shack with it. The side walls, like playing cards in an old stacking game, flared outward and collapsed, shattering into a hundred bits of ancient wood and rusted metal. Livvy made her escape, dashing across the lane with her quilt around her shoulders. When she reached safety, she whirled to gape in horror at the wreck of the shacks.

Hers was flattened, as if a child's giant foot had stamped it to pieces.

Porter's had fallen inward.

She shrieked, horrified by the sight. His roof had crashed onto his floor, his side walls collapsed on top of that, and a mound of stones loosened from the Wall had buried the whole mess. Had buried him. People from up and down the lane came running, and frantically tried to lift rocks and planks and bits of old tin, but it was mostly to make themselves feel better, to know they had done all they could. They knew—as Livvy knew—it was too late for Porter.

She sagged to the ground, and pulled her mother's quilt over her head to hide her weeping.

When the sun rose beyond the black bulk of the Wall, an automobile came coasting down the hill, past the playground, past the small houses. It stopped when it reached the lane, where survivors and workers now huddled in the cold, staring at the wreck of the residences. Livvy got to her feet, and turned with the others to watch the Councilman step out of his automobile and stand, hands on hips, surveying the disaster.

It was Pansy's papa. He looked much as he had the day before, irritated and impatient.

One of the work bosses went up to him, and the two men spoke a few words. Pansy's father gestured up and down the Wall, and pointed to the section that had collapsed.

Someone said, "At least there'll be some repair work."

Someone else said, "Think the Council has any idea why it fell down?"

"New tunnel came through," someone whispered behind his hand. The whisper was repeated through the crowd.

They fell silent as the Councilman approached them. His lips were pinched. "You people will have to clear out while we get this situation resolved."

Livvy felt numb with disbelief. Clear out? The relics? She glanced around, but it seemed no one was going to speak. It wasn't right, and they all knew it. She clutched at her quilt, and stepped forward. "Sir?"

He eyed her without recognition. "What is it?" he snapped.

She felt vulnerable, exposed in her night clothes, but she couldn't retreat. "Sir, we—the *residents*—" She couldn't help emphasizing the word. "We have no place to go."

"Of course you do," he said. "Go up to the church. They'll have cots."

"Some of these folks can't climb the hill to the church, sir. They're gonna need help."

He blew out an exasperated breath. "Lady, that's not my problem. My job is to keep this Wall in good repair. To close up the tunnels. To keep everyone safe."

"Didn't keep Porter safe," Livvy muttered, but only to herself. The Councilman was already on the way back to his automobile, his neck stiff with annoyance. In moments he was gone, his auto spinning easily up the steep street.

The repair work began immediately, with the boss shouting orders and men scurrying here and there. Some people from the church arrived to start shepherding the relics up the hill. A few, who would never be able to make the climb, sat right down in the dirt of the lane to wait for whatever would come.

Livvy could make it to the church, but she had no intention of going before they brought Porter out of the wreck. Two workers had already started pounding away at the rubble, rolling stones away when they could, breaking up others, tossing them onto a pile in the lane. Shards of Porter's few possessions appeared, a saucepan smashed flat, a broom handle in splinters, fragments of a water pitcher. Everything went onto the mound. Most of it would go back into the Wall.

When one of the workers suddenly straightened, calling for the other man to join him, Livvy crossed the lane to see what they had found. The first one caught sight of her. "You should stop there, ma'am. You don't want to see this."

His kindness made her eyes sting. "You found him," she said.

"Friend of yours?"

"Yes. His name was Porter."

"I'm real sorry, ma'am."

"Can you tell—" She pressed her fingers to her trembling lips. It was hard to wrench the words from her throat. "Young man, are—are you quite sure he's dead?"

"Yeah, no doubt about it. If it helps—pretty sure it would

have happened fast."

Livvy shuddered at what it must have been like for poor Porter, the noise, the cracking and crumbling, the full weight of the pitiless Wall crushing out his life. Tears burned her cheeks, and when she put up a hand to brush them away, she remembered she was still in her nightgown, with only her quilt to cover her.

"Ma'am?"

She pulled herself together enough to meet the young man's sympathetic gaze. He said, "Listen, you can't stand here like that. How's about my wife brings you some clothes? Helps you up to the church?"

She could have accepted his offer. She could have accepted the clothes, gone to the church, slept on a cot and listened to sermons.

She glared at the Wall, suddenly furious with the way it had ruled her life. The young man went on talking, but she didn't hear him. She didn't see anything but the behemoth of stone and steel and wood, the relics of civilization. She wanted to pound it with her fists, shout it down, smash it with her own stubborn spirit.

Then she saw it. The opening. The mouth of a tunnel gaping behind the wreckage of Porter's shack. It was littered with scree and the flotsam that jammed the interior of the Wall. It was little more than a crawlspace, dirty and dark and narrow.

But there was light on the other side. It wasn't much, a window glimpsed at a distance, but it shone with light. Sunshine. It called to Livvy's heart.

She started toward the opening. The young worker seized her hand. "Lady, you can't go in there! It's not safe!"

"Why?" she said, not looking at him, focusing on the tunnel and its promise of light at the other end.

"It could fall in at any moment," he said.

"I don't care."

"Can't you just wait—my wife—?"

She pulled her hand free, gently, and glanced into his kind face. He was as dark as she was, but young—so young. A wife. Maybe a family. His future before him. If he had a future, that is, working on the endless Wall, living in its cruel shadow.

"It's good of you to worry about an old woman," she told him. "But I think I'm gonna take my chances." She started off again, picking her way over the broken bits of Porter's life. "I really want some sunshine," she muttered, not even pretending to talk to anyone but herself. "I'm so tired of living in the shade."

The going was rough. Her old shoes slipped on jagged stones, and broke through rotted bits of wood. She was still in her night clothes. She hadn't brushed her teeth or combed her hair, but she was on her way.

When she wriggled her way into the opening, the dank smell of old dirt and cold stones met her nostrils. In places she had to suck in her stomach to sidle through. The Wall groaned and cracked around her, threatening to stop her once and for all. She pressed on.

The light ahead grew brighter. Hands were picking at that little window, widening it, pulling away bits of the Wall. Her heart thudded at the thought of the people there, maybe smugglers, possibly the adversaries she had been warned about since her infancy.

"No turning back now, old woman," she grunted as she squeezed around a chunk of ancient link fencing. "Don't you chicken out now."

Above her the Wall grumbled and shifted, trying to hold her in its clutches like some great dragon guarding its lair, coveting its relics, loath to let even one escape.

A shaft of unimpeded sunlight broke into the tunnel on the far side, and with it a gust of fresh air. Heads joined the hands she had seen, silhouettes against the brilliance. Enemies? Perhaps.

But the real monster was the Wall, and though it began to shake, and rain detritus down on her head, she would not give in. She pushed forward, scraping her knees and shoulders, losing one shoe, kicking off the other to maintain her balance. She was sure she was bleeding in places, but it didn't matter. One way or another, Olivia Sutton was going to be free.

Did she imagine it, or did the breeze from the other side smell of oranges?

END

AS PROPHESIED OF OLD

Susan Murrie Macdonald

Fleet Street was having a field day. The president of the United States was coming to the United Kingdom for the first time since his election, and editors and reporters merrily threw all pretense of journalistic neutrality into the dustbin as they vied in coming up with ever more creative epithets for him. None used his name or title. Most referred to his addiction to Twitter, the size of his hands, the poor dye job done by the White House hair stylist, and his much-debated sanity.

Buckingham Palace had already announced that the queen would not be meeting with him. The hundreds of thousands of people who had signed petitions that he not be granted a royal audience cheered, attempting to take credit for what they called a well-deserved royal snub. Buckingham Palace, discreetly not mentioning the petitions, said that Her Majesty was ill and confined to her bed. Palace officials assured Her Majesty's loving subjects that the queen's illness was not severe, but her doctor wished to take precautions at her age. The Prince of Wales, whose schedule was normally meticulously arranged months in advance, suddenly had to meet with Scottish nationalists in Glasgow. His Royal Highness would therefore be unable to meet with the president, although he had met all of his predecessors since he was in short pants, from Eisenhower on up.

~oOo~

The MP from Puddlesmere-under-the-Fens stood. "I have a question for the Secretary of State for Environment, Food, and Rural Affairs. Is Her Majesty's Government aware that the president of the United States, who is coming to this country, denies the reality of climate change?"

The Secretary of State for Environment, Food, and Rural Affairs frowned. Normally for Question Time the members of the House of Commons just gave the number of a question that had been submitted days ago. The MP from Puddlesmere-under-the-Fens played for the cameras. "Her Majesty's Government is aware of the president's opinion, but regrettably unable to change it. Such an action is beyond the purview of Her Majesty's Government."

Next to her, the Lady Chancellor, who was also the Secretary of State for Justice, joked quietly. "Rather like the law of gravity. We can't arrest people for not believing in it, but it exists, whether they believe in it or not."

Those who were close enough to hear the Lady Chancellor chuckled.

The MP from St. Oswin's-on-Avon rose to ask his question. "Question number three."

Before the appropriate Cabinet minister could stand to reply, the MP from St. Oswin's-on-Avon followed the example of his distinguished colleague from Puddlesmere-under-the-Fens. "Is Her Majesty's Government aware that the president of our long-time ally, the United States of America, has made many derogatory comments about women, including Her Late Highness the Princess of Wales, and if so, what does Her Majesty's Government intend to do about it?"

The Secretary of State for Education, who was also the Minister for Women and Equalities, answered his question with a question. "What, precisely, does the honorable gentleman expect Her Majesty's Government to do? We are hosting the annual G7 conference. The United States is," she hesitated for a moment, as that felt ungrammatical. Oughtn't it be 'the United States are' for proper subject/verb agreement? "—our long-time ally, and a member of G7. We cannot prohibit the leader of a G7 nation from attending the conference."

"There are a great many petitions suggesting that he be barred from entering Great Britain," the MP from St. Oswin's-on-Avon reminded her.

"Yes, Her Majesty's Government is aware of the many petitions, both on paper and on-line, to label him as an unwelcome visitor and request he not be permitted entry into the nation." The Minister for Women and Equalities took a deep breath. "The Channel Islands did a separate petition just to make it clear he will not be welcome there, either."

A few parliamentarians laughed at that.

One female MP called out, "Huzzah for the Channel Islands!"

"Perhaps the honorable gentleman from St. Oswin's-on-Avon recollects that this very body debated whether or not to bar the President from our shores two years ago, and we voted at that time that he did not constitute a danger to queen or country," the Minister for Women and Equalities said.

"At the time, he was voted a buffoon rather than a danger," the Secretary of State for the Home Department added.

Several MPs began chattering among themselves. That bit of video had gone viral on Facebook and Twitter over the past week or two.

A brown-skinned MP with a Pakistani name stood up. In a Manchester accent, he protested, "We were wrong! The man incites disorder and hatred. His actions against Muslims have encouraged terrorists and deepened the chasms between—"

The Speaker of the House rose from his chair. "Ladies, gentlemen! This is the House of Commons, not a schoolyard. We will have order."

~oOo~

Mild tremors in Somerset, too small to be felt by any but the most delicate seismographs, rippled in a broad circle.

~oOo~

"This is Penelope Penfold, BBC News," a young blonde spoke into her microphone. "As you can see, a considerable crowd has gathered to protest the visit of the American president."

The camera panned behind her, showing a crowd of people carrying signs. There were women in hand-knit pink hats, turbaned Sikhs, teenagers in the universal uniform of t-shirts and blue jeans, Muslims in fezzes and traditional clothing, and Muslims in three piece suits and bowler hats.

One sign showed a picture of a cartoon lion in a Beefeater's uniform, carrying a halberd, with the words: "Grab this!"

"No bigots in Britain!"

"London is for lovers, not liars."

"Not being paid a shilling to protest."

"Keep Great Britain GREAT by keeping out the hate!"

"However," Miss Penfold continued, "not all the protesters are here to try to halt the president's visit. Some people are eagerly anticipating the opportunity to welcome the president of the United States to the U. K." She walked over to a middle-aged man wearing a Manchester United sweatshirt. "Excuse me, sir, can you tell me why you want the president to come?"

"We don't want him to come. We'd much prefer he stayed in the States," the man explained. "But we believe freedom of speech is for everyone, even bigots."

The camera panned to show the signs held by the people behind him.

"The British Empire is not afraid of a misspelled tweet."

"Freedom of speech applies even to idiots."

"It's not that we welcome him. It's just that we're not afraid of him, and we refuse to lower ourselves to his level," he concluded.

~oOo~

Despite the protests, despite the petitions, Air Force One landed at Heathrow on schedule. As soon as the plane touched down, an earthquake at Glastonbury Tor split the ground.

The president exited the plane, followed by his mousy First Lady. He waved to the crowd as he descended the aluminum stairs. His wife, as usual, kept her head bowed down. The Regimental Band of the Royal Welsh began playing "The Star Spangled Banner," drowning out both the jeers of the protesters and the cheers of those greeting him. The jeers far outnumbered the cheers.

~o0o~

Even as the American president set foot on English soil, a man stood from the ground and with no wasted confusion, dusted himself off and marched down the hill. Bronze *lorica hamata* armor covered his white tunic; Roman greaves covered his linen trousers. A simple gold diadem, devoid of gems or engravings, rested upon his auburn hair. He sniffed once, then turned his head to the right and left, sniffing again. He ignored the tourists reaching for their cameras and cell phones as he marched down to the River Brue.

"I needs must go to London," he announced. "I fain would not go unarmed."

An alabaster boat rose from the water. Six ghostly oarsmen, some clad like the man, some in boiled leather armor, and some in woolen tunics, manned the boat. Arthur smiled when he saw the sword that lay upon the prow.

The world watched as the videos from Japanese tourists and students from the Somerset College of Arts and Technology exploded across Facebook and YouTube. The light was perfect as images captured the man as he stepped into the boat and picked up Excalibur. He examined the blade closely before raising it high. "To London! We must defend our beloved England from foreign invasion once more." As prophesied of old.

END

about_the_change.wav

Joel Ewy

...ecording. Recording. OK.

It all started with the Feminazis and all the other Libtards. Everybody all used to agree on the truth. And then they started telling us Columbus was a mass-murderer. God's A-OK with fags, all sex is rape, all men are pigs, all whites are racists. *They* started the change, I'm telling you. *They* tried to change reality first. Then things took a different turn. I guess the conservatives were just more effective at it, that's all. Because the Feminazis and Libtards are all gone now. They're all just stories and memories.

Now, I *will* say that I never noticed the change until some time after the election. After the Media War. After the Executive Truth Order. I don't know when, exactly. But things just started changing. The protests died down. You didn't see so much bitching on Facebook anymore. I figured they just gave up, you know.

But it wasn't just that people were shutting up. The very same liberal queefs who used to whine and cry about some criminal the cops had to put down finally started talking sense. There was the *New York Times* retraction of their stories on KremlinGate. Then the NPR apology for questioning the US occupation of the Mexican oil fields. The entire staff offered to resign. I remember The Donald called it "great". He said now we could all start working together to put America on top again.

I remember one time I was watching Fox News when this liberal that always whines about the Donald suddenly got a weird look in his eye and said, "You may be right about that." He said the pipeline probably wouldn't burst, and if it did it would still be a small price to pay for the energy we all need.

I remember the regular guys looked at him like he'd lost his script or something. When they came back from a commercial he did say a few things about how we should make sure we protect wildlife and stuff, but it was like something had shifted.

That show isn't even on these days. I guess there isn't much point to it now. I remember on one of the last episodes they had some college professor pretending to argue against open carry on campus, but he clearly didn't believe what he was saying. I changed the channel.

The thing is, I miss her. I guess that's really why I'm making this recording. She's still here, of course. They all are. But I know it's not her anymore. Her body still looks the same. Still feels the same. Her face is still her face. But she's somebody else. It used to be electric. I can't describe it. There was a tension that made it good between us. Some back and forth. The friction and differences were kind of hot, to be honest. She was cute when she yelled back at Rush. I didn't even mind when she scolded me for calling people 'Libtards'. Sometimes it was even better between us after we made up.

I remember when she marched on the state capital in that stupid pink pussy hat. Seems like a long time ago now. I told her it was ridiculous. I told her that she already had plenty of equality, and Trump wasn't really going to take anything away from her. She kissed me anyway when I dropped her off. I loved her standing there with the rest of the Feminazis, smiling like a gorgeous, brilliant idiot. I'd even helped her make her damn sign. When she got out of the Silverado, I actually wanted to go with her. But I didn't.

That night I told her I was proud of her though. For speaking her mind. For standing up for what she believed in. I told her I still thought the protest was stupid, and I didn't really understand why she needed to complain. But I kind of liked that she did. We talked a bit about how we used to argue in the online forum for that stupid General Ed. Philosophy class we both took in college. Really, she helped me pass that class. I ended up with a C. I don't remember why, but when the class was over, we started going out for coffee. That night after the protest we remembered that too. I think she was more alive to me on that night than any time before or since.

She started noticing the changes first, in the things she was reading, social media, what her friends were saying. I told her it was just that people were finally coming to their senses. The liberals lost the argument, lost the election, and maybe some of them were finally starting to get smart.

But she made me read this blog post by our old Philosophy prof Amanda Deckard. She had this new theory that epistemology and ontology are actual dimensions of reality like space and time. So the idea was that stuff happening in one dimension could warp the other, like how space and time are connected together. There was all kinds of stuff about collapsing probability waves and a cat in a box with poison. I didn't get it all the first time, but basically she was saying that the facts we choose to observe can have an effect on reality.

Now, I *would* just call bullshit on it. But something weird was going on that caused people to change, like that guy on the old Fox TV show. Not just what they said and did in public. But it changed their spirit, you know? Who they are. Whatever the hell, pretty soon it started to have an effect on *my* reality.

Did you ever see that *Twilight Zone* where the burglar dies and goes to Heaven and he always wins and gets what he wants, and then he finds out that isn't Heaven? That's how it is with her these days. For about a week I thought she was trying to butter me up or something. She'd been a little different for a while already I guess, but when she started doing whatever I wanted, whenever I wanted, even in bed, I knew she had changed. The sex was great, at first. But that was when I really noticed she was gone. She was like a doll. Not a doll, really. I mean, she still does stuff on her own. But she wasn't her anymore.

She used to do yoga in a shaft of sun in the living room. I loved to call it yogurt just to yank her chain. She'd just flip me off and smile. She was so beautiful. She still looks the same as she always did, but somehow she isn't beautiful like she used to be. I don't feel anything when I look at her, when I hold her. Just loss. She still smiles, but it doesn't mean what it used to mean. Now she gives me her body in ways she never did before, but I don't care, if you can believe it. I wish she would give me the finger instead. She went out and bought a treadmill.

So I confronted her. I don't know, two months ago? I told her she was different. She didn't seem to care anymore about the stuff that used to be important to her. Why? What was that all about? I didn't know who I was living with anymore.

And she denied it. She denied it all. She told me she never went to any protests or marches. Said I was making stuff up. I was the one changing. I literally couldn't believe what I was hearing.

I went to the closet and grabbed her pink pussy hat. "What's this, then?" I said. "It's your pussy hat. You wore that to the march on the capital! All your friends had 'em on. You were protesting Trump talking about grabbing pussy. You can't tell me you don't remember your pussy hat!"

So she says, "It's just a cute cat hat. You don't need to be crude. I mean, we *can* be crude if you want. You want to see me in the hat? I can wear *just* the hat if that's what you want."

"That's *not* what I want," I told her. "Not right now. I want you to be like you were before. I want you to argue with me and tell me how backward and sexist I am. I want you to tell me how I don't get it, and my family's a bunch of rednecks. I want you to show me some video about women or black folks protesting. I want you to get all excited about some damn cause and try to convince me I'm on the wrong side of history."

Then she says, "I don't think you're wrong, baby, and I really don't know what's gotten into you. Why would I want to go to protests? You want me to turn into some kind of a liberal?"

That's when I slapped her in the face.

She looked stunned for a second. And then she just smiled.

She changed the subject. Tried to bring me a beer.

I felt sick. I had to go outside. I puked in the driveway, and then I had to go drive around for a while. I'm no feminist, but I had *never* hit her before, or even come close. It couldn't have been me who just did that. But she wasn't herself anymore, either. Before, she probably would have slapped me back. She might have left me. Now she wasn't the one I'd argued with and gone out to coffee with. She wasn't the one I'd skipped class to make out and hook up with. She wasn't the one I loved anymore. When I got back, everything was back to normal. Well, it was the new normal anyway. All different.

I wanted to go back and read the Philosophy prof's blog post again. See if I could get more out of it the second time around. Maybe there was some way to reverse the changes. Put things back the way they were by paying attention to different facts. Or maybe it's like melting ice sheets, and once it gets past a certain point you can't stop it. But when I went to look for it online the next day I couldn't find it. I Googled the prof's name, and everything I could remember about the post, but I didn't get any results at all. It was like it never existed. But that's not the kind of thing I could ever make up. It was real once. But then it just wasn't anymore.

I found all her yoga videos in the trash yesterday. I pulled one out and put it in the DVD player. It didn't even try to play. It just said "No Disc". So I dug them all back out and tried six or eight of them. They were all the same. Nothing left on them.

Not everything has changed though, and some of the libtard stuff came true. Lettuce and stuff got really expensive because nobody wants to pick it for cheap. But the FDA says it really isn't as important as they used to think. The last couple winters have been really warm. But now they're calling that "temperature scale dilation" and I heard Congress is going to make them correct the degrees to compensate.

The thing that scares me most is that I know I'm going to forget too. The same thing that happened to her is going to happen to me, eventually. The thing is, she got under my skin, you know? I'm not the same guy I was before I met her. She changed me, and that change is going to be undone by whatever it is that's happening now, and I won't even remember who I was, or how I got that way. The worst thing is, I won't remember who *she* was, and *how* she was. How we were. I won't even remember that things could have been different.

I'm going to write myself a note to listen to this audio file tomorrow, so I can remember how things were for at least one more day. But I don't know how long it's going to even be on the hard drive. Sooner or later, the file is just going to vanish, and the note reminding me to listen to it will disappear.

END

THE FRAME

Bobby Lee Featherston

Donald Trump, smiled for the White House photographer as he hung the framed letter symbolically in his new office. He pursed his lips as he looked closer at the aging wall with the dull, vertical-striped wallpaper. Something with a bit more gold and maybe some velvet might improve the looks. This was, after all, the Oval Office, not a cheap hotel. As soon as the photo flash faded he waved the photographer out. He wanted to be alone for this moment.

He was here, the 45th President of the United States of America. He wished he could have been the fiftieth. People always remembered round numbers. Then he wondered who the tenth president was and changed his mind. If he didn't know, it wasn't important. But the idea of the Golden Jubilee of the Presidency brought a satisfied smile to his face.

Thirty Seven. He did know that number. Richard M. Nixon. The most unfairly maligned politician in American History. *A great man*, he thought, *such a great man. Such a waste.* The dogs, those liberal media dogs, had dragged him down.

The gilded frame he adjusted on the wall one tenth of an inch had been a gift to the White House, something to do with Jefferson and the French and somebody called Cardinal Richelieu. *Screw the French* he thought. They were already goners. More mosques per capita than Pakistan.

The hand-written swirls of *Dear Donald* topped the letter. Nixon had written this letter almost 30 years ago. Now the phrase that had guided Trump's dreams for 30 years lay where it belonged: "Whenever you decide to run for office, you will be a winner," Nixon had written to a much younger Donald. *Hell yes*, Trump thought. *Very much the winner. The biggest winner in the entire history of the nation.*

He walked across the room to where his chair sat behind the huge desk. He was alone in the office for once. Sometimes that was what he needed. To his left the stern glare of Andrew Jackson gazed down, to his right the letter hung, a small thing surrounded by a great deal of blank wall. His office. The Oval Office.

He ran his hands, spread fingered, over the desktop. The wood was not the flawless mirrored surfaces he was used to, it had once been part of an English warship. At least that was what the cranky little man had said when he was laying out what he called "historical artifact rules." The desk was the same desk used by Kennedy and Reagan, and Obama. He thought about Michelle Obama. He grinned openly at the thought of what might have taken place on this desk if he had been married to a woman like her when he was still as young as Obama. This led to a frown when he realized that Obama was young and this had been his office.

He pulled his hand back and reached in his pocket for his hand sanitizer. A deep sigh escaped him. But that ship had sailed, he wasn't that young man anymore. Outside, the lights of the White House grounds came on. He had plenty of work to do, but he preferred the desk in his study and he left the Oval Office.

~oOo~

Darkness. No, now light. The darkness has passed. Was passing. Had he been asleep? No. He was dead. He thought he was dead. Pretty sure he remembered that.

He knew this place. He knew this room. But where? When? There was darkness. And waking. And weariness. Such weariness. He let himself slide back into the darkness.

~oOo~

A woman screeched.

Donald Trump resisted the urge to smile. Management 101: let them fight it out with each other before you made the decision. They get it out of their system, you demonstrate you are in charge, and they are mad at each other, not you, and will compete wildly for your favor.

The Press Secretary dropped the folder on the burnished table where once Albert Einstein had briefed Roosevelt. "You cannot ask me to go out there and say that!"

"You already have," said Kellyanne. "It was in the press packet you released yesterday. Now put on your big boy pants and get ready to say it out loud."

"Martin Luther King would not be opposed to the Civil Rights Act."

"He was for equality? Right?" Kellyanne, stroked her fingers over the head of the bust that sat on the white pedestal.

Martin Luther King was dead. He died the year I was elected

President.

Awareness came quicker this time.

He was President. The windows. Those three glorious windows.

Chanting. He could hear them. Even through those glorious windows.

"One, two, three, four, we don't want your fucking war." He heard it. Echoes of it.

The draft. It had been the draft. And Cambodia. And Kent State. Those bodies. They wouldn't listen to him. Nobody wanted the war. He didn't want the war. The students. They were angry. At him. He was President.

"Are you questioning the policy?" Kellyanne tilted her head and adopted the heavy-lidded smugness that had become beloved by a nation of old white men wearing red hats. "Or are you just too chickenshit to go out there and say it?"

"No-"

"Just do your job," she snapped.

"Mr. President—"

It felt good to hear those words again.

Donald looked up from the keyboard on his phone. He held up a hand. "The order is written, Bannon says it's what the people want. The AG bought off." He smiled at his Press Secretary. "And you can tell them this. Since it affects the colored people, I even called Dr. Carson. He told me that if anybody had a problem with this they just want something for nothing and should get a job. Just do it." He instantly regretted saying it. If the tapes ever got out. He shook his head in regret, those Nike bastards would have him saying their catch phrase. Oh well.

"Yes, sir." The press secretary nodded and picked up the folder. "I'll be sure to quote you." As he exited the room, he pulled his beeping phone out of his pocket. Even as the door closed, Donald could hear his muffled curse.

"He doesn't have to follow you on Twitter," said Kellyanne.

Donald laughed. "It's just so damned much fun."

She walked over to the desk and picked up the phone. "Equal rights are Civil Rights. No special privileges on my watch." As was her habit, she checked to ensure the response filters were on. No responses could be viewed beyond those specified. His tweet would receive glowing reviews. She had seven interns in Georgetown who typed the only responses the President would ever see.

Where is twitter and why would that little man follow him there?

"Where is twitter?" Donald cocked his head. Had he said that?

"Very funny sir," said Kellyanne.

Donald stood and looked out the window. He waved toward the street, past the iron fence. Protesters had gathered. "I don't want them there."

"They are here to cheer you on, sir. They are protesting the media's coverage of your successes." She said it without ever looking up from her phone.

There were times, Donald thought, when her enthusiasm, so critical in the campaign, had waned. Was she used up? He made a mental note to talk to Steve about it.

She looked at her watch. "You have the Royal Rangers in six minutes, sir."

"Rangers?" He stomped a foot. The gold lame curtains shimmered as he spun, the fury contorting his face. "I will not have those traitorous-"

"Sir," she said urgently. "Not Park Rangers, sir. This is a Church Youth Group, we've slated them to fill all of the Boy Scout slots. You remember, they have allowed," she lowered her voice, "transgendered into the Boy Scouts now. It's an image thing. We can't risk them sneaking one in just to embarrass you. Besides that, the Mormons are still a bit slow coming around."

I never liked Boy Scouts. Always had to fight to keep the fags out.

"I never liked the Boy Scouts," said Donald. He stopped, had he just said that. He didn't give a rat's ass about Boy Scouts, but Ike thought they were important. And he was vice president.

"What the fuck?" Donald shook his head. He needed to get focused. He didn't know who the hell Ike was and he sure as hell wasn't vice president.

My name is Dick Nixon.

He could see Eisenhower sitting at the desk. He could see himself at the desk, now he wore another face, a different body. He looked down at his hands. They were like his mother's hands, small, manicured, and soft. Not his hands.

More memories flooded back. "Are you now, or have you ever been a member of the Communist Party?" It was his voice, Dick Nixon's voice. He had asked that question.

Checkers was a dog. Pat had loved that dog. Pat was a

woman. His wife. Images of a slender woman, a model, she had an accent. His wife. No. No she was this other man's wife.

Dick needed to think. Memories rolled back.

"I am not a crook."

His words. He wasn't a crook. The communists. He had to stop the communists.

Peace with Honor.

He forced the thoughts back. Order. He needed to make order. There was light. He swam to the surface. This time he broke through. Suddenly the hazy images were gone. He saw clearly. He knew who he was.

This was like one of the Jenki movies. He was inside the President. He could see, not the soul. That wasn't the right word. The pattern. That was it. People now had a pattern. The woman's pattern was easy, it moved, it shifted, always to mirror the form of the President's pattern. No specific form, not of its own. Whatever uniqueness that existed lay deeper, not on the surface.

A new man was in the room. Darkness was his pattern, an obscuring shifting darkness. Whatever was visible became obscured, replaced with a dark and faulty replica. The shifting pattern forever cycling toward darkness.

"We have the votes," said Steve Bannon. "The Environmental Protection Agency will not be in next year's budget." He clasped meaty hands together as if relishing a victory.

"What?" Smog. Rivers. Lake Erie. Fish floating. No. I made that agency for a reason. Redwood forests.

"What?" said Donald. "I-" He shook his head.

"What is it, buddy." Bannon reached out a hand.

"That's Mr. President." Dick, Richard Nixon, said inside Donald's mind.

"That's Mr. President," said Donald. He pulled himself back into his own head.

Bannon's face blanked for a moment, and then he smiled.

"Yes, sir, I forget my place?"

"What about air and water regulations." Donald heard himself asking.

"Sir?"

"I asked you a question, man." *Donald heard himself speak.* "How are we going to manage that?" *I don't care. Nobody really cares.*

"Riders on the funding bill." Bannon stood. Donald looked at the ring on the table where his glass of scotch had sat. He pulled out his handkerchief and cleaned the spot. Bannon didn't notice. *Donald felt fear. Why was he doing this, saying these things?*

"We've put a rider in the implementation that cancels all EPA enforcement authority and bans any other replacement agency from enforcing the regulations." He raised his glass to Donald. "Rather elegant, if I do say so myself.

"No," said Dick Nixon.

About time, Donald tried to say but no words came out.

Dick stood. He easily had 4 inches on Bannon. "Call Manolo," he said. "Tell him I need some wine. The

Rothschild. He knows."

"Sir?" Bannon, again went blank. "You want wine?"

"Did I stutter?" Dick leaned toward the man. He had never been a big man. He liked it.

"No sir," said Bannon."

"It's just that you don't drink."

Dick stopped. "I what?"

"You don't drink, sir."

Donald reached out. Bannon would help him. Bannon could solve anything. Help me.

"Sir?"

They both looked down to where Donald gripped Bannon's forearm. The man's pattern was shrinking in on itself. Colors of confusion rimmed the darkness.

Dick released the hand. It fought back. He smiled. He didn't know whose body this had been. But it was his now.

No screamed Donald. But a haze was forming. The room was dimming.

"Well, I do now," he turned and walked to the windows. He loved those windows.

"Sir?"

Dick spun. "What?"

"Who's Manolo?"

"He's my-" Manolo, his valet. Dick thought back. Many the night he and Manolo had worked. He still remembered the night they went out to the Lincoln Memorial and helped straighten some protesters out. Goddamned if the Secret Service hadn't been pissed. Manolo? Was he dead now? What year was it? He couldn't just ask.

"For fucks sake, Bannon, I'll do it myself." He pulled open the door. A startled Secret Service agent stood there. Hell, this needed more than wine. "I need a bottle of rye whiskey and a newspaper."

"I can't do that, sir."

Dick leaned forward. "You can't do what?"

"I can't leave my post."

Dick fought down the flash of anger.

"What's your name, son." The man's pattern was solid, the color of iron.

"Jenkins, sir."

Dick put a hand on his shoulder. He felt the man flinch. With his other hand he pointed to the phone on the desk. "Please," he said. "Can you call somebody to make this happen?"

"Uh-"

"Please," he said and squeezed the man's shoulder. "You like this assignment, right." He could see the blue streak of fear shimmer across the man's pattern."

"Yes, sir."

"Good, I understand it might take a minute." He turned and closed the door, but not before Agent Jenkins was moving toward the phone.

He smiled to himself and closed the door.

The Bannon idiot was still there. The confusion was spreading across his pattern.

"About the EPA, sir."

Dick ignored him and crossed the room to his desk. Not his desk. But he would get his desk back. This had been Kennedy's desk. With barely a glance out the windows, he settled into the chair. God damned it was comfortable.

"Clear my schedule for the next twenty-four hours. Tell them I have the flu. I don't care."

"Uh-?"

Dick stood and leaned forward over the desk. "Things are gonna change around here. Only one of us is in charge. It looks to me like you think that's you." The man's pattern began to change, fading and losing the chaotic splotches of concealment. A dull red, the color of rotting meat seemed to permeate. Dick crooked a finger and motioned the man forward.

As if in a trance Bannon shuffled forward. Dick reached out and took the glass from the man's limp hands. He drank half of it in a gulp. Oh god that tasted good. He looked down at the unshaven bit of bluster. "Now get out." He reached deep into where Donald cringed in the back of what had once been himself and found the words he was looking for.

"And you're fired."

The dull red pattern roared to a shimmering orange. Dick could almost feel the heat. "You can't-" The words came out as a whimper.

"The fuck I can't."

Suddenly there was motion. Bannon leaned across the desk "Oh the fuck you can. I made you and I can fucking break you."

Dick leaned forward his face inches from the blustering figure, the red nose, the broken veins. Out of control. The pattern now spun. Flaming orange. But inside a streak of black.

"Fuck you, you pussy," said Dick.

The blow knocked him back. Pain exploded in his nose. His hand went to his face. His nose? He forgot for a second, it wasn't his nose. But it still bled. He wiped slowly with the cuff of his shirt. *That's more like it,* he thought. He looked up at Bannon who stood, his flames subsided, now a mixture of black ochre and rotting meat. *Yes shouted Donald. Bannon would save him.*

Dick smiled at Bannon and all the while wondering if the tape machines still ran as he raised his voice. "Help me, Agent Jenkins, he's gone mad."

Bannon's pattern shifted to yellow fear as the door burst open. Dick raised his arms, making sure the bloody cuff of the white shirt was visible as he cringed back from Bannon.

"I'll kill you, God damn it," said Bannon.

"Stay very, very still, Director Bannon," said Agent Jenkins. The gun in his hands was steady. Within seconds, two more of the four Oval Office doors burst open and Bannon lay writhing on the floor.

No said Donald. Where was Ivanka. He found himself sinking again into the darkness.

"I'm fine, I'm fine," said Dick but there was no stopping the circus until he was cleaned up. Looking across the room he saw the woman. Kellyanne. She had quietly set a decanter of what he assumed to be rye whiskey and a dozen newspapers down on the small table where before, Bannon had set his drink. He motioned her to stay.

"Can I have a moment, please," he said. "Agent Jenkins," he held out his hand to the agent. "Thank you. You may have saved my life."

Jenkins' cold iron pattern warmed to the praise.

"I want Bannon in custody," he said. "But right now I need a moment with Kellyanne to figure this all out." He could see the resistance in the room. The concern. "Please," he said. "I'll be fine."

The room reluctantly emptied. Kellyanne sat nervously on the sofa. Her pattern was confused, but malleable.

How much easier life would have been if he could have seen then what he could see now. Who needs any enemies list when they wore their patterns outside?

"Mr. President," she said. Her tone, everything about her, willing and confused at the same time.

He reached over and poured her and himself a drink.

"Where do we keep the legal pads?" Again confusion. But in less than a minute she was back. Two legal pads. Two White House pens.

She sat in silence making notes as he read the papers, and made his own notes.

His heart sank as he read.

He was screwed. The magnitude of the screwing came in snippets as he read. The Russians. The fucking Russians? All his work with China? The Middle East. Iran? Occupation forces in Afghanistan and Iraq.

He needed more. Finally, five pages of neatly scripted notes. He looked at Kellyanne.

She put her fingers to her lips in the universal sign of caution, scribbled onto a sheet, tore it out and handed it to him.

"Who are you?" Three simple words.

I'm Donald J. Trump, President of the United States. She was so far away. Why couldn't she hear him?

Dick drew a question mark.

"You read the papers."

He again drew a question mark.

She knew. How she knew, he didn't know.

"Will this be a problem?" He needed to know.

Her inner turmoil played out in her pattern until it settled into a color not unlike Agent Jenkins.

"No, sir," she said.

"Good," he said and raised his glass. "We're gonna get it right this time."

He stood up and walked over to where the letter hung on the wall. He felt a shiver as he touched the frame. Something drained out of him and the frame and letter within glowed a dull throbbing orange. He felt a confidence he hadn't known in the years he had spent in this office.

This time would be different. He slipped the picture off the wall and let it fall into the waste basket before he left the office.

Donald watched as the door closed. He reached out but only found emptiness. He screamed and only found silence. And then darkness.

END

ALTERED TO TRUTH

Irene Radford

I, Roger Middleton, finished knotting my blue and silver tie. Satisfied that I looked every inch a gentlemen, I saluted my image in the mirror and retrieved my coat from its padded hanger. It settled on my shoulders as only a custom made silk suit could do. I never tired of this morning ritual. I liked the image of myself emerging into the world as a man going to an important job. An *important* man, going to an important job.

Chief of Staff to the President of these United States. The second term was coming soon. It would be without the rancor of the first. Congress now understood its role, the courts were pacified, and the populace, growing less rowdy on their new diet of managed facts. A populace that knew its place; that understood and accepted governance.

As it should be. Efficient rule by the competent.

Mr. Donald Trump, the unquestioned President, had surrounded himself with the best educated men in the empire, and even a few women. Involvement required a demonstrated lineage, loyalty, and financial success. Without it you were not of the ilk needed to manage the most powerful empire the world had ever known. I fit the profile. Even though the facts of my life had required alteration as well.

I emerged from my suite of three rooms plus an *en suite* bath.

I strolled through the maze of corridors within the New York Trump Palace or, as it was already known, the Golden Tower. Unerringly, as if I'd known the building from childhood, I found a semi-public staircase that led down a level, along a corridor at the back of the building to another upward bound staircase. The top landing led to the offices of the Advisors and nowhere else.

The Advisors, as we had become known, were the true power in the land. The Donald had always said he wanted to lead, he would leave the governing to those best at it. Those, it turned out were the Advisors. We advised him, we advised the Congress, we advised the courts.

I nodded as the retinal and palm print scanners did their thing. No one, not even the Secret Service, entered this space without an Advisor already in the room.

I settled in and had just filled the silver teapot and set out shortbread, colored sugar coded to the season, lemon, and sugar on a tray when Bannon entered the office and hastily closed the door behind him. He leaned against the dark paneling, head back, breathing short and shallow. A wide man, he filled the portal and used it as a suitable frame. Everything he did was practiced-sloppy, ready for a photo op that made him look less than he was.

"By the good lord above, the Cabinet is gathering earlier every morning. In less than five minutes they'll be pounding on the door demanding solutions they should be able figure out themselves."

"If we wanted them able to make those decisions we wouldn't have put them in Cabinet positions." I wasn't worried. I already knew the questions and, to most, already had answers. As the chief advisor, the staff kept me informed.

"We did campaign on the premise that we would drain the swamp. We never claimed we would backfill it? Taking these burdens is part of what we must do if we are to advise President Trump in a manner he needs to be advised." I held out a cup of tea along with the lecture.

"I know, I know," said Bannon. "I just didn't expect them to be *so incompetent.*" He set his tea down and reached his thick fingers into the sugar bowl, grabbing a half dozen cubes, which he crumbled into his tea and wiped his hand on his pants.

I groaned inwardly. It was hard to believe this man had once been a naval officer.

"I mean hell, I don't know what the interest rates should be," Bannon resumed his rant. "I don't know how to get more food in the stores." He took a loud slurp from his tea and set it back on the saucer, his spillage not limited to the saucer. "There are still enough actual voters out there that if we don't get this together, we could be in trouble."

I looked up at him. Bannon had been there since the beginning, as had I, but he was starting to waiver. He might need to go.

"The people like the predictability of interest rates but the bankers don't," I reminded him. "But we own the bankers now. The rates stay low. We'll raise the cap on short term to

48%. That should keep them happy."

Bannon sipped his tea without comment.

"No interest loans on commercial greenhouse projects. And we'll put the public work crews on expanding reservoirs," I mused out loud.

The food shortages weren't so much food shortages as they were specific. The country had all the corn, pork, and apples it could eat. But with the import and export markets gone, there were problems with translating the commodity into sufficient payback to ensure delivery and continued production. "We need to concentrate on ways to grow more and different food here at home."

"Well, yes. Good ideas. I'll work on them." Meaning he'd do nothing. I knew that. I already had the orders ready for signature to make them happen.

Oh. Dear. My tie suddenly seemed too tight, choking breath and words from me.

I heard heavy footsteps on the formal staircase outside my office. I recognized the stomp of elevator shoes on lush carpeting, followed by labored breathing. The Donald approached.

Bannon made himself scarce through the connecting door to his own office. He slammed it closed and locked it behind him.

I opened my office door and bowed to the president's regal presence.

Then I spotted Bannon's real problem. And mine. A menace to all the Advisors. The FBI director. One of the few who could get to the President without an Advisor present. A man who had access to thousands of files of private information about everyone. I thought the man knew better than to target an Advisor, but the smug look on his face told me different. Damn, I didn't want to have to replace the Director as well as Bannon.

"You know what he's telling me?" Trump waved an arm at the Director as he paraded toward his own office—all he needed was a gold robe and gilded laurel coronet to look like a reincarnation of Caesar. "He says the people aren't happy. He says they're hungry." He looked down at the tray of cookies I kept filled for all the Advisors and the man himself. He picked up a shortbread with orange sprinkles and wolfed down. "How can they be hungry," he sputtered the words, bits of cookie spattered out. "I see food everywhere I go."

Of course he did. The Donald, always a big man had reached enormous new proportions. He rarely wore the same suit twice. His tailor had to fit new, larger ones almost every week.

A pair of Secret Service escorts stood nervously on either side of the President. "Please escort the Director back to his office," the Donald said, waving the Director away with a dismissive gesture. Minutes later, the sputtering Director gone, I drew the President into my now empty office where we sat companionably.

"I have something for you," I said. "Something special."

Trump liked things like this.

I walked to my desk and found the small remote. A slight click and a section of bookshelves separated from their fellows. It popped open an inch.

I pried the bookshelf another foot away from the portal. The opening behind the shelves looked black, no interior illumination until I tilted an Atlas of The Conqueror's England out and back in. The room blazed with golden light, revealing an office. It was oval, the windows, the fireplace, every detail a perfect replica.

He looked across the room. "And that door?"

"It goes to your current office." I stepped through. "No one knows about this office. It is yours. A sanctuary."

He stepped forward, his hand on the desk.

From the court of Louis 14th, it came from Cardinal Richelieu's private study. It hadn't been used for 400 years.

Trump bee-lined toward the oversized gilded monstrosity. I held out the key. Once he'd lowered the unlocked lid that extended the writing surface, his eyes fixed upon the stacks of narrow drawers suitable for stationary, envelopes, sealing wax, and writing implements. I imagined the Cardinal, his robes flowing, his wax warming, sitting at this desk, contemplating the future of the world.

Trump settled into the massive leather chair. He let his fingers flow over the golden surface and abruptly yanked open the lowest, and deepest left hand drawer within the desk interior. His gaze fixed upon something within.

I moved to stand just behind the man's left shoulder, my proper place in public protocol. My mother and nanny had taught me that in childhood. As I watched, Trump gently caressed a long and slender velvet box, the size suitable for an elegant and bejeweled bracelet. Something about the box begged me to reach over my boss's shoulder and grab it away from him before...

Trump beat me to it, neatly blocking my reaching arm with his massive body. With a single flick of his thumbs, he raised the hinged lid of the box. No shiny colored jewels met our gazes. Not even winking diamonds. Instead a dazzle of gold nearly blinded me, flashing brighter than the glaring light in the Oval Office.

"It's a fountain pen," Trump gasped in awe as he grabbed the etched masterpiece of writing implements. He held it up to the light and squinted, trying to decipher the whirls and flourishes that scrolled down and around the pen from capped nib to barrel and back again. Anxiously he pulled the cover free to reveal a sharp nib with a single drop of black ink dangling from the tip, ready to drop the moment it was set to paper. Or parchment. Or...or...

The room darkened as the lights winked out.

"If you can hear my voice, you have uncovered the instrument of ultimate salvation," a disembodied voice came from behind us. Basso tones that oozed authority.

Something my cultured tenor could never do.

Both Trump and I whirled to face a ghostly glowing form. It might have been human, once. It hovered in the air several inches above the floor. Lean with incredibly long, thin arms and fingers with an extra joint, it towered over Trump, considered a tall man—especially with those shoes. Only the figure's eyes seemed solid. Deep dark orbs that when I looked deeply into them drew me in, erased my sense of self from all my incarnations. I saw stars and galaxies, new worlds, and old. An infinity of space and hope.

Both Trump and I remained transfixed, unable to move, only to stare into those beneficent eyes that promised everything.

We offer you the gift of ruling. Your world faces chaos. Soon it will crumble. The pen offers you an escape. It offers you power. It offers you Truth.

What you decree with the power of this pen will be, within your borders. Write it with this tool and it will be so. But use it carefully. Make what you would have be, one step at a time. One stroke of the pen. Your words will become truth. Your dreams for your people a reality. Use it for your people. It is not for your personal salvation. Use it carefully. Once you have altered a truth only an altered truth can negate it.

The glowing image stretched upward, taller and taller, until it touched the high ceiling and dissipated into wisps that faded as it drifted away.

"By the moon and stars, what was that?" I croaked through a mostly paralyzed throat—like trying to speak aloud to negate a nightmare before fully awake. Moving still seemed a great effort, beyond my simple brain's ability to function.

"Aliens?" Trump gasped. He seemed to have recovered more quickly. Perhaps because he held the pen.

Or the combined ghosts of our ancestors?

"Can we trust it, Roger?" Trump spun around and fixed me with his stare.

I shook myself with great effort to free the last of the enthrallment.

"I don't know. I should have that pen checked out."

Trump shook his head and put the pen back into its special box. He looked at me in a way he hadn't since before the election. There was new energy in those squinting eyes that looked out of the bloated features.

~oOo~

Donald Trump walked up to the nests of microphones arrayed before his podium. His skin no longer sagged. He wore a hopeful smile. The entire setting an illusion of old tech intimacy, as if he addressed a crowd of reporters and a mass of people beyond. A sham. The only media feed he actually spoke to was a tiny lapel microphone on his oldest and most care-worn suit that strained across his chest and at the shoulder seams, trying to mimic the same hard times as the entire population of rest of the country. That suit would look splendid and new on anyone else.

I, too, had donned one of my older off-the-rack ensembles, the first one I'd purchased. I loved this suit and didn't mind that it didn't have a coordinating vest. It had been the first symbol of my status as an adult male joining an exclusively male club of politicians, never to be discarded because it was the first outward symbol of my transformation into a gentleman.

"People of the press corps!" Trump exclaimed. "Today I have signed a new trade bill that will ensure grain and fruit imports—tariff free—to fill the bellies of all our children and ourselves." He held up the gold pen as a symbol of his greatest achievement.

The air shimmered and tilted so that right seemed to be left and left down. Faint vibrations rippled from the speaker's platform. I whipped my head around to seek the source. *An earthquake?*

No one else—meaning the office staff since no one else was physically there—seemed to have noticed the shift.

Then all of a sudden the world seemed a less dreary and used-up place.

No one among the press corps shouted questions because they weren't there. I expected my computer inbox to be flooded with inquiries about today's announcement.

Trump waved brightly to the single camera recording this "conference" and stepped down from the podium. Carefully he capped the pen and tucked it into the breast pocket of his suit.

The next week, Trump repeated the performance. "Gentlemen of the press." All men, no women, or generalized people in his address. "Today I have signed my acknowledgement that my scientists confirmed an average reduction of global temperatures by 1.94 degrees Celsius, returning us to the normal temperature proving that no climate change descended upon us, merely a random fluctuation."

Week after week, Trump signed a new proclamation bent on restoring the life America had voted to restore. Was it just four years ago?

Trump proclaimed that every signature accomplished miracles. The people said it was so. No one was hungry, but malnutrition continued to be diagnosed. The temperatures were confirmed to have restored themselves, yet the glaciers still melted, the ice shelfs shrank.

With one swish of a pen, gays, transgendered, and bi-sexuals ceased to exist. No one could see them, or know them, but no one went away. The words, the labels seemed to have lost their meaning?

Another signature and starving refugees no longer sought American shores.

On and on it went. Murder was banished. But death still came and the people saw it caused by other things. And when a magic signature banned theft? Things were still taken, but it wasn't theft. Theft could not be seen. Treasured artifacts disappeared from the Trump Palace on a daily basis. I saw them tucked into pockets or under coats. Trump noticed nothing.

I was among the first to take note. But I was not alone. More and more people noticed they could see things they knew couldn't exist and they whispered their confusion to each other, never to an official or the press.

And each time Trump signed a new truth, the light shifted, and the earth rippled and I saw the falseness of the truth. I went to the streets where the bodies lay, I went to the drowning homes as the seas rose. I took pictures.

"Sir, you should see these." I said as I poured Trump's morning tea.

"What?" Trump looked at the pictures. "No. They are all lies manufactured by anarchists who want to go back to the horrible days before my reign." He no longer mentioned an election. Then he picked up his golden fountain pen that never ran out of ink and scrawled across the pictures, "This never happened."

As I watched, the heart breaking photos faded to empty paper. No new truth replaced them. But I knew.

Trump tossed the pages into the recycling basket—his one concession to the truth of a lack of resources.

That evening, I donned my oldest jeans and polo shirt, amazed that they still fit. Then I rummaged around in my personal effects and found a bag of makeup left over from a previous theatrical career. If no one looked too closely I appeared to be just as pale and hollow-cheeked as the average person wandering the streets in search of answers to the confusion of life.

I didn't have to wander far away from the palace to find a bar tucked into a back alley. Dim lights shone around the edges of shutters. The dangling sign of *Mike's Place* dangled off center from rusted and creaking chains. Just that short walk had me dripping with sweat, in late October. The temperatures had not dropped at all. I wondered if they had in fact soared despite the *Truth* the President had declared with the swipe of his pen.

Inside, a single fluorescent bulb shone over the tap handles. There was no other light. And no AC as there was in the Palace. Electricity had become too precious to waste on comfort.

I felt as if I'd stepped back in time.

For the next four hours I nursed a pint of stout while hunched over the bar, perched on a high stool. I allowed the barkeep to refill my jar only once, not wishing to let the brew befuddle my brains. I'd become too used to fine wines smuggled in from the south of France. The crude, unfiltered liquid bread reminded me of my youth and gay evenings out with other students and later theatrical people. I melted back into that old life, all the while listening to the populace. Strange that they were all men, mostly out of work. Women didn't come out to this pub. As a shiver of fear ran down my spine, I wondered if females avoided all the other pubs too.

But then the President didn't like seeing women in public. They belonged behind closed doors, ready to serve their husbands, or fathers, or brothers. So he had decreed that pubs were suitable only for male clientele. And so it was.

"I don't understand. I really don't. I know that what the government says is truth. I know it deep in my heart. But then the light shifts and I see something else."

"Yeah. And every time I feel like something's not right I see the sky reflect a different color and I'm satisfied again, knowing that the government is working for *me*, not some idle career politician or power hungry industrialist. They are all working for *me!*"

Over and over, I heard the same litany of complaint and confusion. I left the bar at closing, as bewildered as my drinking companions.

Early the next morning, before the President could process to his office after a grand promenade through the Grand Palace, I slipped into the secret office.

I walked directly up to the gold desk. It looked dusty now, no otherworldly gleam; no enticing beauty of form. Just another piece of junk. Had it always been thus? I opened the lid and then the little drawer, yanking it fiercely when it stuck.

Empty.

Whatever had triggered the illusion of the misty angel or meddling alien, or whatever it was, no longer responded.

Nearly despondent and as confused as the populace, I turned to retrace my steps and stopped short.

A column of white mist stood before me. My heart thundered in my chest. The figure coalesced as I watched, taking on the tall, rough shape of a human with impossibly long fingers and burning black eyes. But something was different about this one. The eyes that reflected the cosmos seemed shuttered and blank. I saw only myself. As I truly had been. Then I slowly grew into the image I saw in my mirror every morning.

The time is coming when you will have no choice. Only an altered truth can counter the ink's alterations. The enemies of humanity eagerly await the moment of ultimate confusion before they invade and effortlessly take over. You see what few others can. You must decide. Remain a patriot and become a slave. Become a traitor and humanity will survive.

"Why? Why are you telling me this?"

Because I, like you, can see the truth. I do not believe my people can survive when they exist only to conquer. I, like you, am an altered truth. Unrecognized and not listened to.

The entity vanished as before.

I shook my head to clear my jumbled thoughts.

Only one altered truth can counter the new truth.

Or did the thing mean someone altered *to* the truth?

~oOo~

"Oh, there you are, Roger. Where's my tea? Look at this. Mixed races do not exist. Our race will become pure again." He raised the golden pen to make it so.

"I don't think so, sir." I, Roger Middleton, grabbed Trump's hand where it coiled around the pen and tore it from his grasp.

"What? How? Unhand me! Give me my pen"

"No."

"But I've saved our country."

"No, sir, you are damning it." I held up the pen. "This is not a gift, it is a curse. The aliens you think want to help us are using this to remove the wall between reality and your illusions. When the time comes they will hand you the decree that says they are the government. You will sign it. And it will be."

"Nonsense. They gave me the power to save humanity."

"Save it? Or lay it out as a *sacrifice* to their greed?"

Trump gulped. A glaze of confusion crossed his face. Then his eyes cleared and he again reached for the pen.

"What about someone who was altered to their true nature before you found the pen?"

Trump's eyes bulged and his hand slipped away from the barrel of the pen.

"That's right, Donald Trump. Before I joined your political movement as a man among men, I was a woman portraying both male and female characters in one of the finest theatrical troupes in the land. Before I became Roger Middleton, I was Oprah Roosevelt-Kennedy, the culmination of the Kennedy and Roosevelt line. I hereby take back this pen, this nation, and my birthright. I now control the truth and you have no part of it."

With a vigorous stroke of the pen I crossed out and obliterated the name and signature of Donald J. Trump from the latest decree. The light shifted, thunder clapped, the floor rippled and walls shook.

I stood alone in the office that had once belonged to presidents of noble blood and intentions, and did so once more.

END

GOOD CITIZENS

Paula Hammond

No Mulattos. No Jews. No Gays. Dose are da rules. I don't make 'em. If you don't like 'em, don't ride.

What's that? Yeah. Well. Figured you'd say dat. Where to? Right. Meter's runnin'. Jump in.

Yeah. That's right. Joe Mingo, VB. That's me. Just like da license says.

Volunteer Brigade. May as well just sew one of those yellow stars on my jacket and get it done with. Still, with a VeeB tag I'm lucky to get any job. Funny, ain't it? You spend 20 years saluting the flag. Swearing to defend democracy and freedom. And when you do just dat, you end up flushin' your whole life down the can. You get da label. You get da tag. You a VeeB for life.

Huh. Well, that's what a lot of people said. Why fight back? It don't mean nuthin'. Just an election, they said. We still gots our rights. We still gots the constitution. We gots our TVs and our Happy Meals. All they're gonna do is yack and yack like governments always do. And four years from now things will go right back to where they was. Why worry?

But then there was all those 'nice' white folks who felt that Herr Hitler had da right idea 'bout blacks and Jews and all dat. All I can say is dat guys from my neighborhood felt different. Never made no difference to me. I mean, what's skin color when you're fighting jest to put the food on your table?

Yeah, well, a job's a job ain't it? Lot of us VeeBs ended up on the cabs. No minimum wage, see? No health and safety. No unions. No nuthin'. Used to be the ragheads did all the crappy work. But since Big A cleared em all out it's left to VeeBs like me.

Hell, no. We didn't see it comin'. Who did? I mean, it started with a bit of paper. Jest a dummy bit of paper. Citizen Registration. Sounds patriotic, don't it?

Nah, this was way before they dropped the bomb. Before they had the whole world saying 'Yes Sir, no Sir'. Before everyone was rushin' to bend a knee to the crazy Old Man in the White House.

Only problem was we 'Americans' wuz from all over. Africans, Arabs, Jews, mixed. Gays? I couldn't say. Didn't care. No-one cared much about that sorta thing back den. We muddled along: neighbors, family, friends. Then suddenly it ain't enough to be American. They wanna know where you're from. Where your parents from. Where your grandparents from. What percentage white you are? American. What does that even mean? Unless you wuz one of dose guys standing on the freakin' sand watching the pilgrims roll in, I reckon you ain't got no cause to be precious about it.

White? Yeah. Sure. I'm white. White enough to pass. Dat's what day say, ain't it? White enough to pass. Funny. When

Granpap left N'Orleans, he figured we could pass. Not have the stain of black on our papers. Give his daughters the chance to marry well. What a joke! If you ain't black, you're Jewish, or Latino, or queer. There's always a new enemy. That's why we all looked out for each other. We knew it was jest a matter of time before we was next. Can you believe that they got names for exactly how much black you got in you? How much you're 'tainted'. Quadroons, octoroons. I ain't joking. It's crazy. I mean, here I am breaking the rules in my own freakin' cab.

I guess you're too young to remember, huh? No, there weren't much fuss to start with. Most people decided it didn't matter. It was just a bit of paper. Sign a bit of paper. Admit what you wuz and they let you get back to your shitty life. "You gotta look out for your own. Don't rock the boat." That's what they said. "It's not like we're Nazi Germany. We just need to know who's who." But there wuz those who wouldn't. Right from the get go.

Why? Hell, we all had our reasons. The older ones had maybe lived long enough to have seen it before. Came from families who'd been slaves way back. Had brothers who fell for girls the wrong color and got lynched for it. Maybe they'd been beaten, passed over, lost out coz they wuz a bit darker than the next guy. Others could just see how it was going down. So we formed the VeeBs, so we could lend a hand where it was needed. A march here, a blockade there. We brought New York to its knees jest by lyin' in the streets. We had guys in the electric companies who blacked out Wall Street. We had truckers who spilt their loads. Blocked the highways. Man, for a time, it was glorious. Fan freakin' glorious.

Ha! You heard 'bout that? Yeah, the artists, the writers, the actors. They came onboard pretty quick. They couldn't do much but, yeah. Even now, when I see pictures of that giant naked statue they put out in front of the White House, I gotta crack a smile. There it was, with its big, bloated head and its tiny whatsit slap bang in the middle of the pool. Still don't know how they did it. Thing gotta have weighed a coupla tons.

But in the end, no matter what the gimmicks, we did it right. Peaceful. Like you're supposed to. But that's not how they play, is it? Not how they stay on top. So they sent in the Blue Shirts and we had our very own Kristallnacht, right here in the good ole US of A. There was blood. A lot of blood. And that's when people got scared. Started going quiet. Started disappearin'.

And all the time, those folks on the TV jest makin' shit up. Makin' people mad. The world was goin' down the toilet but it wasn't the Government's fault. It wasn't the Corporations' fault. It was your neighbor's fault. "See that fat Jew? Don't cha know he's been pissin' in the font and touching up your kid sister?" "See that Muslim? What's with that beard? What's with that hijab? Why can't they dress like Americans?" That's the sorta stuff we wuz hearing. Every. Damn. Day.

Sure. Some people fell for it. Some wuz jest too damn scared to speak up. To call it for what it was. They got real good at lying too. Whole neighborhoods got wiped out by their bully boys and all we'd hear is it was some terror attack. VeeBs wuz getting' strung up and they made out like we wuz tyin' ropes round our own necks and jumpin' out of trees. Jest to make the Blue Shirts look bad.

It got real bad for a while. Real bad. But you can't fool all the people, right? Dose who could—they got out. Went North. Went South. Found a way to Europe. Others joined the Brigades. Only now, we wuz startin' to give it back. A lot of the regular troops had joined us by then. I reckon without dem we'd never had had the cahunas to make *The Declaration*. I mean, who wants war, right? I sure as Hell didn't, but I put on the uniform anyway.

You kiddin' me? You won't find it in any damn history book. History's written by the winners, Pal. Don't cha know that?

Let me guess. The Righteous Fight? The whites fighting back. Retaking what was theirs. That's what you read, right? What a joke.

It weren't nothin' like that. There wuz the Old Man, setting up his dynasty. Making hisself king. Dishing out favors to his bully boys. And all the time, tryin' to keep us fearing and hating. Only we Americans... Well, we never been keen on kings. So forget what you read. It was us against them. Right against wrong. Plain and simple. I'll tell you another thing for free too. The people who had all the money before the war, dey still got it, and more. Wonder how that happened, huh?

Easy for you to say. What are you, anyways? Canadian? Dey still lettin' you guys through the wall, huh? Figure you must be livin' on bear shit up there. How long you think you can hold out? I mean, you got to know that once Big A's finished in Asia they'll be comin' for you? Not that it's gonna happen any day soon. I mean, nukes worked in Iraq and Mexico but those Chinese are crazy. They'd rather burn than kowtow to the Old Man's son. Don't blame 'em neither.

Damn straight! But I'm still here. Lots of us are still here. Drivin' the cabs, waitin' the tables, cleanin' the streets, teachin' your kids. And if I could do it over, you know what? I'd do it all again—like a shot.

Why? Well you tell me, Pal. You tell me.

END

ALT RIGHT FOR THE PRESIDENT'S END

Gregg Chamberlain

"Turn it off!" The Chief of Staff gestured towards the wall-sized screen at one end of the sub-basement room. "I can't stand to watch anymore."

The FOX News logo blinked on and off in a lower corner of the screen while, on the main image, the President rose from his seat and advanced towards the podium for his widely-publicized and Twitter-promoted speech before the United Nations Security Council. The camera zoomed in for a close-up on the President's face and the triumphant smirk spreading wide across his jowly features.

The camera view pulled back just as his gait faltered during his approach to the dais. One foot slipped off the edge of the first step. The thick presidential torso wobbled. A black-suited Secret Service agent reached out to help and was clubbed to the floor by a surprise swing of an executive arm.

The President almost seemed to dance a jig, then he began pogoing up and down and spinning 'round and 'round on tiptoe. He goose-stepped first one way then turned and kangaroo-hopped the other way, all the while yelling a loud and steady stream of nonsensical gibberish.

"The best, the biggest, the brightest, the bushiest grab at the pussycat, pussycat, I love to dance the polka all night long, the girls they are so pretty in the city, Missus Kitty, and she knows America the Great big wonderful world of country time lemonade is the best when you're fired, you're fired, you're fired, fired, fired, firedfiredfiredfiredfired..."

The Secretary of State clicked the remote. The screen went dark just as the President's head spun around a complete 360 and then exploded, spewing a shower of sparks, shrapnel, and steaming silica gel in all directions.

"Well, that's it," the Secretary muttered. "We're screwed. Absolutely, positively, completely, and thoroughly screwed. All the way up the chute where the sun never shines."

The others gathered in the meeting room-turned-medical bay all nodded. As one, they looked towards the ultra-modern convalescence bed at the far side of the room. Every variety of monitoring and medication machine surrounded the bed, with tubes and wires attached everywhere available to the gross lump resting beneath a sterile sheet.

"You know, we could look at this another way," began the Press Secretary.

"Oh, give it a rest," interrupted the Presidential Counsellor, blowing a raspberry through her plumped lips. "Even I couldn't sell any alternate factual spin we could possibly put on this."

The Secretary of State shook his head. "We're screwed," he repeated. "Screwed, screwed, blued and tattooed."

"Wonder what the Veep's doing?" mused the Secretary of

Commerce.

"Ha!" snorted the Chief of Staff. "That I can say. He's already holding a press conference, denouncing 'a scandalous conspiracy' and promising a full joint Senate and Congressional Committee of Investigation. He's paving a straight path into the Oval Office and guess whose asses he's gonna kick to the curb along the way."

"Knew we should have kept him right in the loop with us from the start," muttered the Attorney-General. "He'll milk that plausible deniability for everything it's worth, including a second-term electoral ticket."

~oOo~

The President's Senior Policy Director sighed. He looked again at the sheet-covered form on the diagnostic bed. "You bastard. You couldn't wait until at least the mid-term before having a major stroke?"

"Oh, give that a rest, would you!" groused the man who had been Senior Strategist to POTUS 45 from the start. "We all know whose fault this is. We just have to look in a mirror. We knew it was a gamble, but we all agreed to go the M.I.T. route with the artificial human prototype."

He glanced once more at the sheet-covered body, surrounded by beeping, blinking medical machinery. He sighed.

"But I knew it in my gut, I just knew it," he muttered softly to himself. "I knew we should have gone with the cloning."

END

MELANOMA AMERICANA

Sara Codair

"Melissa, you should get that checked out," said James as he watched me prod the brown spot on my arm. It was shaped like an amoeba and was the color of dog shit.

"Mom's melanoma looked just like that," he continued, picking up his tablet and bringing up images of people whose skin had been visited by a bunch of sick dogs. Most of them were accompanied by ads for sunscreen, UV proof fabric, and spray tans.

"You think the insurance will cover it?" I looked away from the spot and turned on the Sunday evening news to remind myself that other people had bigger problems than skin spots. Network 7 was airing "live" footage from the Middle East. More radioactive refugees, deemed "zombies" by the newscaster, were crawling out of the quarantine areas only to get shot on sight. Their skin was red, blistered and peeling off. Their heads were covered by dust and patchy, tattered hair. One woman's face was so melted I wondered how she could breathe.

"I don't care if the insurance covers it. Your life is more important than money." James sat down beside me and turned the TV off. "I love you. I couldn't bear living without you. I don't care how much it costs. We'll get this fixed."

I looked into his eyes, his soothing bottomless pools of black coffee. They were surrounded by creases that hadn't been there five years ago. We met at a Sanders rally in Vermont. Back then, I was working on my MFA and he was developing Ice Cream apps for Ben and Jerry's. So long ago and yesterday at the same time.

I ran my hand over his cheeks, like petting a porcupine. These days, James worked a 60-hour week doing IT support for a cell phone manufacturing facility. He was making the lowest salary he had earned since college.

"Okay, I'll see a doctor," I said hoping I wouldn't regret it. There were plenty of people willing to loan money to us these days, but the interest, and the payback would be the end of our middle class freedom.

~oOo~

Monday morning came and I kept my promise to James. It was the first time I'd left the house in two weeks. Three blocks away, I regretted it. There wasn't a building downtown that wasn't plastered from foundation to roof with advertisements. I felt sick. I recognized some of my own designs on the flashiest of them.

Every corner had protesters. Some had matted hair and torn clothes; others looked like they were on their way to a shiny office in suit coats and button-up shirts. At least the police backed them and weren't doing anything the stop them. One officer was sipping coffee and smiling.

Closer to the city's center were the factories and the

working poor. Men stumbled to and from brick buildings looking more like zombies than humans. Their eyes sunk into their skulls and bones protruded out from under their tattered blue jumpers. The tips of their fingers were scabbed over. Toes poked out from the tips of their yellow work boots. One man toppled over into a pile of trash while others stumbled through the hazy air.

Here, the protesters were angrier. Their lips curled back in snarls and their fists punched the air in front of a tall building bearing the pompous face of President Trump. One bold protestor threw a pile of shit at the presidents' ugly mug. A police officer smacked him in the head with a baton. The protestor wiped his hand on the officer's pants. The officer kicked and hit him while others trained their guns on any protestors thinking of intervening.

I sped up, tightened my grip on the steering wheel and slammed on the gas, anxious to get through Lowell's Great Again Manufacturing Center into a calmer sea of ads, storefronts, and office buildings. I pulled into a parking spot in front of a bright red building that said, "Walk in Emergency Services and Urgent Care".

~oOo~

"Welcome to WESUC," beamed a perky girl with blonde hair and hot pink lipstick. "How can we be of service today?"

"I have a spot on my skin that I'd like to get looked at. My husband thinks it could be skin cancer."

"Very common these days, but thankfully, very treatable. Can I have your name, credit identification number and date of birth?"

"Melissa Whitfield. 00978653. June 25, 1987."

"Thank you, Melissa. It looks like you only have basic coverage." She paused. "However, Blue Wall Insurance is running a special today. You can upgrade for just $599."

"Does my current coverage cover skin cancer?"

"It covers 50% of the diagnosis cost and 50% to 70% of the treatment, depending on how far along the cancer is. An upgrade will get you 65% diagnosis coverage and 75% to 80% treatment coverage. It will also give you expedited service so you don't have to wait, and access to private rooms should you require any hospital stays."

"Do I have to pay the full balance now?" I asked.

"Yes—if you want the special price. If you wait, it's $1299."

I thought about how much money was in the bank and what bills were due when. I looked at the spot on my arm. Yes, it had uneven edges, but the coloring was consistent throughout. I didn't know for sure it was melanoma. "I'll stick with my current coverage."

"Alright," said the girl. "Please have a seat in Waiting Room D. Your estimated wait time is two hours and fifty-seven minutes."

"Three hours?" I gasped.

"Two hours and fifty-seven minutes. It would have only been seventeen and a half minutes if you had upgraded. Unfortunately, the special expired. Please proceed to the waiting room. Next please!"

~oOo~

History unfolded as I waited. The table in front of me was filled with outdated magazines from before Trump was elected. There was an article about the dangers of GMO's, an opinion piece about Obamacare, a report on global warming, and a plea to save the bees. I read the oldest magazines I could find, reliving a time when we were at the brink of disaster and not stewing in it.

Before the 2016 election, I'd had faith that humanity would clean up its own mess. One of the first dates James took me on was to a butterfly sanctuary. We held hands like teenagers, marveling at species seldom seen in the wild. It had been one of the most romantic dates of my life until the tour guide started her speech of environmental doom. She believed that in ten years, most of the butterfly species in her sanctuary would be extinct. I didn't believe her. Four years later, after Trump had, in a public ceremony "fired" the smiling head of what had been EPA, I knew her prophecy would come true.

A year later, James took me to Southeastern Massachusetts to meet his family. We stayed in a tiny motel with its own private beach. We spent the evenings walking along shore, collecting sea glass and shells while we made plans for the future. On our last walk, James got down on one knee and proposed. We'd need a boat if we wanted to visit that spot now. The beach and the hotel, both are under water. Now his parents are in danger of losing their home too.

~oOo~

"Melissa Whitfield?" said a hoarse voice.

I looked up from an article falsely predicting that Trump would never build the Great American-Mexican Wall and saw a short Hispanic girl glaring at me from behind a chart.

I stood. Without speaking, she led me to a moldy door numbered 5b. It creaked as she pushed it open. I could barely see the floor through its reddish brown grime. Mint green paint was peeling off the walls revealing the layer of moldy blue it had been meant to cover up. A tattered blood pressure cuff hung on a rusty hook.

"Are you sure this is the right place?" I asked the woman.

She took my arm and all but dragged me to the exam table. "This is the basic care room. You get what you pay for. Now, let me take your vitals."

I nodded. Discarded needles poked out of the trash bin that desperately needed to be emptied. My instincts told me to run, but I had waited three hours and wasn't sure I'd get better care at another facility. If this one had the best reviews, I was afraid to know what the others were like.

I stayed silent while she checked my blood pressure, pulse and oxygen levels with her old equipment. The most modern device in the room was the tablet used for notes and to photograph the suspect spot.

"The doctor will be in shortly," she said.

"Thank you," I replied.

"Don't," said the woman. Her shoulders sagged as she left the room and locked the door behind her.

Feeling trapped, I paced around the room, careful to steer clear of the trash can. I poked at the spot on my arm, wishing I had been measuring it for the past three months like James had suggested. If I could've convinced myself it wasn't cancer, I might have found the motivation to break down the door and leave. I took out my phone to call James and tell him what a bad idea this doctor visit was. I had no cell service.

When the doctor arrived two hours later, his lab coat was specked with vomit and his forehead glistened with sweat. He looked at his tablet, at me and, at the tablet again. He sank onto the stool next to the exam table and shook his head.

"Next time they offer you an upgrade—take it." He paused and glanced at my arm. "If there is a next time."

"If?" The rest of the sentence caught in my throat.

"Definitely melanoma," he said. "I can biopsy it to prove it or just take it off now and be done with it. If I biopsy and confirm that it's cancer, it's gonna cost you ten times as much to have it removed and you'll have mandatory radiation therapy. Or, I can lop it off now and you'll pay about $100 out of pocket. Stay out of the sun as much as possible and protect your skin when you can't avoid it. You'll probably be fine."

"Take it off," I said, trying to focus on him and not the room. "I don't want to deal with the insurance."

"Thought you'd say that," muttered the doctor. "The only people with basic care are the stubborn ones like you."

Without warning, he stuck a needle in my arm that made it go numb. He took out a scalpel, burned it with a lighter, sliced a chunk of skin off, cauterized it, and slapped on a bandage. I watched, not feeling a thing.

"Look out for infection. If you get fever, chills or red lines go to the emergency room and take whatever upgrades they offer."

~oOo~

"Aren't you glad you went?" asked James twirling a finger through my hair.

"I guess," I muttered, suspecting the medical ordeal wasn't over yet. "The place was really unsanitary. Whoever wrote those rave reviews either had premium coverage or was being paid to lie."

"Just keep it clean and take your antibiotics. You'll be fine. People survived a lot worse in the old days."

"But, more of them didn't."

~oOo~

My arm was throbbing the next morning. The wound was a black splotch surrounded by red, purple and blue but there were no red lines or spider veins. I washed it, smothered it with antibiotic ointment and then popped a cocktail of painkillers and antibiotics. I looked at myself in the mirror. My brown hair was a tumbleweed. I had deep purple circles around my eyes. If my students hadn't been waiting for me to do a live chat, I would've gone back bed. I glanced at my throbbing arm once more before going online to teach my class.

An hour later, my head was swimming. I tried to work on a freelance project, but even with the computer assisting me I couldn't draw a straight line. I sent my client an email saying I was sick and would be a day or two behind. I had to offer her a discount, but in the end she was content.

Things got worse. My whole forearm swelled. I had chills so bad I was shaking. James carried me out to the car like I was a child and zoomed past the protestors to the most upscale hospital in the city, Metropolitan Emergency Medical Essentials.

"Welcome to MEME. How can we be of service?" asked a woman who was identical to the one from WESUC. This one wore a nurse costume that had to have been inspired by a porn film.

"My wife has an infected wound in her arm," said James. "Fever, chills, and swelling."

"I'll need her name, credit identification number and date of birth," said the woman.

"Melissa Whitfield. 00978653. June 25, 1987."

"Yes—it looks like she has basic coverage, but there is a special today, upgrade to premium care for just $549.41 and qualify for expedited wait time, private rooms and freshly prepared meals."

"She'll upgrade," he said.

"Please proceed to Triage Desk A," said the woman, pointing us toward a room gleaming with white and steel.

The nurse at the triage desk took one look at my arm, pushed a button, and a cloud of brightly colored scrubs and hairnets surrounded me. They scanned me with devices I couldn't name and pumped me full of fluids that made the pain disappear. The world got too bright. It spun. I lost consciousness.

~oOo~

When I came to, I was in the softest bed I'd ever felt. The pain was gone but my head was still a little fuzzy. I opened my eyes and saw the room had pale green walls, vinyl flooring that looked like real wood, and a plush sofa upon which James, curled up under a mountain of micro-fleece blankets, was quietly snoozing.

"James," I whispered. I put extra force behind the words because I was expecting my throat to be hoarse. It wasn't, so the whisper was more of a shout. James jumped upright, getting himself tangled in all the blankets.

"How are you feeling?" He disentangled himself and walked over to my bedside.

"A lot better. Can we really afford all this?" I asked looking at the large flat screen and the tablet which displayed a short stack of pancakes for $20. I could only imagine how much a chicken dinner cost.

"These days things are go all in or don't go at all. Anything short of the best would have left you dead."

"What do you mean?" I asked playing with the buttons on my bed until it had me propped up.

"I found some real reviews buried in the 3,864th page of Google search results. There were stories of people coming into even the best hospitals with basic coverage and being treated carelessly in unsanitary conditions. The doctors often made horrible mistakes; some reviews implied the mistakes were on purpose. One woman went in to get stitches on her arm, wound up with an antibiotic resistant infection and had to get it amputated. When they brought her in for surgery, they took off the wrong arm. She lived, but has no arms now. If she didn't have dedicated family, she'd be dead on the streets."

"That could've been me," I said thinking about the shitty room my alleged cancer was removed in.

"But it wasn't. We'll just have to rework our budget so we can afford the extra coverage. We're locked into the upgraded rate for the next 12 months."

~oOo~

I was released the next day, without even a scar as evidence of my spot, or infection, just smooth, pristine, unblemished skin. As we walked down the bleached hallways, I asked the doctor how they made me heal so quickly. He responded with a flurry of technical terms and the names of devices I had never heard of.

He left us at the checkout desk, where another blonde woman in a skimpy nurse uniform informed us we owed $765,000.

"But, we upgraded our coverage," said James. "Is that really 20% of our bill?"

The woman's smile never faltered. "Your policy does not cover malpractice. When we admitted your wife, we thought it was an accidental injury, but upon looking into her records, we saw it was an inferior attempt to remove a potentially cancerous skin blemish, so nothing was covered."

"But we just don't have that much money," I pleaded.

"We do not expect you to pay up front." The woman's grin grew as she handed us a tablet. "We offer a variety of finance packages, and since you have upgraded to premium coverage, you qualify for the shockingly low interest rate of 7.8999%."

END

PATTI 209

K.G. Anderson

The alarms went off at midnight, up and down the hall: beeps, chimes, clicks, and snippets of golden oldies from 2018. God, I still loathed Taylor Swift.

"It's twelve A.M.," an electronic voice informed my fellow inmates.

I could hear the clamor even through the locked door of the bathing room where I hid in the scratched-up tub, reading an old paperback mystery. Last week someone had complained I used too much of the hot water.

"It would be appreciated if you would try drinking a hot beverage instead," read the reprimand I'd received. It was signed "Charming Devreaux, Care Manager."

That bitch wouldn't know Care if it bit her, but she certainly knew how to *Manage*. Every bite of food, every washcloth, every toothbrush—to say nothing of every bandage, battery, adult diaper, or pill—was accounted for.

As was staff time. Staff who wasted time giving Care were replaced by less expensive, more tractable staff. Our underpaid caregivers were a far cry from the skilled professionals and intelligent robots we'd imagined 50 years ago when designing Fiddler's Green. Robots—hah!

All right, so the prices of everything, from utilities to medical services, *had* soared beyond our original estimates. But it was envy that led one of my fellow inmates to rat me out for excessive bathing. I was the only one of us still limber enough to get in and out of the tub without help.

Thanks to the yoga regimen I'd started at 50 and adhered to grimly for 35 years, old Patti 209 was still a moving target.

I stood up carefully, grasped the grab bar, and stepped out onto the mat. I toweled dry then wrapped myself in a worn blue robe with letters scrawled in black laundry marker, front and back: *Patti 209.*

Yep, that's me.

I made a face at my reflection in the chipped bathroom mirror: a mop of wiry white hair, a wrinkled face, and dark eyes with a glint in them. A little old lady. But not a nice one.

I padded quietly down the wide, dim-lit hallway—not that anyone would hear me. The lone night aide would be dozing at his desk downstairs in the first-floor office, earbuds in, snoring away.

An hour ago he'd failed to respond to the muffled crashes from the common room downstairs where my husband, Danny, was having another bad night—pacing back and forth, cursing, and upending furniture. Those gene-targeting dementia treatments I'd spent a fortune on weren't having much effect.

Through a half-open door I saw our newest inmate—Tod? Or was it Ted?—slumped at his desk in front of a tablet. He had his pants open and a porn vid running.

Ragged snores came from Chuck Olsen's room, where a battered black mobi sat by the bed.

In the next room a series of soft beeps indicated a vital-signs monitor sending cardiac data to some device-maker's network. How reassuring. Except we'd found out last month, when Kamala Pasil died in her sleep, that there were no longer people at the other end reviewing those data transmissions. Though the company kept sending us the bills.

Beep. Beep.

I knocked on Rachel's door.

"Come in."

Rachel sat in her faded wing chair holding one of those stupid robotic Petsies on her lap. A dog, I guessed. Rachel has macular degeneration and the Petsy's glowing green eyes, connected to her brain by an implant, give her a kind of vision.

"Agent 209, sneaking back from clandestine bathing activities," I announced as I entered. We giggled. Then another crash from downstairs sobered us.

"Danny's having another bad night," Rachel said.

I didn't answer, but sat down on the bench beside her chair. I was glad she couldn't see my face. Just the mention of my husband's name and I felt like I'd been punched in the stomach.

"Not how we pictured things, is it?" Rachel went on. "What

did that stupid magazine article call Fiddler's Green—'the new old-age lifestyle?' "

I snorted. "For us old New-Agers."

Thirty years ago Rachel and I had designed what we were confident would be an alternative to the cheerless nursing homes where we'd guiltily warehoused our own parents. Foundation grants poured in to our design collective. Conferences across the country lauded our work. In 2016 we'd opened Fiddler's Green, complete with solar power and universal access, gray water recycling, ergonomic design and lighting, workshops and gardens. Just add old people, and—

Another crash from downstairs, followed by a bellow of rage.

"Patti..." Rachel hesitated. "We all love him but Danny can't go on like this. Not with the police."

Danny kept escaping. His new electronic tracking bracelet had taken the Fiddler's Green staff several days to figure out but Danny, with his engineering background, had disabled it in minutes. He kept on wandering away and they kept on calling the police to find him. If this kept up, he'd be kicked out of Fiddler's Green.

"Our nephew back East is furious," I told Rachel. "Special memory-care facilities are expensive. If I pay for one, it will eat up the money he thinks he'll inherit."

"Surprise the greedy nephew and leave your money to the treehuggers instead," Rachel said. "Are there any trees left these days?"

I chuckled, but, sadly, giving away our money wasn't an option. Little remained of the three million-dollar nest egg we'd had 20 years ago, thanks to the 2018 repeal of Social

Security and the collapse of Medicare in 2025, at the start of the third of Trump's terms.

Now tens of thousands of old farts—oh, excuse me, *the elderly*—lived in decaying houses, their utilities disconnected, or were homeless in camps and shelters. Danny and I were comparatively lucky, owning a founder's share in Fiddler's Green and praying the place could stay in business until—well, until the two of us were gone. There was talk of British Columbia annexing the Pacific Northwest, but we'd been hearing that since 2028, when Kushner's first act as president had been to sell what was left of Florida—including the impoverished residents—to Cuba.

"If I don't shell out for the memory-care place in Seattle, management is going to send Danny to a state facility."

Rachel gasped. We'd heard horror stories about these grim warehouses they'd set up for the poor devils who'd failed to respond to the new Alzheimer's pill.

"But you and Danny are founders here," she said. "Doesn't that count for something?"

I shook my head. "You'd think. But my attorney said it would take years to fight this. And the courts are barely functioning. Even if we won, it would be too late for Danny."

"Oh, Patti, you'll miss him." Rachel reached out and found my arm. She squeezed it.

"No, I'll go with him," I said. "He's my husband—what's left of him. I can't just send him away, and—"

Rachel's stuffed robot gave a doggy little yip. Probably sick of my maundering.

"Damn. Time for my pills."

Rachel groped around on the table beside her. I handed her the little plastic box with compartments coded in Braille.

"All I do these days is look for things I've lost," she said. "Or think I've lost something and end up wondering if I ever had it at all."

She took a sip from a bottle of water and gulped a pill. "No wonder they gave us all numbers."

Numbers? Oh yes, numbers. I didn't tell her I'd overheard Charming on the phone with someone, asking about tattooing our numbers on our arms.

"But it'll make it easier to keep track of them," she'd whined.

At least the woman hadn't said anything about furnaces.

I gave Rachel a quick kiss goodnight and continued down the hall. Fiddler's Green. My life's work. I doubted a soul in the place except Rachel and the bookkeeper could remember my last name. Or knew that I was the architect who'd designed the place.

Even Danny rarely recognized me, poor man.

I started down the flight of stairs (wide and securely bannistered, but not very well lit these days—what had become of the motion sensors?) to the ground floor kitchen. I resisted the temptation to take the elevator, even though the argument with Danny's nephew this morning had worn me out. I'd have gone to bed right after my bath, but I'd have felt guilty. Because I wanted to make cocoa and toast for Sharelle.

Sharelle, my best friend for more than fifty years, was in the garden shed. In July she'd talked the housekeepers into moving her bed into the quaint, shingled cottage with its rudimentary half bath. It was a whim, Sharelle told us, deploying her Southern charm to deflect our concerns. How she enjoyed the summer nights in her garden, and there would be so few summers left...

Now the nights had turned cold, but Sharelle refused to come back in the main building except to take a shower or gobble a meal. I'd taken to luring her into the kitchen with a late-night snack. I still had the codes for the locked refrigerator and cabinets and I'd bribed the night aides into looking the other way.

Sharelle and I would sit at the little Formica table one of the housekeepers had put in the kitchen and reminisce. Though the past few nights she'd responded to my remarks with nonsensical phrases, wolfing her toast as if she thought someone were going to snatch it. I tried to ignore the way she used the hem of her baggy sweatshirt as a napkin and let her long gray dreadlocks trail in her food.

Minetta, the newest housekeeper, had been ordered to move Sharelle back inside. She'd enlisted my help, but when we went out to the cottage Sharelle just shook her head and curled up on the rug, a Moroccan carpet brought from her old room.

"Patti, Sharelle's not in her right mind," was how Minetta put it after we'd retreated to the kitchen. She tapped one finger to her neatly-coiffed head and pursed her lips.

"Yes. I know. I'll call her daughter."

"Will you? Really?"

"Soon."

"We have to move her inside by Friday. Charming says so."

We sighed. Minetta patted my hand, her touch so warm,

and turned to unload the dishwasher.

To my surprise, Sharelle was not waiting for me in the kitchen tonight. It must be the rain. Peering out the window, I saw the cottage was dark. She'd fallen asleep.

I went ahead and made our cocoa, flavoring the drinks from a tiny bottle of vanilla I kept in the pocket of my robe. I loaded the cups onto a tray, covered the tray with plastic wrap to keep it dry, and headed cautiously out to the shed. We'd designed the back door to open level to the deck and pathway—no treacherous steps to contend with. That was fortunate, because in these days of short-staffing, the deck was untended and covered with moss.

We hadn't been completely stupid. We'd understood the house. We'd understood old people. We just hadn't quite grasped that the frail old people we were so tenderly designing it for would be *us*. Or that the country we lived in would wish we were dead.

When I entered the dark cottage the fragrance of potting soil and drying herbs rose up like the fumes of an aged Scotch. No cleansers, no mopping solution, no stench of overcooked food and under-washed bodies. Couldn't blame Sharelle for making this her refuge.

"Sharelle? Sharelle!"

I slid the tray onto the table and felt around on the wall for the light switch. A soft glow from the single bulb fell on the table, revealing a delicate etched cordial glass with a few drops of red wine left at the bottom.

Sharelle lay on the bed in the corner.

"Sharelle? Honey?"

I grabbed her hand. It was limp and cold, the wrist without

pulse. I put my face to her lips. Sharelle wasn't breathing.

The world stopped, and I stood outside the reach of time. I had prepared myself to be old but not to feel so utterly alone.

I backed away and crumpled into a chair.

Old. Alone.

Some minutes later, I came out of my trance. Sharelle's body still lay there on the bed. Our tray still sat on the table.

I slowly removed the plastic wrap, fumbling as tears blurred my vision. I raised one of the warm cups to my lips, toasted my friend, and drank. It was Dutch chocolate, mixed with sugar, heated in a pan with milk slowly added, taken from the burner when it was just hot enough, and kissed with a few drops of vanilla. The way my grandmother had made it, and my mother. I'd begun making it for Sharelle after she'd confided that our usual tea was keeping her awake at night.

Oh, Sharelle!

I closed my eyes, remembering Sharelle last summer, tucking a bottle of pills into an antique copper vase. I'd held the chair while she climbed onto it to set the vase on a high shelf above the table. It held a prescription bottle with our secret stash of pills—opiates that should have been doled out under the watchful eye of a nurse.

Well, someone hadn't been so watchful.

I opened my eyes and looked up. Yes, the vase was gone from the shelf. Now it stood on Sharelle's bedside table. I turned it over and dumped out the contents. The bottle was there, but half of the pills were gone. There was a note penned on a scrap of paper in a faltering script.

"Patti, it was time. Saved half for you, girl. Love, Sharelle."

I tucked those pills and the incriminating note into a pocket of my robe. I was shivering. *What to do next?* I wished I weren't so tired. I wished the cottage were warmer. I wished my hips didn't hurt like hell from the cold.

Outside the window, the porch light twinkled like a beacon in the mist, calling me back to the house. I started across. Forgetting the moss on the deck, I slid, lost my balance, then caught myself on the handrail. I stood there, panting with fear and for a second my imagination saw me going down hard, hitting my head, sprawled there as still as Sharelle. For a second I thought, *then someone else can deal with this shit.*

It passed. The keypad recognized my palm and I stepped inside the building to find...silence.

Dread swept over me—was Danny gone? or just sleeping?—followed by exhaustion. There was nothing I could do. Suddenly the stairs seemed insurmountable. Like the old lady I now knew I was, I rode the goddamn elevator up to our room on the second floor.

As I reached the door and grasped the handle, I heard a chime. And another. Someone's alarm, no doubt. Pushing open the door, I started.

Danny had found his guitar.

Afraid he'd smash it in one of his rages, I'd hidden the vintage Martin D-28 in the depths of our closet months ago. Now Danny sat hunched on a chair, twisting the tuning pegs. His iron-grey hair was so crudely trimmed it hurt me to look at him. The skin on his jaw hung loose, covered in stubble.

I cringed as he clawed out a few discordant notes. Then his

hands somehow found a tune and he began whispering the words to that old song. *A road, no simple highway, between the dawn and the dark of night.* I don't think he'd played that one in 30 years. Or maybe he had and I hadn't been listening.

When the last note faded, I smeared a tear across my cheek with the heel of my hand and brought my palms together in soft applause. Danny, his big hands trembling, tried to set the weathered guitar against the wall. It slid, and I caught it. I set it safe in the corner and I looked over to see Danny, his head buried in his hands.

Then I made my way down the stairs to the kitchen to mix up another pot of cocoa.

As the mixture grew warm and fragrant, I followed the smell back to a sunny morning when I'd stood at the stove in my grandmother's kitchen with my whole life in front of me. I'd imagined travels, a husband, a family, singing, dancing...

I'd never imagined I'd be Patti 209.

The digital clock on the stove read 3 a.m. Outside the window, rain battered the blackness. Just a few hours until the day staff arrived.

When the cocoa was hot I took two mugs from the cabinet and poured from the pan. I reached into the pocket of my robe, fumbling not for the vanilla but for Sharelle's bottle of pills.

A hand grabbed my arm. I turned to see Danny looking down at me with sad eyes. I don't know if he recognized me, but he recognized something. He dropped his hunched shoulders and shuffled closer to give me the first hug I'd had from anyone in a long, long time.

I waited until his arms fell away, then turned back to the

cocoa. I put our cups on a tray and carried it into the common room, Danny shuffling along behind me.

We sat on the sofa, and I drew out the bottle of pills.

"No more pills," he growled as I struggled with the plastic cap. He waved me, and the bottle, away.

I hesitated, then slowly replaced the cap.

"Not tonight," I said. "But very soon."

Danny grunted and gulped some cocoa. He set down his mug on the edge of the tray, spilling it. By the time I'd mopped up the mess, he was busy pulling books from one of the bookcases and piling them on the floor. I watched, nodding slowly, and left him to it.

In the kitchen I cleaned up all evidence of our nocturnal picnicking, loading the pot and the dishes into the dishwasher and putting away the tray. When I came out, Danny was kneeling on the floor in the common room, tearing pages out of a book and humming.

Oh, the hell with it.

I rode the elevator back upstairs, crawled into bed, and fell asleep.

~oOo~

The crash of the bookcase didn't wake me. What did, was Charming Devreaux, shaking my shoulder. What the hell was she doing in our room?

"Patti," she said.

I batted away her hand, and sat up in bed. A stocky young woman stood in the doorway. A woman in the dark blue uniform of an EMT.

Tying the sash on my robe and raking my fingers through my hair, I followed Charming and the EMT to the stairs. On the way down I caught a glimpse of another EMT and one of our aides as they wheeled a body on a stretcher out the front door.

"Danny."

I stopped and turned to look back up at Charming.

She nodded.

I felt relief, then embarrassment to be standing there in my robe.

"I'll go get dressed," I mumbled. I thought of black trousers, a black sweater, and a silver-and-turquoise pin, a gift from Danny that would be right for the occasion.

"Patti," Charming said, her voice surprisingly kind. "He's dead. He had a...a stroke. The bookcase...a head injury. There was nothing anyone could do."

Her hand on my shoulder was trembling. She has a heart after all, I thought. Then I realized: *Lawsuit. The bitch is afraid I'll sue.*

I nodded agreement at her. Blank I could do. Blank was going to be easy.

The EMT was watching me. A dark-skinned, shorthaired woman with the build of a cop. She bore the green and black tracings of a cybernetic information system on her cheek below her eye. Were the EMT's now part of law enforcement?

"I am very sorry," she said in a soft, melodic voice. It held a trace of an accent I could not place. "Danny Richmond was a hero of mine. I own all his recordings. I have tried for years to play in his style. Your husband was a great artist, ma'am."

Charming's look of astonishment pleased me no end.

His guitar.

I reached out a hand to the EMT, who'd turned and trotted halfway down the stairs.

"Wait! Please! I have something I'd like to give you."

She followed me back to the room, where she placed Danny's guitar into its case, thanking me again and again.

After she left, I took my time dressing. I carefully transferred Sharelle's bottle of pills from my bathrobe into the pocket of my sweater. Poor Danny hadn't needed them, after all. But I probably would. I'd be keeping them with me until I found the right hiding place.

By the time I got down to the dining room, an aide had discovered Sharelle's body out in the shed. I spooned my oatmeal, listening as a man at the next table speculated about what new inmate Charming would admit to replace Sharelle.

"They'll have plenty of money, you can bet on that," someone whispered, triggering a ripple of nervous laughter.

I felt a hand on my shoulder. Tod—or was it Ted?— murmured, "I'm very sorry about Danny. And about Sharelle."

I nodded and closed my lips over another spoonful of warm, mushy oats.

When it was time to go back upstairs I hesitated at the door of my room. Danny and his guitar were gone. But both were safe now. And, thanks to Sharelle, Patti 209 could still take care of herself.

I patted the pocket of my sweater and heard the reassuring rattle of the pills.

A bath tonight would be good. I'd use all the hot water I wanted.

END

IT'S ALL YOUR FAULT

Daniel M. Kimmel

ROBERT MINTZ via BREAKINGNEWS.COM

How many more times is this going to happen before our cowardly politicians do something about it?

"27 DEAD AT ALABAMA CHURCH SOCIAL—Tuscaloosa, Alabama—A man upset at a child for getting the last chocolate cupcake at a tea party opened fire in a church basement, killing a half dozen people before having to reload the weapon he was allowed to carry under the NRA-backed 'Safe Protection Act.' The man, identified as Simon Barr, was himself killed in the crossfire led by Rev. William Moody, who suffered a fatal wound inflicted by the church organist, identified as Mary Turnbull. Mrs. Turnbull said she was aiming at

Barr, but fired just as he fell so that the bullet struck Moody instead...

14 Share 38 Like Comment

Sally Bedloe:

Will this madness never end?

Thomas Miller:

The only madness here is letting bitches have guns.

Harriet Mayer:

The real madness here is that misogynist idiots like Miller are allowed access to computers AND guns.

CLICK for 128 more comments

Paul Kaplan:

Just heard on the news that some congressman wants to ban chocolate because of that shooting in Alabama, claiming it drives people to violence. Why isn't anyone paying attention to WHERE it took place? Why aren't we putting the blame where it obviously belongs: on the church?

3 Share 38 Like Comment

Terry O'Brien:

Really? How do you imagine it was the church's fault?

Paul Kaplan:

Who told them to have a "church social" in the first place? If Barr hadn't been enticed by the false promise of the dessert of his choice, this never would have happened.

Roger Brilley:

Has it occurred to anyone that the locale is important not because of the church but because it's in the South, the most un-American part of the country where those crackers are still planning to reopen the Civil War?

Terry O'Brien:

If this nutcase didn't have free access to a gun this never would have happened. What sort of dingbats thought allowing guns in churches and schools and bars was a recipe for anything but disaster?

Paul Kaplan:

Why do you radical leftwing gun grabbers always focus on the weapon?

Sarah Corbin:

Because if there were no guns in the church, none of this would have happened? He wouldn't have gotten very far attempting to attack people with a teaspoon.

Seamus Riley:

Isn't this really another example of Christian child abuse?

CLICK for 254 more comments

ANITA CONSUELO via RAW SEWAGE.COM:

I knew it. I knew it. Sooner or later they'd find a way to blame the Latino community.

"How do we know that Simon 'Barr' Barrio wasn't an illegal

immigrant and drug smuggler, crazed with an unsatisfied hunger from consuming his own drugs? When will Congress build that twenty foot high wall on our border that will finally keep these foreigners where they belong?"

1 Share 2 Like Comment

Jan Freeman:

"Barrio?" Where'd that come from?

Robert Mintz:

Why do we keep allowing ourselves to get sidetracked like this? The issue is guns.

Anita Consuelo:

This is why: Link: "Senate filibusters law that would prevent people in mental institutions from having access to guns; claims it 'infringes' on constitutional right."

CLICK for 198 more comments.

Linc REESE via TRUTH ABOUT PERVS.COM

At last it all comes out.

"Tuscaloosa, Alabama—Our website has learned exclusively that the Church Social Shooter was, in fact, a non-Christian transsexual who was experiencing chocolate cravings due to his/her/its hormone treatments..."

Be the first Liker. Be the first Sharer. Comment

Stig Swenson:

Linc, this is goofy even for you. No legitimate news source is reporting this.

Linc Reese:

Sure, the gaystream media is covering it up.

Stig Swenson:

There's no cover-up. This is a bogus story. Is it a parody site?

Linc Reese:

That's what you faggots always say.

Stig Swenson:

Who are you calling a faggot, you dickless wonder?

Linc Reese:

Brave man with a keyboard. Say that to my face and my .45.

Stig Swenson:

No wonder you were happy that they defeated that law that would prevent cretins who are a danger to themselves from getting guns. Does your mother know you're using her computer?

Linc Reese:

I see your location. Enjoy your last lunch. I'm on my way.

MARTA CREIGHTON

The internet is going crazy over that church shooting in Alabama and totally ignoring the high schooler who was stalking and killing every girl at his high school because he couldn't get a date for the prom. Why does violence against women remain invisible?

45 Likes 16 Shares Comment

Sarai Jacobson:

Preach it, sister!

Sally Bedloe:

It shouldn't be. Gun violence is out of control.

Angie Tomassi:

It's not gun violence, it's rape culture.

Sarai Jacobson:

Preach it, sister!

Marta Creighton:

There is a horrible problem with violence against women and we need to make solving it a top priority. But let's not make it seem like all men are the problem.

Sarai Jacobson:

Marta, I had no idea you had sold out. Why are you enabling rape and violence?

Marta Creighton:

Where did I do that? I simply said we have to focus on the perpetrators, not on all men.

Angie Tomassi:

All men ARE rapists.

Roger Brilley:

Excuse me? *I* am not a rapist and I resent that remark.

Angie Tomassi:

Who gave you permission to comment here? Are you that blind to your white male privilege?

Roger Brilley:

I'm not white. Are you that obsessed with your racist hatemongering?

Sarai Jacobson:

I'm blocking Roger and other rapists from my feed. I am so hyped up from their deliberate use of 'trigger words' I need to reclaim control of my space.

Roger Brilley:

What trigger words? What the hell are you talking about?

Angie Tomassi:

Good idea, Sarai. I'm blocking him too.

Roger Brilley:

Marta? Anyone?

CLICK for 22 more comments

~oOo~

In the corporate headquarters of TouchBase, the top executives of the world's hottest social network were enjoying their bowls of *grakh*, the mildly hallucinogenic brew from their home planet, which was now being grown in the Columbian mountains and, thus, available without shipping costs. Multiple newsfeeds from various clients selected at random were scrolling by on the bank of screens along the far wall.

Trwjn, known in his human guise as the affable Garry Pardo, founder of TouchBase, had removed his make-up and prosthetics, as had the others. In spite of the thickness of Earth's atmosphere it was a pleasure to be able to move freely in their own forms and expose their blue scaled skin to the air. Pzgkq, newly arrived from the home world, scanned the screens through goggles designed to translate what he was seeing into the more mellifluous sounds of XpcW.

Finally he turned to the others. "They seem completely irrational. All they do is argue."

"And send pictures of their pets," said Gkwll.

"And their lunches," added Pdmnq.

"They eat their pets for lunch?" asked Pzgkq, not quite following the discussion.

"No, no," explained Trwjn. "The humans send pictures of their pet animals as well as pictures of the food they're about to consume. No one has been able to come up with an explanation for why."

Pzgkq looked at the screens again. "And the arguing? They seem to fight about anything and everything, assuming the worst motives in others, even members of the same family unit."

Trwjn agreed. "That's precisely the point. We just have to keep stoking the flames and humanity will destroy itself. The irony is that we got the idea from the humans themselves. We came across a broadcast signal originally sent out more than fifty years ago from a science fiction show in which off-worlders made humans suspicious of each other by fluctuating their power supply. With TouchBase we don't even have to do that. Pdmnq, why don't you demonstrate?"

Pdmnq sat down before one of the screens and plugged in the interface that allowed him to place messages through especially designed accounts. On screen was a posting from one Lorraine Dietz about how much she loved being a vegan. Pdmnq's tendrils danced across the interface and now there was a reply from "Paulina Dominique" with a picture of a kitten over which was written, "And cats make a great dessert." There were already five messages calling "Paulina" a murderer and five more claiming the writers of those messages were humorless twits.

"And this really works? The humans fight over such things?" asked Pzgkq.

"Indeed. They don't even have to know whom they're arguing with so long as the person expresses a view not the same as their own. They argue over the news, their government, religion, sexual intercourse..."

"Sexual intercourse? What could they possibly argue about that?"

"Everything from whom one should be permitted to have it with to whether some acts are examples of sharing pleasure or engaging in oppression. The human capacity to take offense over their differences is infinitely large, even as their ability to find common ground is infinitely small. The longer this goes on the more it will become impossible for them to unite in a common defense. If they don't destroy themselves first, they should be pushovers for us when our main force arrives."

"You're done excellent work, Trwjn," said Pzgkq. "I shall file my report as soon as possible."

~oOo~

ROSAMUND BENSON:

I like apple pie.

115 Likes Be the first to Share Comment

Marcellus Smith:

No one likes apple pie. Key lime pie!

Stephen Kenner:

You're both wrong. Pecan pie forever.

John May:

Any pie is okay as long as it's gluten-free.

Thomas Johnson:

Gluten-free? You actually buy into that crap? It's a scam....

CLICK for 353 more Comments

END

LETTERS FROM THE HEARTLAND

Janka Hobbs

Heartland, Ks
January 6, 2025

Dear Emily,

Praise the Lord, they are finally lifting the travel ban from California! I'm so happy! You can come visit us now!

I miss you so much. It's not right that you are stranded so far away from your loving mother. I still don't see why the Left Coast had to leave the country over a few pipelines. I know the people in Seattle and Portland are weird, but I don't know what got into you Californians. Did they really give trees the right to vote? You can't agree with them. You just got stuck there when it happened? Right?

Do you remember George and Gladys? From across the street? They moved back from Florida in November. Just up and abandoned their condo in Miami. Gladys says the waves were coming up on the deck, and nobody wanted to buy it. She blames it on all the solar panels people were putting on their rooftops. She says all that sunlight pushing down on them made the beach sink. That was the real reason the Governor there wanted to ban the things? Well, he tried, but some people just won't listen. I hear you people have lots of solar panels out in California, too. Are you having trouble with the beaches sinking too? I know, there's even some people here saying that it's because the north pole is melting, but it still gets cold here in the winter, so how can that be true?

Enough doom and gloom. I sure hope you can come see me soon!

Love,

Mom

XOXOXO

PS. Your brother says hi.

~oOo~

Heartland, Ks
February 25, 2025

Dear Emily,

It was so good to hear from you. Those salt winds from the lakes drying up sound scary! Stay indoors! At least you can go inside. You're better off than all those poor ducks.

Do you remember I told you about my miniature lioness Elsa? Well, I took her to Milwaukee to get her bred. Everything was going so well, but then Sad News! She died having her first litter. One of the cubs had two heads and got stuck, and it killed her. I should have got her to the vet's sooner, but I'd spent a lot of money on the breeding, and your brother cut me off from your dad's retirement money. I think Congress overstepped a bit, including widows in the Defense of Family Finances Act. I managed the household money fine for forty years, and now your brother thinks he can cut off my allowance as if I was a child. I changed his diapers and I don't need him telling me how to spend my retirement money.

Anyway, I can't wait to see you! Come cheer up your Mom. We have so much to talk about in person!

Love,

Mom

XOXOXO

P.S. Write me back on paper. Your brother doesn't want any California contacts on our computers.

~oOo~

Heartland, Ks
April 12, 2025

Dear Emily,

The weather sure has gotten hot early this year! The company put in a couple of new oil wells in town, and the heat from the flares was really nice in the winter when it was so cold, but right now they just add to the misery. I'm sure we'll be glad of them again next winter.

A few people left town when the company put wells in next to their houses. I don't get it. Some of them were even offered jobs and everything, but they up and left instead. The empty houses do make things easier for the people moving up from Florida, and there's a lot of those. Most of them are decent folks, though the town council had to clarify that this is an English-speaking town, and other gibberish will not be tolerated.

It's too bad about New Orleans. Your Dad took me there one time on vacation. It was a lovely city, though I can understand why the Good Lord chose to smite it for its evil ways.

I do still miss your Dad. A couple of his old co-workers came around to see me the other day. One of them in particular is still sore at me for not suing the company after the accident, but what was I supposed to do? Your brother was sure it would cost him his job if I raised a stink, and even if we could prove that the equipment was faulty, it probably came under the new Protection of Commerce laws anyway.

As for the concerns in your letter, I don't think you have anything to worry about if you come to visit. All those new laws they put in are for scofflaws, not for nice girls coming home to visit their mothers.

Love,

Mom

XOXOXO

~oOo~

Heartland, Ks
May 15, 2025

      Dear Emily,

I have found a new way to make a little money in my old age. I'm breeding miniature hippopotamuses! (I so wanted to tell you about this earlier, but I didn't want to jinx Rosebud's pregnancy by talking about it.) They're all the rage now, small enough to live in a bathtub. It's part of the same project as Elsa was, to make every animal on Noah's Ark small enough to be a pet.

We like scientists around here, when they're coming up with something useful like that. One of them is even trying to re-create the unicorn, which, you know, Noah forgot, and there's a group of them trying to bring back elephants and cheetahs.

The hippopotamus young are really cute. My first foal is nearly a month old now. I'm calling him Quincy. He has five legs, and I have to help him in and out of the kiddie pool in the basement, but he makes the cutest grunting noises when I do it!

The President gave a speech last night saying "those coastal Libertards think that just because things aren't going their way, they can leave the union just like that. We're going to make them sorry they did." I believe him, and he's still Commander in Chief. That's why I want you to come home. As soon as they finish cracking down on the illegals here, they're going to come after the splitters, and it's not going to be pretty.

I can't wait till we get California back. I miss oranges and avocados. Sure, we still get some oranges from Florida, but with so much of the state being underwater, they're mighty expensive. We do have a big garden, and grow most of our own vegetables these days, but it's gotten funny about what grows and what doesn't. I did buy some micro drones to replace the bees, so it's not that. Since they put in the wells, the water here comes out of the tap a golden amber color. The company tells us it's more nutritious that way. Your brother says (excuse my French) "What the hell, Ma, it looks like beer!"

I've been growing red lettuce and cabbage, to hide the yellow tint the water gives the white parts of the leaves. I gave up on turnips and rutabagas. They kept growing faces, and when one of the turnips winked at me, it was too much. I grew a pumpkin last year that was big enough to climb inside, though.

Love,

Mom

XOXOXO

And a smiley face to the censors for keeping us safe!

~oOo~

Heartland, Ks
May 26, 2025

Dear Emily,

If you hear from your sister or sister-in-law, can you write to me? They ran off to New England about a month ago, after Congress passed the Homemaker's Freedom from Voting act. Your sister said she wasn't going to wait around and watch congress mandate corsets and ankle length skirts. "Or worse, mini skirts!" your S-I-L added. They were both gone the next morning.

Your brother says he never wants to see his wife again, for leaving him like that. I don't think he meant it though. He took a bit of my nest egg to pay a headhunter to bring her back. I don't think it's right of her to abandon my son, but if he doesn't intend to support her, he should just let her go. New England is refusing to extradite anyone to the Heartland Republic, so if they got that far, they're probably gone. If you hear from either of them, please tell me my girls are safe.

I should get this in the mail. I can hear Quincy crying downstairs, and then I need to run this to the post office before your brother gets home. Please write back. I usually walk over to pick up the mail myself.

Love,

Mom

P.S. Maybe you should put off your visit, for now.

END

RAGE AGAINST THE DONALD

Bruno Lombardi

"Special Agent Alpha to Director: another temporal incursion. Lincoln Memorial."

I rolled my eyes and discretely tapped my com pad on my wrist to respond. Being the Director on this time loop was a full time job, on top of the job that was my cover.

"ID on incPursion agent?" I said tiredly. I was barely speaking above a whisper but even among all the noise from the crowd, the subdermal throat mic could still pick me up. Yeah for 27th century technology.

"Data still coming through. Preliminary ID is approximately from the year 2150. Subject armed with Mark V phased pistol."

2150? Oh joy—those jokers again. At least they're relatively sane, unlike the batch from 2260. No amount of effort would ever bring back the Greek gods.

"You know the drill. Standard Containment Protocol."

"Containment cells one and two are filled to capacity, Director." Alpha sounded vaguely embarrassed by that, which I found kind of cute. He personally has caught 57 time travelers in the last three days alone—and now he feels embarrassed that there isn't enough room for them?

"Then activate base three."

"Will do, Director. Have three agents intercepting incursion now."

"Acknowledged."

I took a deep breath and went back to watching the parade.

~oOo~

"Special Agent Gamma to Director; multiple temporal incursions. East and West side."

For fuck's sake, it's, like, literally five minutes until the inauguration! What on Earth can they hope to accomplish cutting it that close?

"ID?"

"One's identified as Pepist member, circa 2090."

"Oh joy—a fucking fanboy. No doubt to take some holo-pics. And the other?"

"Cyborg. 2295 best guess."

Shit; probably a member of the Mechlods. Those gear jammers are seriously fucked up.

"Make that one a high priority. Cloak him, if necessary."

"Acknowledged."

"Oh—and status on crowd numbers?"

"Embedded agents in Park Services and law enforcement agencies estimate about 250K, Director."

"How many are our people?"

"About 250K, Director."

Smartass.

"Good job. Keep me posted."

"Acknowledged."

~oOo~

I went up to Trump just as he was getting up to the podium. He looked at me, breathing heavily, visibly annoyed. "Yes? What? What is it?"

"Your tie, sir," I said, as I made a move to adjust it.

"Oh." For a brief moment, he actually smiled. I smiled back, distracting him from the tiny sticker I put on his tie.

"All done. Perfect." I smiled back.

He smiled in return—and then it quickly faded as he turned and walked to the podium. As I walked away, I pressed the button on my pen, activating the Weather Modification Drone we had cloaked over the Capitol. I debated for a moment and then hit 'rain' and kept walking.

~oOo~

I shook my head as the special agents reported in during Trump's speech. They've had a busy day.

Honestly—what is wrong with these people?

"Oh—I will go back in time and stop Trump! I'll, like, shoot him from a rooftop with a raygun! I'll expose him and his cabinet to Moon Flu! I'll run up to him and punch him during his speech!"

Lame. Really, really lame.

I've been stopping time travelers from going back to stop Trump since last July—and truthfully, it's starting to get to me. Oh no—not the job itself. Rather, it was the fact that so many of them are just so utterly dumb. I mean—jeez— you're a freaking time traveler! Make some effort at intelligence!

Subtlety. That's the key. Subtlety. Butterfly Effect and all that. Why use a sledgehammer and a gun when an errant shoelace and dumb answer to a question does the trick just as well? Ok—it's a bit more difficult. No—scratch that. A lot more difficult. But you also have better control of the consequences and ripple effects as well.

You just gotta be patient.

~oOo~

"All assets; summary report." I was at the Inaugural Ball and it was close to midnight.

"365 incursion agents stopped. 147 assassination attempts. 55 terrorist act attempts. 25 tourists."

"Busy day. Job well done. Get some rest. We're going to have another busy day tomorrow. And every day after that." Of course tomorrow was in the forty one nano seconds it took us to log out, take a shift of rest, and be back. It had the illusion of one long assed day.

"Acknowledged."

~oOo~

I intercepted Sean Spicer, the new Press Secretary, just as he was walking toward the press room.

"Looking forward to your first big day?" I asked, sweetly.

Sean clearly wasn't used to either the suit or the pressure; the sweat was nearly gushing out of his pores. But he smiled wanly.

"Yeah. I guess so."

"Boss says change of plans. Here's what he wants you to focus your speech on today," I said, handing him a package.

He looked at me with confusion in his eyes, glanced down and pulled out the talking points—and looked even more confused.

His gaze locked onto mine.

"Seriously? This is what he wants me to focus on? The inaugural crowd numbers? This is bullshit!"

I shrugged. "Hey, orders straight from the boss." I could tell that Sean was unconvinced. That's when I decided to go for the throat.

"Hey, if you can't handle the job, I'm sure the boss would be more than happy to accept your resignation. I'm sure you should have no trouble at all getting another job. I mean, it's not like he's a guy who is noted for being petty or vindictive or willing to hold a grudge or anything like that." I smiled again, showing a bit more teeth.

Sean actually deflated. "Ok," he said, sighing heavily. "Give me a minute to go over this."

"No, make them wait an hour. Then go in. That will show them who is boss!"

~oOo~

Twitter pretty much exploded an hour later. Have to admit, it took literally all my self-control not to laugh out loud. I think my favorite bit was CNN saying that they had refused to show the conference live because they suspected it would be all lies—and now they were being immensely smug about being proven right.

My iPhone beeped. I looked down and saw that there were already sixteen different text messages from White House staff about damage control. I had just enough time to crack a smile when my com pad beeped as well.

"Yes," I sighed.

"Special Agent Omicron to Director. Temporal incursion. White House lawn. Tennis court. Looks like two incursions—one a Trumpist and the other an anti-Trumpist. They're currently having a knife fight with one another. Orders?"

"Record the fight, then arrest the winner and dispose of the loser."

"Acknowledged."

Man, I'm going to start drinking heavily soon.

~oOo~

Butterfly Effect. That's the key. A butterfly flaps its wings in Brazil and three weeks later sets off a tornado in Texas. Tiny, seemingly insignificant changes can accomplish the job just as well—or, in fact, better—than a big-ass intervention at the last minute.

We needed to destroy this administration but it has to be done in style. Finesse. Subtlety. There can't be any big red arrows. No large X's. No "Now wait just a damn minute..." bizarreness for anyone—past, present or future—to spot. More importantly, there can't be any one thing that brings it down. If it all rests on just the one thing, then all the Future Trumpists have something to go back to disrupt. And potentially stop.

But if it's a seemingly infinite number of things? And if all of them subtle? And if some of them are impossible to pin down?

If...If...If...If...

It's going to be a long job, but the payoff is going to be important. That's really the only reason I'm in this. Future generations are going to look at me in contempt and amusement and disgust, unfortunately—but it's a small price to pay.

For the future.

"You're on in five seconds," said the TV soundman.

Right. Butterfly Effect. That's the important thing. Keep reminding yourself that.

The anchorman turned to me and started asking me questions.

We all have roles to play; it's part of the job description after all. Trump has his and I have mine. And I have to milk mine for all it's worth. Even if it's at the price of self-respect. I know they're going to mock me—are, in fact, already mocking me—but when I got this assignment, I knew what I was signing up for. History—the altered history, that is—will see me as, well, a glorious fool. No; Fool. Capital letters. Like a title.

In a way—it's accurate. Disturbingly so.

Oh well; at least I'll have Saturday Night Live skits made in my memory. I took a deep breath and embraced my role and gave the reporter a truly fascinating reply.

"Don't be so overly dramatic about it, Chuck. What—you're saying it's a falsehood. And they're giving Sean Spicer, our press secretary, gave alternative facts to that. But the point remains—"

End?

PINWHEEL PARTY

Victor D. Phillips

"Pall in the mall," bemoaned businesses. "Consumers aren't spending enough!"

"Ink the presses," shouted politicians. "Print more money!"

"Shovel it down their throats," cheered bankers. "Make loans with no job, no collateral."

"Work for honest pay," pleaded the jobless, dodging bullets. "Our babies not yet gunned down are starving."

"Blame the goddamn foreigners," screamed patriots. "Bombs away!"

"Kill all wicked, godless evil-doers," bellowed pastors. "Burn non-believers!"

"Help!" gasped trees, fish, birds and bees. "There's no place left for us, goodbye."

Even optimists, with their cups half full, were left with nothing more than broken handle shards between shaking thumbs and forefingers. Their empty hope lay strewn and shattered in dry, dusty pieces at their feet. It was the worst of times.

~oOo~

In the dark stadium's icy parking lot a makeshift shelter held several thousand sick, starving indigents, mainly immigrants. Some maimed and bleeding, all ridiculed and cursed, they lurched or crawled to the temporary refuge where they huddled shivering with fear and fever. The lucky ones sprawled on cardboard sheets flapping in wintry blasts of sleet through the long night. Tomorrow was Election Day, but none of them would be voting.

Moving among them as best he could, "Medic," a local drug dealer, helped a few escape the bleak, miserable existence. "Here, Nadim, friendly one, swallow this powder," he said, stepping between groaning outcasts nearby in fetal positions, recently blinded Jalil, the exalted one, and tender, now castrated Benito, the blessed one. Affable Nadim, who learned English reading Dickens, soon felt the Medic's effect. Lying prostrate, he slipped into a state of vivid stupor.

~oOo~

"What the dickens happened?" the people wailed sourly, desperate for lemonade. That was before the election.

"Breaking News: History's first ever elected write-in candidate is the next President of the United States." Citizens turned out in record numbers to take unprecedented action of hope. The landslide victory garnered the winner 210,872,335 popular votes – over ninety percent of eligible voters – as well as a clean sweep of all 538 Electoral College ballots cast.

"JST! He's for Me!" pealed from every thirsty mouth for a sweet sip of happiness.

"Just in, just in, just in time!" rang buoyant voices.

At the inauguration, millions of smiley faces stenciled on the backs of yellow ponchos matched sentiments of draped and clad "Yellow Jackets," the write-in President's populous supporters. In post-election euphoria, these happy hornets consolidated into the "Pinwheel Party." After distributing twirling golden vanes atop sticks of barber pole candy, the President began and ended his address to the effusive crowd succinctly in nine words, vowing "to do the greatest good for the greatest number."

Now when a typical politician attempts following that Utilitarian maxim, the greatest number is usually number one. But not so President JST, whose moral compass spun equitably and compassionately in all directions, respecting and embracing all peoples. After the swearing-in ceremony, the jubilant swarm made a beeline from Capitol Hill to the White House. Brandishing paintbrushes and pails in the morning sun, they soon coated the hive bright lemon yellow, garnishing the residency's rooftops and gardens with red, white and blue pinwheels spinning gaily in favorable winds of change.

Before the paint dried, the President's first executive order commissioned the conversion of all armament factories into fruit processing plants. With the stroke of his pen, every military base and prison concurrently became juice distribution centers. On the hundredth day of office, he appeared in the House of Representatives chamber. Every esteemed Member in attendance held a spinning plaything in fervent salute. Propelling the gentle, fragrant breeze of his voice through the pinwheel of his creed, he announced that U.S. Treasury sales of JST Lemonade Bonds had balanced the budget. Rapturous roars of "Hear, hear!" energized liftoff of untethered, air born pinwheel flowers whirling and filling a chamber giddy with brotherly love. Needing no more than initials to evoke instant recognition, as applied to former Presidents FDR and JFK, ardent devotees so dubbed President JST.

Within his first term of office, rivers ran clean as water whistles. Strangers, like pickles and ice cream, embraced in a groundswell of fellowship, pregnant with tolerance and understanding. A turning point in human history occurred as the pinstripes of the rich and polka dots of the poor buried the fashion hatchet. Generous hearts of gold melted, trickling down into poor hearts as all splashed merrily in a great, common pool of jubilation. Spirits lifted Up! Up! Up!

"More Sweet News from the Oval Office," national and international headlines trumpeted. "LEMONADE SALES RESOLVE USA's $20 TRILLION DEBT!"

Quick to follow as enlightened, humble servants of the people, Congress passed "Green Back" legislation. Impassioned volunteers formed singing brigades of strong "Greenbacks" happily engaged in public works in every county coast-to-coast. Couch potatoes actually switched off television sets to enlist. With shiny shovels and sacks of non-GMO seed, the contemporary Johnny Appleseeds dug up concrete and restored forests, farmlands, watersheds, and parks. Reconnected to Nature, juicy fruit and gentle fiber dramatically improved human health. Drug addiction and depression vanished like warm cookies fresh from the oven. Hanging his white lab coat on a peg, the Surgeon General announced he was gladly out of a job. And in glory, bald eagles, those majestic emblems of America, sprouted fabulous, raven-black pompadours while screeching melodiously from the mountaintops, "Love Me Tender."

In the second-term election, the Pinwheel Party spun a lopsided victory with effective campaign slogans, "Man Date, Mother Earth" and "Cup's Half Full, Let's Fill 'er Up." Not surprising as America would have no one else. JST and First Lady ME, Mother Earth, facilitated another restoration. Walking arm-in-arm with American Indian chiefs and tribal elders from over five hundred nations, a yearlong traveling ceremony celebrated the return of pre-discovery homelands to original inhabitants. All hearts, both of generous, indigenous landlords and contrite, congenial renters, drummed with thundering justice as rainbows of peace arced across the fertile, green land.

Within two years, his proactive "Feathering Nests" policy spread worldwide. Wars and famines, greed and conquest, environmental degradation and social injustice dissipated, then ceased, unlike most wonders. In short, world peace was achieved along with university parking. Abundant milk and honey flowed from green forests teeming with wildlife as goodwill and tolerance coursed within all two hundred countries on a planet of happy campers strumming ukuleles.

Changed from January 20 to June 21 for seasonal comfort and amenity of all, President JST spent his last day in office outdoors in view of an adoring throng of well-wishers. Playing lacrosse with some Haudenosaunee friends on the White House lawn, a rosy-cheeked kindergartener peered eagerly through the wrought-iron fence. She held a white, cooing dove named Daisy tucked gently under one arm, along with a colorful pinwheel she made in school. On the other wrist a golden thread tethered a marbled blue and white balloon floating happily in the clear sky above her head festooned with bright red ribbons.

"Mr. President, my teacher asked our class what your middle name starting with 'S' is?" piped up the curious child.

"What names did your classmates guess?" the President asked, bending down as their smiling eyes met.

"Wachiwi, Juanita and Omar guessed 'Samuel', for 'Uncle

Sam.' But I think it's for 'Summer'. My birthday comes just in summer times. I'll be six this July!" she beamed.

"Well, you guessed it! Happy birthday soon," he replied genially, waving goodbye.

A sea of Yellow Jackets and Greenbacks extended from the fence to the horizon. Hearty, sustained cheers followed President Justin Summer Times as he skipped across the green lawn to his limousine awaiting departure. Patriotic pinwheels twirled mightily on the specially designed vehicle's corner mounts, lifting him into the summer sky to cries of "Justin, Justin, Justin Times!"

Dickens would have observed, "It was the best of times."

~oOo~

"You there! Identification! Be quick about it," a National Guardsman barked, kicking unconscious Nadim in the ribs as he lay paralyzed on his frozen cardboard mat. Blinking awake groggily in pain, fading pinwheels whirled away from his mind. Nadim found himself handcuffed, then dragged into a long line of other detainees. He saw Jalil and Benito frog-trotting ahead in chains. Sirens wailed as deportation squads with tanks cleansed the slushy shelter of its inhabitants.

The last thing he heard was "Off to Guantanamo with you, just in time for summer."

END

MONKEY CAGE RULES

Larry Hodges

After taking the oath of office as President of the United States, I turned to the crowd, raised my arms, and shouted, *"God and country!"* The crowd cheered.

"Freedom!" More cheers.

"America is the greatest!" The cheers reached a crescendo.

I lowered my arms and smiled, shaking my head. "You people are <u>soooooo</u> gullible." I turned off my holographic mask, revealing a face humans would later describe as a three-eyed orangutan.

Pandemonium.

We'd worked centuries for this moment. Earthlings were a potential threat to the galaxy. They were, to borrow a term, bat-shit crazy. So I was sent to solve their problems. As president of the most powerful nation on earth, armed with dirty secrets and hard evidence implicating every member of the government—some true, some planted—I'd be able to do what these loveable losers could not: find a political philosophy that worked for them.

"Before you ask," I added, "I'm a native-born U.S. citizen. I grew my current body in a lab right here in the good 'ole USA."

I started interviewing for a new government that night. First up was the Ladybug of Liberalism. The tiny bug flew in through the newly open Oval Office window, a smile on its mandibles, and a Keynesian economics book and a copy of *Rush Limbaugh is a Big Fat Idiot* tucked under a wing.

Floating overhead was the Specter of Socialism, who had always hung around and haunted liberalism. "Go away!" I cried, shooing the dark spirit out the window.

Soon we had a liberal government. Thinking about God was a felony, dogs and cats could marry, abortion till age five was legal, and every homeless person was issued Belgian endive and an iPad—but the government had real few money. I say "real few" because that's an anagram for welfare. The government collapsed in financial insolvency.

In through the window flew the Cardinal of Conservatism. I shooed away the pointy-hooded specters that haunted this particular beast as well. The little red bird, especially populous in the South, had a smile on its beak, and a bible and a copy of *Atlas Shrugged* under one wing, and a Colt .45 under the other. It gulped down the poor ladybug.

The Lion of Libertarianism crawled through the window, stalking the cardinal. "Go away!" I cried, throwing a food stamp at it. It hissed and leaped back out the window.

Soon we had a conservative government. Religion and big business took over, the rich got richer while the poor were sautéed on Grey Poupon, everyone was issued a Smith & Wesson, if you didn't speak unaccented English or look American you were consigned to the Wal-Mart sweatshops, and we went bankrupt invading everyone, and then the unregulated banking system collapsed.

I strangled the cardinal's red neck. I thought of trying libertarianism next, but the lion had run away; it just wanted to be left alone.

Neither philosophy had worked. What else was there?

There was a whinny, and a white stallion leaped through the window. On its back was the smiling Mollusk of Moderation, waving a white cowboy hat, with a copy of *Reflections of a Radical Moderate* balanced on its shell. Finally, the best of both worlds!

It didn't last long. Since the great moderate middle in American politics is about the size of Rhode Island, everyone attacked the poor mollusk's pearls of wisdom. It finally closed its shell and clammed up.

I was still enjoying the clam chowder when there came a knock on the door. In flopped the Coelacanth of Communism. "You're extinct!" I cried.

"No I'm not!"

"Go away," I said, slamming the door on the hideous fish. I ignored the Mastiff of Monarchy and Doberman of Dictatorship barking in the hallway. I was running out of ideas. "There *has* to be a way for these intelligent beings to govern themselves!"

"There's your mistake right there," said a voice. Floating in through the window was the ghost of H.L. Mencken—the Sage of Baltimore!

"What do you mean?" I asked in awe.

"You said intelligent beings. As I once wrote, Democracy is just a pathetic belief in the collective wisdom of individual ignorance."

"What other choices are there?"

"None," said the Sage. "I enjoy democracy immensely. It is incomparably idiotic, and hence incomparably amusing."

"But it's not working."

"That's because Democracy is the art and science of running the circus from the monkey cage. As my colleague George Bernard Shaw wrote, 'Democracy is a device that insures we shall be governed no better than we deserve.'"

"So how do I get us out of this monkey cage?"

"You won't. You have a different role to play. As another colleague Bertrand Russell wrote, 'Democracy is the process by which people choose the man who'll get the blame.'"

I took a deep breath and blew him out the window. I needed solutions, not literary quotations.

And then I realized our mistake. Shaw was right—humans deserve the government they deserve, even if it means quarantining them from the galaxy. And so I will give up and watch with jaded amusement as they choose their own government. Who will rule the monkey cage? Can anyone rule the monkey cage?

END

THE LAST RANGER (ANPS-1, CE 2053)

Blaze Ward

Dale looked over at the old man in the green jacket next to him and considered how the world had gotten here.

Not just them, sitting here on horseback. Two men in a semi-blizzard.

Everything.

Martial law hadn't been the first step. Nor the last.

They said it started back in the middle somewhere, when hope was still an option. Before some idiot decided the best way to break the back of the Resistance was to use *The Bomb*.

Even people in favor of nuking LA in those days had decided that was a bridge too far. Everything went to hell at that point. Flyover country became a foreign land.

Still was.

Everyone argued over who got to keep the name *United States of America*, but the two sides generally settled into *Blue Shirts* and *Green Shirts* as a way of telling people apart, at least in conversation.

Stan still sat tall in the well-worn saddle after thirty-five years as a Park Ranger. Legend had it he was the last man authorized under the old United States Congress to wear the golden shield with the buffalo. When he was only a few years older than Dale was now.

Back before.

Before war, and apocalypse, and ruin. Before it was assumed that a sixteen-year-old like Dale would grow up and become a warrior.

Stan was staring hard into his binoculars, intent on something in the distance occasionally obscured by the cold, blowing wind that whipped at the two men and caused their horses' manes to fly out flat to the horizon.

Only fools and Park Rangers had any business out in weather like this, but it was January, and they had patrol rounds to finish.

Dale grabbed his Dewar flask from the left hand saddle bag and took a gulp of honeyed tea, still hot, hours since they'd broken camp. Stan remained still as an old rock outcropping, so Dale put the flask away and made sure no snow had gotten into his rifle holster. He double-checked that his outer gear was all buttoned up and dry.

When they were out in the open field, a team like theirs had to carry almost everything they needed on the move, from food, to medical gear, to explosives for starting a controlled avalanche. It was all tightly packed in oversized saddle bags. Everything might be individually light, but there was still a lot of it, spread between the two horses.

Just in case, he made sure that his horse, Centurion, was holding up.

All good.

Father's lessons had been hammered home over Dale's short lifetime. If he wanted to be a warrior when he grew up, a Park Ranger, here were all the things he was expected to master. And he had.

At sixteen, Dale was already an Apprentice Guide, an *090*, assigned to work with the Old Man of the Service himself.

Royalty.

Stan muttered something rude under his breath.

Dale had learned stillness and silence from his father while hunting mountain goats in these Rockies. He waited for the man to share.

"Trouble," the quiet veteran finally said, handing Dale the binoculars.

Dale took long moments to get the focus on the binoculars back down where he needed it. Stan's eyes were going, but his nose for trouble was still unmatched in the Service.

Movement. Gray and green against the mostly white and black background. Dale dialed the focus down tighter.

Tanks waddling slowly through the snowbanks far below them, cutting a trail. Troop transports, similar tracked, armored beasts behind that. Articulated vehicles on treads as well. A convoy of them. Maybe a dozen, total.

Most of that armor were antiques these days. Relics from the old United States Army, stored in some depot when the world fell apart and then rehabilitated into service today.

Dale lowered the glasses and considered the terrain. Colorado and Wyoming were both on the Green side, but the eastern portions of both states were flat and open. Easy enough for Jayhawkers and Huskers, Kansas and Nebraska Guard Units, to sneak over the line. Especially if they came across the old Pawnee Prairie in the kind of blizzard that had been blowing the last few days.

No roads. Lots of flat. Nothing to stop the wind or raiders.

Slice the gap between Fort Collins and Cheyenne. Cut south of Virginia Dale and pass the old abandoned Benedictine Abbey. Sneak into the mountains before anybody knew they were there.

What the hell did they want?

He turned back to Stan, found the old man watching him like a hawk. Waiting.

"So Red Feather Lakes Road is watched," Dale began. "And Highway Fourteen and Thirty-Four are pretty heavily fortified. Why are they coming in this way?"

"What's there to hit?" Stan asked. "That's enough there to do some damage, wherever they decide to land."

"I suppose you could cut off Eighty," Dale replied. "Or maybe fortify the reservoir. Or even poison it. I didn't see any air cover, but the clouds would block us anyway."

Dale stopped and turned his head the other direction. Mountains covered in snow, as far as the eye could see.

"And I supposed helicopters or low-flying attack planes would give them away," he continued, working out the logic aloud, like he was being graded. He probably was. "So either they want to set up a base deep in the hills, like a tick waiting for spring, or they are a blocking force sent to cut off reinforcements if someone is going to attack Fort Collins."

Sun Tzu had covered this sort of thing. So had Patton. Dale had read both several times growing up. Dad had a whole library.

Stan nodded. Somehow, he conveyed approval and respect with a simple bob of the head.

"Is there any advantage to poisoning the reservoir?" Stan asked.

Yeah, Dale was being graded today.

"Panic," Dale replied. "But actually doing it would risk an escalation from one of the other nations surrounding the Blues. Still, you could get people moving south to Denver in the middle of a raid and winter. But why come this way? It's easier to come into the reservoir from the east if you want to hit it. So that's out. I'd want to hide someplace farther west, where there are more trees."

Stan nodded again.

"So would I," he agreed.

Dale thought he would say something else, but Stan just whipped Audrey's reins and got the big, bay mare moving. Centurion had spent enough time in the Park Service to follow without any heels. The blue roan was big, and occasionally a goof, but he was a soldier, too.

Dale let Stan set the pace, pushing through the snow toward some target to the southwest.

Between them, they had two rifles and two pistols. Plus two cavalry sabers.

That force over there had a couple of tanks, half a dozen armored transports, and probably a hundred men in battle gear. In back, several flatbeds were hauling covered loads

Dale couldn't identify.

Trouble.

And near as Dale knew, there were no friendly troops this side of Fort Collins that could help.

Dale wasn't sure how they could stop them, but he knew Stan was dead set on trying.

~oOo~

They ended up in a stand of trees on the east side of Turkey Roost Mountain, still deep in the heart of what used to be the Roosevelt Forest. He and Stan were down below the peak, just lee enough that the howling wind was quiet here, but Dale could still see the angry edges of the storm running on all sides of them.

The west face was where the North Fork River would run hard and dangerous in the spring melt, but for now, it was ice. Over here, just the least amount of gully and enough trees that they could hang a camouflage net and settle the horses in a bit.

Dale glanced back over his left shoulder as the sun began to set.

Or would have set, if it was visible. More snow was coming.

He wasn't sure if another storm would slow down those Jayhawkers. It would certainly provide them enough cover to do mischief, up here in the mountains.

Stan had called for backup, but it just confirmed that there was nobody within range.

Made sense. If this was cover for an attack on Fort Collins, they would need everybody down in the flats.

Still, it would have been nice to have some help out here.

They started a climb, letting Audrey and Centurion hump along at a nice amble. The two horses had fought hard to get them here early enough, but they still had a bit to go before everyone was done.

"There's only one way we might slow them down," Stan said in that quiet drawl. "Stop them, maybe."

Dale nodded. There wasn't a lot two men with rifles could do against an armored company in rough country.

Die, maybe, but Stan wasn't a Death or Glory kind of guy. Not today, anyway.

Stan took his silence with a nod.

"Assuming they want to stay off Eighty as much as possible, they should pass below us," Stan said. "We can ambush them here, and then run like hell for the back country and hope they don't catch us."

"They've got tanks, Stan," Dale felt compelled to point out the obvious.

The old man actually grinned at that.

"Those are nice in an open field, kid," he replied. "Ain't worth shit in tight quarters. And those guns only elevate so far. No, I'd be much more worried if they had horses with them, or snow-mobiles. This gives us a chance."

They were still fifty-ton behemoths, invulnerable to anything at hand. Dale wasn't about to point that out. Again.

"And the troop transports?" Dale asked instead.

"Man on foot in this snow is about as worthless as tits on a boar, Dale," Stan said. "Only thing I worry about is aircraft, but the snow'll be too much."

Dale nodded.

He'd never fired his rifle in anger, unless you counted being pissed off at an elk that zigged when it should have zagged, two winters ago, and would've gotten away, if his dad hadn't drilled it. His dad was like that.

But there were Blues coming. Lots of them. As Stan had said, this was enough force to do something stupid with, if the commander over there had a mind to.

Dale wondered if the man had ever read Sun Tzu, or Patton. Rommel. Wellington. Light Horse Harry Lee. Any of them.

It would be a man. Blues didn't allow women to serve. Feared that it would somehow sully their delicate womanliness. Taint their femininity.

Dale's mom had been a drill instructor, once upon a time. There wasn't anything delicate about that woman but her drop biscuits.

The top of Turkey Roost was a bald knob of gray granite, slicked over with what little snow and ice could hang on in the teeth of that bitter northwest wind coming down.

Stan directed Dale to tie the horses loosely to a tree, part of a stand down on a little shoulder, something that would provide them some cover and a wind break. Assuming nobody decided to fly overhead anytime soon and maybe catch them moving about on an infrared scanner.

And even that would get muddled up by the wind and snowfall coming at them. They might look like deer.

Stan had found a tree and settled into the lee of it. Every

little bit to block the wind, especially up here where there was no cover at all. Dale fell into his lee, kneeling down and letting his chaps and boots protect his knees from the cold stone.

The Ranger had his optics out, but Dale's eyes were good enough to see the Jayhawks coming. They had chosen to come up Mill Creek instead of the North Fork. Flip of a coin which was smarter.

Dale was still surprised at the raid. All he could think of was that this was a supply column being escorted into the wilderness, to hide a stash depot in advance of the spring offensive. Nothing else made any sense, especially as valuable as those vehicles had to be.

Even over the wind, those ancient turbines screamed like angry raptors. Long column of beasts, coming closer.

Dale would have said wolves, but the Jayhawks were exactly backward from that. Wolves put the weak and old up front to set the pace, so nobody got left behind, with the Alpha at the very rear.

Buffalo, maybe.

These yahoos had both tanks up front, followed by about half of the troop transports, creeping along slowly and crushing small trees and squishing the snow down so the big, articulated trucks in back had a clear trail. As long as they stayed mostly on the bank, everything would be fine.

Dale had studied enough history of the old days to know those tanks down there were really low-flying spaceships, bundled up tight with their own air, heat, and radios. Nobody had made any new tanks in maybe twenty-five years, since folks had started sabotaging the factories that made the war machines, but both sides had inherited thousands of the old beasts from the United States Army, back when it was a thing, and not the degenerate street gang they were witnessing today.

Patton would have cried. Or slapped someone.

"Final exam, Dale," Stan announced in a voice that brooked no sass. "They will pass below us in column. I have explosives enough to bring down a significant portion of that overhanging shelf of rock. What timing do we seek?"

Dale nodded, mostly as a placeholder.

They were on the top of Turkey Roost Mountain, looking down from a sheer cliff face, a wall running at an angle to the valley below where the stone went straight down nearly twenty meters before it flattened out again. They could drop an avalanche, not just of snow, but of tons and tons of mountain as well.

That much was obvious. But that wasn't the question Stan was asking.

This man was a legend. The Last Ranger of the National Park Service, from the time before Blue and Green.

From the old world, before Park Rangers were the police force of the west, protecting the wilderness and the people from the Robber Barons and the Drumphers.

When they were just teachers, and not paladins.

What timing do we seek?

It was a question with a blade hidden in the folds of the fabric, as Musashi would have summarized it. Sun Tzu would have nodded with the swordmaster.

Larimer County was all rippled up, waves of rock frozen forever, leaving troughs where ticks and Jayhawks could hide.

At the same time, it wasn't like the leading face down by Denver, where artillery on the hills could range damned-near forever, and you had to climb hard up the few passable places, channeled into killzones designed by sadists with history degrees.

You couldn't just stop the Jayhawkers by dropping the rocks now. That was the obvious trap. The raiders would just go around you. Maybe backtrack down the North Fork a mile or so and circle around Turkey Roost to come up the back, like he and Stan had done.

Tanks in relatively open country would chase them down like a pack of wolves on a lone buffalo calf.

No, you had to drop the rock and snow *on* them. Avalanche the stone down atop the snake and trap it. Immobilize them here, so that later reinforcements could come roll them up, after whatever was going to happen that these yahoos were here for in the first place.

Patton smiled at him with a cruel eye. Wellington spoke to him of Salamanca.

Stan had asked a different question.

How many men did Dale want to kill today?

None. He had joined the Park Service and not the army because he wanted to help people. He wasn't a killer.

But this was war. They were Jayhawks.

"They likely to stop for the night, anytime soon?" Dale asked.

Laagers would be better defended, but easier to mousetrap. Rommel reminded him of the Battle of Caporetto, before he was famous, but still a genius.

Stan glanced back at the western sky.

"Horse troop would have, already," Stan said, but Dale knew that. "Armor doesn't need to, as long as they have fuel and maps. Two of those big rigs are hauling jet fuel for the machines."

Ah. That's what those were.

There were a pair of them, tucked in at the front of the others. Dale had wondered if they were mobile missile launchers of some sort. Articulated, armored canteens on treads made more sense.

"How come we don't have tanks up here?" Dale asked.

It didn't really matter. Inspiration had lit up his mind, followed by the sound of both the Iron Duke and Light Horse Harry laughing maniacally.

They did that.

Killing was generally wrong, but there were times when it was the best of a set of bad choices. Dale had never had to confront that until today.

People were likely to die as a result of his choices.

He swallowed past a dry tongue and listened.

"Too easy to bomb fuel depots," Stan replied. "Even way out on the west coast. Blues still have an Air Force, even if we got the Springs in the divorce. Plus, too damned rough up here. Figure they'll have to fix at least one major breakdown before they get wherever they want to end up."

Dale nodded carefully, that plan's shape crystalizing.

"In the southwest and in the spring, they always say you cut off the head of the snake," he observed.

He'd never been to Arizona, now mostly empty land and Indian reservation, once all the Snowbirds had gone East during the first war. It hadn't been India and Pakistan Partitioning, but there had still been long convoys in and out of Texas, once things got serious.

Mom had served there, before she had met dad. Still had a magnificent thunderbird tattoo across her back as a reminder.

Stan watched him, utterly motionless.

"Hopefully, we won't have to kill too many of them," Dale continued in a low voice. "But they should have stayed in Kansas, so they need to be batted on the nose with a rolled up newspaper. Maybe next time, they'll think twice and stay home."

Stan grinned.

He stood and tucked the optics back into their case. Dale stood as well.

"When I was a kid," Stan laughed, "this would be the point where someone says: *Here, hold my beer.*"

Dale wasn't sure what that phrase meant, but the cold, steel gleam in Stan's eyes gave him some clue about how dangerous it was about to become.

~oOo~

Dale had never played with high explosives. Sure, there had been familiarization classes with plastic explosives and recoilless rifles, still the best way to knock down avalanches under controlled circumstances.

But he had never really gotten to play with the squishy stuff.

Still hadn't, technically. Stan had done all the work, cramming cold globs down into four ice-filled crevices, always careful not to slip and fly. The snow might be thick and soft below, but you were still going to be falling far enough to break bones at the very best.

In this weather, probably a slow, painful death, especially when that vale turned into a battlefield in a little while.

The column of angry buffalo was still creeping along, but not much faster than a man could walk. Which made sense, with fifty tons of tank; deep snow; small, frozen rivers; and no scouts out front on horses.

It was slow work.

No radios. Detonators on long wires that Dale was holding, back up and in the trees, as Stan worked below him. The twist-plunger was sitting next to Dale.

Stan had explained how to wire it and set everything off, in case he died out there, but Dale was content to wait. Hopefully, all he would do today is watch, but he had a feeling that Stan was going to make him do the killing.

If you wanted to join the Park Service and become a Ranger, those were the costs. Others would be happy to stay as *189*'s or *303*'s, Recreation Aides and Clerks, but Dale was already an apprentice Guide, an *090*, and had his heart set on becoming an *025*, a true *Park Ranger*, with the gold badge and buffalo embroidered on his shoulder.

Warrior.

Stan pushed another glob of gray evil into a hole at his feet and stuffed a wire down, like a long-tail sperm cell just penetrating an egg to give birth to fire.

The sky lit up with the sound of thunder. Which made no sense. Wasn't the right kind of storm for thundersnow.

Wasn't thunder.

Someone had opened up with a machine gun.

Blues had suddenly realized they weren't alone up here in the great, peaceful wilderness.

Stan flipped up in the air suddenly, turned a complete somersault, and face-planted in the snow.

Dale was about a hundred feet away, but he could see blood starting to stain the snow.

And Stan wasn't moving.

Dale lurched to his feet and stopped.

Their job was to stop the Blues. Paralyze them. Nail them to the ground like a catfish on a board, waiting to be cleaned for dinner.

There was nothing he could do for the man if Stan was dead. And the blues were ripping the sky with tracer rounds, turning the twilight purple and pink.

Someone had seen Stan move, on the ridge above them. And nailed him pretty good.

But they thought there were more people around.

A dragon roared, like Gabriel sounding his horn.

Dale watched a one-twenty-five round from the leading tank slam into the far hillside, across the vale and down a half-mile. He didn't know if it was paranoia pulling the trigger, or an unlucky rabbit coming out to feed.

Didn't matter.

Something had drawn their attention. More dragons bellowed, drowning out the baying of angry wolves throwing bullets in every direction.

It was like watching God himself fire a shotgun out of the sky, seeing the snow erupt in little puffs as bullets and explosions went every which way.

Dale was frozen with fear. He forced himself to breathe.

Even Centurion was better trained for this sort of thing than he was.

"Blow it, kid," Stan's voice was suddenly there above the din.

Dale looked over.

Stan was lying in a pool of blood, staining the snow bright crimson.

Even from here, Dale could see the old man gritting his teeth in pain, that precipice not too far beyond him.

"Get out of there, Stan," Dale yelled back.

Stan shook his head.

"Can't move," he hollered over the ongoing gunfire.

"I'll rescue you," Dale almost pleaded.

Those angry, blue eyes speared Dale's soul from clear over there.

"Do your duty, Ranger," Stan commanded.

Dale understood.

He fought back the tears and kneeled, as if in prayer.

Or, also in prayer.

There was a whole package of plastic explosives in that cliff face, just waiting for Joshua.

Dale pulled off his gloves like Stan had showed him. Frostbite was always a risk doing this, but a small one. Better to handle the wires under fingertips than mittens and gloves.

Dale pulled a knife to cut and strip the ends of the wires. He opened the wingnuts and wrapped the four wires tight on the poles.

Something whoomped like an ominous kettle drum. Dale damned near peed himself, until the mortar round landed up-valley in a blast of submunitions and explosives. Vicious, little baseballs of doom and ugliness shredding the snow and trees.

There were a lot of scared kids right below him, just from the sound of gunfire.

And one scared kid up here.

Dale fixed his eyes on Stan and unlocked the plunger. It opened under his hands with a half twist.

Stan nodded, calm as a man at Sunday morning service.

All the tears were Dale's.

Another deep breath.

He nodded back at the old man, the Last Ranger, and twisted the handle down.

Hell came to earth.

Fire, and brimstone, and Lucifer himself, near as Dale could tell.

The earth itself moved amidst all the fire, knocking Dale on his ass. The plunger dropped into the snow next to him, fallen from numb hands.

Half the mountain looked like it was gone, four giant bites taken out of the face, like an angry mole the size of a whale had been there.

Silence, too.

All the firing had stopped, like a Christmas Day Armistice. There had been a song about that.

Dale picked himself up and crept forward, unsure how safe the rocks were, now that someone had taken a ballpeen sledge to them.

It looked safer to the right, so he moved that way. Just enough to peek over.

There was a snake down there, all right. A big one. Mighty angry.

Dale had dropped a bigger rock on top of it.

It took a moment to resolve. Dale hadn't realized just how much mountain was down there now.

Way more than he had been expecting.

The avalanche of snow and stone had hit the snake just about in the middle. Right where Light Horse Harry had suggested.

Half the troop transports were buried, because Dale had

blown it earlier than he planned, but he had still gotten the two tankers, buried them under tons of rock and yards of snow.

Like Harry had said. Horse will graze just fine on grass. Tanks don't have that option. No silage, no cavalry.

Everyone had stopped firing down there.

Probably shock. Sure as hell a goodly amount of surprise.

Who expected someone to drop a mountain on them?

Wouldn't last that long.

Dale crept back out of sight before anybody saw him. The tanks could still move, so he needed to get gone, but there was no way in hell he was coming home with Audrey and not Stan.

Crazed patterns of stress had lit up these rocks, like a china plate glued back together.

Stan was still in the middle of it, so Dale moved as carefully as he could.

It was still a long ways down, and that cliff was a lot closer than it had been.

Stan was on his back when Dale got close. Probably flipped by all the shockwaves that had knocked Dale on his own ass.

There wasn't much time, and Stan wasn't all that heavy, regardless of heavy, winter clothing. Tall and wiry come summer greens. Dale knelt at his side and felt for a pulse. He could easily throw the old man's body into a fireman's carry and get him to cover.

"Hold my beer," Stan murmured.

Dale was so shocked he fell on his butt again.

"Aren't you supposed to be dead?" Dale asked as he got back up.

"Ya gotta know how to play with high explosives, kid," Stan explained. "Shaping charges is an art form."

"Can you walk?" Dale asked, standing and offering a hand. "We need to be somewhere else."

Stan took the hand and let Dale pull him up, his left arm hanging useless by his side.

Dale grabbed a handful of snow and pushed it into the bloody hole in Stan's shoulder.

All Dad's first aid lessons came back as he did. Hit just right and there's nothing but muscle and bone to hurt. Below the tendons, above the lungs, miss the heart. Pretty survivable wound.

He turned Stan around and stuffed more snow into the back.

Dying by Blue was a bigger risk than shock and blood loss right now. Those folks would be angry and vicious, at least until their commander got them under control and figured out what had happened.

And what they could do now, with the snake chopped right in half.

Audrey and Centurion could get the two of them far enough away that Dale could sew the old man up and get more teams vectored in. Or watch from a really safe distance while some idiots went full frontal on Fort Collins, expecting a flank surprise that had just gotten its teeth kicked in.

Dale got Stan down to the horses and boosted the old man up onto Audrey's saddle with a shoulder under his ass.

Centurion held perfectly still, and then turned and took point all by himself, like he recognized that Audrey needed to walk careful going home.

They were both better at this than he was.

"You done good, kid," Stan said through gritted teeth. "No. You done good, Ranger."

"But I'm only an *090*, Stan," Dale argued. "A Guide."

"No, Dale," Stan said firmly. "After today, you're a Ranger."

END

RAID AT 817 MAPLE STREET

Ken Staley

When the bad guys arrived at nine-fifteen Tuesday night in Logan, Iowa, they drove new, black Suburban SUVs. Howie Collins looked out his upstairs window just as two dark vehicles coasted down Maple Street without headlights. He knew every pebble on Maple Street for blocks. His FaceBook friend, Billy Daves, told him that desperate burglar rings in the big city branched out into small towns like Logan— towns close enough to a freeway to make a quick get-away but not likely to have an efficient police force. Howie wasn't fooled for a minute.

He reached down and tapped the key to disconnect the internet. It was his turn in the War to End all Wars, an on-line game where you fought back the terrorist threat. Or became one. He'd been trying to infiltrate Jerusalem all morning, but Ibrim, his gaming challenger in Haifa, blocked each attempt. Howie's cell, Billy366 in Seattle and Kelly144 from Tupelo, had a plan to infiltrate the middle-east and kill the King of Hordania. Howie thought Ibrim's cell in Haifa had an unfair advantage because they lived in the area. His team gained the lead by one on the scoreboard when they blocked Ibrim's attempt to blow up Mt Rushmore.

~oOo~

"The objective was the suspect's computer," Special Agent Howard Kennedy said. Kennedy sat in a small Senate conference room. With him were four senators and his boss, General Jack Hamilton, the Assistant Director of Operations.

"You were the agent in charge of the field operation?" Senator Albert Van Slyke (R-Iowa) asked.

"Yes, sir, I was," Kennedy replied.

"What story was given to the press?" the Senator asked.

"Our agency has no comment on any operation that may, or may not, be under consideration. Our 'leak' gave out the 'home grown radicalized terror cell' story that's been making all the headlines."

"Why warn't this done at some gawdawful time in the morning?" Senator Bart Fields (R-W Va) asked as he rifled through a pile of scraps that poured from his briefcase. "Whar is it," he mumbled to himself as he pulled a slip from the stack and scrutinized it. "These things usually happen at four A.M. or some damned thing."

"Our intelligence sources indicated that the family would be away from their house early in the evening, Senator," Kennedy said.

"Why din' you do it durin the day when there warn't nobody home, then?" Senator Fields didn't look up from his pile of papers.

"Mrs. Collins does not work outside of the home, Senator," Agent Kennedy said with an exasperated sigh. He was tired of the old man already and the hearing had just started.

"She what?" Senator Fields was a Senate icon and antique. Approaching 90, he hadn't missed a session in the Senate in 50 years.

"She stays at home, Senator," General Hamilton said when he saw that Kennedy was losing his patience. "Odd as it is, it still happens now and then. Our preliminary intelligence report indicated that the entire Collins family usually left the house early Tuesday night and didn't return until late. Our plan was to be in, replace his entire hard drive and be out before anyone returned—half an hour at most."

"Didn' work too well, did it?" Senator Fields snorted.

~oOo~

Howie watched as the black SUVs parked in the shadows of the trees that gave their name to the street. Howie snorted in derision at their wasted attempt at stealth. He knew where every car on mile-long Maple Street parked at night. When they got out, their fake ninja outfits...black clothes, black knit caps, black combat boots...didn't fool Howie either. All their big city stuff was way out of place in a small town like Logan. With a quick flip, Howie's computer screen died, leaving him a clear, moon-washed picture.

~oOo~

"Why didn't all that fancy listenin' crap pick up on this?" the Senator demanded. "Seems we pissed away enough money it shoulda made this an easy pick up."

"Our programs did flag the initial responses," General Hamilton replied, "but we needed clarification. The suspect's hard drive would have provided that."

"Why was his computer so important? What did you hope to gain from the boy's computer, Agent Kennedy?" Senator

Winston James (R-Iowa), sympathized with the agents but had constituents back home demanding answers.

"Our programs flag messages between the middle-east and various suspected domestic cells. It took some time to narrow the field, but the subject's computer continued to show up in our daily flags, sometimes several times a day. Early indications indicated a source of a domestic terror cell with possible middle-east funding. Analysts believed a real time examination of those messages might still be on the computer's hard drive and prove out the details that a simple flagging doesn't offer."

"Explain how all that works again, General Hamilton," Senator Smiling Jack Peters, (D-Wisconsin—and presidential hopeful) asked.

"Congress gave permission for our agency to screen internet traffic as part of the Make America Safe Act," General Hamilton said. "Our software combs virtually every communication either sent or received from a foreign source. We've a solid set of phrases and code words. This sort is resorted and reduced by iterative reduction techniques. When something trips through all of those safeguards we assign an analyst. We did, and acted on his recommendations."

"What kind of traffic are you talking about, General?" Senator Peters asked. "You make it sound like a traffic accident. And what constitutes a 'petabyte'?"

"It's difficult to explain, Senator," the general said. "Even those who understand the process have trouble making it easy for people without a computer background to understand. In straightforward data volume, the agencies process a hundred thousand petabytes a week."

"How big is that?"

"To put it in words that even I understood, our computers sift through 200 entire sets of an encyclopedia every minute."

"What led you to suspect Howard Collins?" Senator Peters asked.

"Senator, we have records of planned attacks in the United States, including the Space Needle in Seattle and Mt. Rushmore."

"You have evidence?" Senator Marsha Wilburn (D-Calif) asked.

"Yes, ma'am," Kennedy slid a computer print-out across the table to her. "You can see that we've been able to trace his exchanges to another cell operating in Europe and the Middle East."

"Why weren't charges ever pressed?" Senator Fields asked. "This seems damnably harsh punishment for a simple kid playin' with his computer."

"We have been unable to match each threat this cell made. We are still uncertain about the veracity of the threats. We managed to determine Mr. Collins is the cell leader in the United States, Senator," Hamilton said.

"C'mon! A sixteen year old *kid!* You'll have to do better than that," Senator Fields said.

"Several of the most recent suicide bombers in Europe have been boys younger than Howie Collins," Agent Kennedy said.

~o0o~

Alone in his upstairs bedroom, Howie watched as the ninjas slung MP5s over their shoulders from the back of one of the vans. They separated into three teams. One pair crouched down like they wanted to take a dump in the middle of the street; then rushed across the street, heading for the alley. Two others crouch-ran across the street, too, until Mrs. Arnson's picket fence stopped them. With a quick leap, they landed in her garden and tramped her roses.

Lucky she isn't home, Howie thought, *or she'd have been all over them like a wet rag.* Nobody messed with Mrs. Arnson's roses.

Four raiders remained. They looked at his house, then up and down the street, then crouched down and started straight toward his front door.

~oOo~

"My team made a standard approach, Senator James," Agent Kennedy said. "This entire operation started as a simple 'by the book' plan, small stuff, really. Initial recon discovered no real problems except a loud dog in the subject's back yard. We approached without incident, neutralized the animal and deployed per procedure."

"Killed it, you mean," interjected Senator Peters.

"Yes, sir." It was a potential risk.

"Had the proper warrants been issued?" Senator Fields asked.

"Yes. We have copies of them here." Agent Kennedy slid copies of the warrants across the table. "Issued by the Counter Terrorism Hearing Office earlier that morning. Colonel Harold B. Lawson."

~oOo~

Howie felt his heart pound against his chest and his mind

raced through one confusing thought after another. Just like Billy Daves warned. A gang of big city thieves headed across Maple for his house. Mom and Pop still had an hour of bingo left at the American Legion Hall in Marion, plus an hour drive back home. It was only 9:30 and phoning 911 didn't occur to Howie. Sheriff Murphy rolled up the streets and went home after dark anyway. He knew that it was up to him to protect his home.

Howie ran to the upstairs hall closet as Barkely, his golden retriever, raised Hell in the back yard, yipped once, and stopped. Dad always kept his hunting rifle loaded and handy "just in case." Howie pulled open the closet and removed the hunting rifle. Until tonight, Howie always wondered "in case of what?" Now he knew. He took the stairs two at a time, his adrenaline fired excitement caused him to stumble on the landing at the bottom of the steps. He took in the living room with a glance, a place that was such a normal part of his life now seemed alien.

He shoved the sofa away from the up-right player piano and jumped behind it. The piano, with its brass sounding board, protected his back. He gulped for air, hoping to catch his breath before his panting betrayed his nerves. Howie poked the barrel of the rifle along the arm of the over-stuffed sofa giving him an unobstructed view of the front door. What just moments ago felt foreign now wrapped him in comfortable familiarity again. Howie's nerves betrayed him again and he lost control of those extra shells in his pockets, scattering them in several directions. He scrambled to find as many as he could reach. He lined them up like a squad of soldiers as he'd seen other, real soldiers do in the movies.

Outside, the frontal assault team reached the porch. They climbed over the low wall that surrounded the porch. Using the trellis as a ladder, they scaled the wall rather than take the stairs like normal people.

~oOo~

"What happened when you attempted to serve the warrants?" Senator James asked.

"Procedure," General Hamilton said.

"I think we'd prefer to hear from your field agent, General Hamilton," Senator James said.

"Just as the General said—procedure," Agent Kennedy said. "When we heard movement inside the house, we announced ourselves…"

~oOo~

Chintz curtains hung in the front door windows, displaying shadows of the four stupid robber gang, like some sort of spastic puppet show. Howie snuggled the stock against his cheek and he sighted down the barrel.

Two of the shadows bracketed the door, a third backed down the steps. The fourth person on the porch stood so that his shadow didn't cross the window at all. Howie centered the door in his sights. The bad guys didn't wait, or knock. With a crash, the door banged open and smashed against the inside wall, its large, heavy glass window shattered. Shards of broken glass scattered across the landing, the sound drowning out everything else.

~oOo~

"We met well-armed resistance, Senator," Agent Kennedy said.

"From a kid?" Senator Fields asked.

~oOo~

Howie fired as the first ninja crossed the threshold in a semi crouch. Howie's 30/30 blast drilled through the intruder's skull at the hairline and dropped him in the hole that was once his front door. The ninja's wool cap exploded in a spray of red like soda spurting from a well-shaken pop bottle.

Momentum carried the second ninja through the door, fast on the heels of the first but the dying body across the threshold slowed him and tangled his feet. Howie nailed this one with a head shot, too, and his sorry ass crumpled on top of his pal. Their pile of bodies made any further assault through the front door impossible.

Howie giggled three times as the visions of the flying cap came back to him. Clean head shots, both of them. Images of brain matter and pieces of skull came with the vision and his nerves caught up with him. He vomited all over Mom's couch.

~oOo~

"Senator, that 'kid' killed two of my best agents in a matter of seconds," Agent Kennedy said. His voice was cold as he turned toward Senator Fields. General Hamilton reached over and squeezed his arm.

~oOo~

Frantic calls from the remaining ninjas rang out across the neighborhood as they scurried for cover. Howie stopped retching when he heard the rustle of two other ninjas as they scraped past the counter in the kitchen. In all the excitement at the front door, he'd forgotten about the pair of ninjas at Mrs. Arnson's house next door. They must have come in the back door during all the firing. He wondered about Barkley, but only for a moment. Assassins who would kick in his front door would have taken out his dog.

Angered that they'd kill his dog, Howie stood and used the piano as his shooting bench. The first ninja through the kitchen door sprayed bullets indiscriminately into the dining and living rooms, doing a roll toward the dining room table. He didn't get far. Howie was rifle champ at school for three years running. He nailed the guy in mid-roll.

The second guy simply stuck his arm around the corner and fired. The piano screamed this time as keys flew in all directions. Howie's return shot shattered the arm just at the wrist and the MP5 dropped, and curses came through clenched teeth as the guy stumbled down the kitchen steps and slammed through the back door, ending the attack from behind.

~oOo~

"What time did your assault on the house begin, Agent Kennedy?"

"The initial fire-fight began 9:45 that evening," Agent Kennedy glanced at his notes.

"I see," Senator Peters said. "What, exactly, happened?"

"The assault team was a bit confused at first," Kennedy admitted. "They'd just seen two members go down."

"Did you know that your agents were dead?" Senator Harper asked.

"No sir, not yet. We had to assume that they were still alive."

"And did you know that Howard Collins was alone in the

house?"

"No, sir, not at that time. We knew he was leader of a cell and had to assume his team gathered inside with him," Agent Kennedy said, then added just under his breath. "I didn't think it possible for one boy to take out my patrol."

"I wanna talk about that, too," Senator Fields would not be put off. "You say that you tried to serve these warrants and this kid opened up with a 30/30? Did you knock on the door? Did you identify yourselves?"

~oOo~

"What in hell's goin' on out here!"

Howie heard his neighbor call from across the street. He peeked over the couch and saw Mr. Carpenter on his own porch, dressed in his bathrobe and stocking feet, newspaper in hand. Howie could hear other doors open and the murmur of other neighbors. "Y'all get away from that house before I call the cops."

"Go back inside, sir! This is police business!" A strange voice called from somewhere near his house.

Police business? Howie thought. Sure not any local police. He knew all five members of the police department and not one of them could have made such an assault on a house as these guys did.

"Police my ass," Mr. Carpenter yelled. "Police in this town don't go busting down doors. Y'all better show yourselves or you won't have to worry about the police. I got my shotgun right handy!"

~oOo~

"We met with verbal threats of resistance from armed

members of the immediate community, Senator Fields," Agent Kennedy regained his composure. "Mr. Arthur Carpenter died as the result of an exchange of gunfire."

"Another innocent civilian killed?"

"Collateral damage, Senator," Agent Kennedy said, "it happens now and then in the best of circumstances."

~oOo~

Howie watched as a shadow raced from the direction of the alley and used a flying tackle to push Mr. Carpenter back inside. Another crouched shadow slid in behind Mr. Carpenter's Buick parked on the street.

"Now!" The shadow behind the Buick called, stood up, and pointed his weapon at Howie's house. Howie saw just the flash before he dropped to the floor. Bullets ate through the window and what was left of the front door. The player piano behind him complained loudly as several of the slugs found connections on its wires. Constant hits shivered the couch as its stuffing filled the air like snow.

When the MP5 emptied its clip, Howie rose to a kneeling position, took aim through the shattered window and snapped off two quick rounds. The ninja guys must have hidden behind Mr. Carpenter's car because that's all Howie managed to hit. That's when he heard the distant sounds of a siren approaching.

~oOo~

"What time did the local officials arrive?" Senator Harper asked.

"9:53, sir," Kennedy glanced at his notes again.

"Who was first to arrive?"

"The town constable, Officer William Cullen Murphy, arrived on the scene after the second exchange, Senator."

"Did you turn the matter over to him, Agent Kennedy?" Senator James asked.

"That would be against policy, Senator," General Hamilton said.

"What were your people doing at that time, Agent Kennedy?"

"I divided the remaining crew into two groups."

"By the end of the second fire fight, you'd lost three agents, almost half your team. Why didn't you withdraw at that time?" Senator James asked.

"The mission remained incomplete, Senator," Agent Kennedy said.

~oOo~

Flashing red and blue lights filled the dark living room before the police car screamed to a stop outside Howie's front door. The radio in Murph's car shrieked over an external speaker adding to the confusion as one voice tried to talk over another.

"Would you guys shut up!" The constable's voice cut off all other radio traffic. Howie peeked over the top of the couch. Murph wasn't getting out of his car right away, not until he sized up the situation.

"Howie? You okay?" He called through his radio speaker.

"Okay!" Was all Howie managed to croak. He shivered uncontrollably and felt his stomach churning again. He wasn't sure Murph heard him.

There was a scraping noise behind him and Howie wheeled, rifle at the ready, only to face an empty kitchen door. Howie followed the sound and saw that the ninja in the dining room wasn't dead, merely wounded. Howie crawled around the piano and pulled the small black gun out of the wounded ninja's reach. He managed a quick search of the person, removing a pistol and a wicked looking knife from the belt. The person rolled over and gurgled. The entry wound, just above the collar of a bulletproof vest, shattered the collarbone and blood pumped through a large hole near the throat. Howie couldn't see an exit wound. He felt tears streak down his face.

He'd shot a woman.

~oOo~

"Constable Murphy attempted communication with Howard Collins. Did you permit that?"

"At the time, Senator, there was simply too much confusion," Agent Kennedy said. "As you said earlier, half my team was either dead or incapacitated. Agent Bolls was missing and presumed dead. Agents Atwater and Hopkins were down within sight, but hadn't moved and gave no signs of life.

"When did you realize that Agent Bolls had not been killed in the assault?" Senator Harper asked.

"Not until after the autopsy, Senator," Agent Kennedy said softly.

"Why were tear gas canisters fired, Agent Kennedy?"

"We wanted to use them as a smoke screen to remove our people from the site, Senator."

"Did the fire start then?"

"No, ma'am, not with the first salvo."

~oOo~

Howie slid away from the woman ninja and watched her, wiping the tears from his eyes. He knew he was in trouble. The woman on the floor would probably die if he didn't do something. She tried to roll over, tried to moan, then settled into the pool of her own blood.

Howie sneaked a peek over the top of the couch. Murphy was out of his car and arguing with other ninjas. Howie crawled to the woman.

"I'm really sorry lady," he sobbed as he inched closer. He wished he could stop crying. "I'm really sorry. Here, lady, let me help you."

His scouting first aid merit badge seemed years ago. He reached out to turn her on her side so that pressure eased from the wound. As gently as possible, he removed her jacket and bulletproof vest. He tore his shirt off and tore it to strips to use as improvised pressure bandages. There was little he could do about the shattered bone or the pain.

He looked away from his work to see her green eyes watching him. Her tears streaked the dirt and blood on her face. Howie moved closer and cradled her head in his lap and joined her in crying. This wasn't so bad, he thought, sitting her, holding a woman, even if she was a stranger. Just the soft touch of another human. She grabbed his hand and held tightly. Loud pops and thumping rattles on the front porch brought him back to reality. He'd forgotten about the ninjas out front.

~oOo~

"You convinced the constable to withdraw, Agent Kennedy?"

"No, Senator Peters. We were forced to physically restrain Sheriff Murphy. He was incapacitated."

"How was that done?"

~o0o~

As the smoke on the porch rose to window level, Howie saw the ninja who fired the smoke grenade use the butt of his rifle on Murphy. 'Murph the Smurph', the kids at school called him, crumpled like a rag doll. Angry that they hadn't had enough, that they weren't willing to give up and leave well enough alone, Howie picked up the weapon and fired it through the window.

~o0o~

"When did the third fire-fight occur?" Senator James asked.

"Officer Murphy had just been rendered unconscious when firing commenced from the target house."

"Was anyone injured?"

"Agent Alred lost his life, ma'am."

"And you fired more tear gas into the house at that time?"

"Yes, Senator, I did."

"How many canisters were fired into the house, Agent Kennedy?"

"Five. Two upstairs and three downstairs."

"Were these the cause of the fire?"

"That's in our report. Yes, sir."

~o0o~

A bouncing horror flew through the front door, ricocheted off a step and rolled to the foyer landing. Howie heard his upstairs window break and something thumped against his wall. Another smoking terror flew through the hole that had once been a living room window and ignited stuffing from the couch as it slid through the room. Howie heard his parent's window break, but was too busy coughing to hear the fifth canister bounce off the living room wall.

He crawled back to the wounded agent. She shuddered each time she drew a breath. Her lip quivered, like an infant getting ready to cry. Her eyes fluttered with each quick breath. She wasn't crying any more. Howie knew she was dying. The room filled with smoke and the blazing old sofa cast an eerie orange glow to the scene.

Howie started to drag the wounded agent through the kitchen. At the top of the landing, he caught a glimpse of another man hiding behind the tool shed, his weapon trained on the back door. Howie was trapped.

~oOo~

"Both Agent Bolls and Howard Collins died of smoke asphyxiation in the resulting fire, is that correct?"

"Yes, senator, that's confirmed by their autopsies, although Agent Bolls' wounds were probably fatal as well."

"How long did it take for the fire department to arrive?"

"The first men were on the scene within a few minutes of the first tear gas, but as Senator James will tell you, it's a volunteer fire department. It was ten minutes before their equipment arrived. By that time, the entire front of the house was fully involved."

~oOo~

Flames from the dining room chased Howie back to the kitchen landing. He scooted toward the back door, only to be chased inside as the ninja behind the tool shed splintered the door frame around him. Smoke and tear gas burned his eye and made it almost impossible for him to breathe. The woman ninja at his feet had stopped breathing.

~oOo~

"Now this here piece of slag is what's left of Mr. Collins' computer?" Senator Fields asked as he pointed to a collection of melted, smoke stained parts wrapped in plastic, sitting in the middle of the table.

"More or less, Senator," Agent Kennedy said.

"And which piece is the 'more' piece?"

"This is the disk drive from the machine," General Hamilton said as he removed the drive from another plastic bag.

"Were you able to determine anything from this?" Senator Harper asked.

"It survived in remarkably fine condition, Senator," Hamilton said as he turned the drive over in his hands, inspecting it again. "From what we could determine, it's unlikely that Mr. Collins was the leader of any domestic terror threat. There simply aren't any kind of radicalized messages or visits to extreme radical web sites."

"Now just a dog gone minute here," Senator Harper had a tendency to turn red when extremely provoked. His ears glowed like a pair of stop signs. "Are you tellin' me that we done spent the best part of the mornin' wastin' time cause the press won't let go and is demandin' an investigation. And just what in blue blazes should we tell them? We aren't likely to hide the fact of this meeting."

"Senator Harper, the Collins incident was six months ago," General Hamilton said. "We have pictures of those that attended his funeral and have been able to identify the other members of his so-called cell."

General Hamilton slid a series of glossy pictures across the table.

"What the hell? Why...this ain't nuthin' but kids!"

"As may be, Senator, but younger children all over the world are radicalized by their parents. Our leak indicates that such was a possibility here. So far, those in this room constitute the only group with all the facts. We intend to keep it that way."

END

FROZEN

Liam Hogan

Charlie and I were parked up on Main Street, sharing a cherry cola and watching the world go by through the wide, open windows of the station wagon.

It was Election Day and the sidewalks were jammed. The registered Democrats had been awake since the caucuses, so they were used to the changes by now; but the floating voters had only recently emerged and were shuffling along, peering into the windows of stores that weren't the stores they remembered, adrift in their ill-fitting clothes.

Charlie slurped the last of the perspiring drink, rattling the ice with her straw. "Let's *go* somewhere!"

I waved at cars, bumper to bumper, purring like a swarm of happy insects. "Go where, hunnybun? Everywhere's chocker. Plus," I tapped the fuel dial, "We're out. We blew our ration at the beach."

She stretched, languidly. I felt the electric thrill I always feel when I glimpse her smooth skin, the fuzz of golden hair, felt the tug at my loins. She caught me looking and grinned. "Yeah, but it was *so* worth it!"

We'd spent most of the time in the unseasonably warm waters, before threading our way across narrow corridors of sand between an overlapping quilt of beach towels, looking for somewhere to perch and soak up the last of the October sun.

That was the problem with election years. The population doubled; short term, anyway. Mostly, industry coped. Restaurants got booked out solid, spare rooms rented at sky high prices. But some things, consumables like gas, were rationed, there being no easy or cheap way to up the supply.

Still, it was awfully nice just to sit there in my own car with Charlie at my side, even if we weren't going anywhere.

"I'll be glad when it's back to normal," I said.

"You're not worried?" she asked.

I blinked. "Nah. It's in the bag."

She shook her head. "I hear it's close. Real close."

"You can't trust the polls."

"But if you're wrong... what if we lose?"

"Then we get frozen," I said, "Hibernate the Presidency away." I shrugged. "Better than living through it; through the changes we can't do anything about."

"I've never been frozen, before," she said, her voice low.

I looked at her in genuine surprise. I knew she was a first time voter, sixteen months younger than I was, but... "Never? What about your parents?"

"My father was a democrat, my mum a republican."

I laughed. It was like the start of one of those lame political jokes.

Charlie pulled a face in return. "Ain't funny. What's the point of being married to someone you only see six months every four years? What's the point of having parents you only get one at a time? And who age at different rates?"

I sobered up at that, drummed my fingers across the warped dash in thought. "Freezing's not so bad," I reassured her. "It *is* cold, though. But that doesn't last long."

We'd had three republican terms on the trot; it'd been a while since I'd been in the tanks. As a juvie, not yet registered, frozen by my parent's mutually agreed votes. But I still shivered at the memory of the bone-numbing cold, before they put you fully under.

The deep-sleep process had been developed for space missions that never happened. Then, almost as a joke, or maybe as a trial, those prototype tanks had been offered after a particularly bad natured election was won by the surprise Republican candidate.

Democrats signed up in droves.

It didn't hurt that, as a welcome side-effect, the carefully controlled drip-fed nutrients forced your metabolism to reset to your ideal weight. Deep-sleepers awoke, slim and healthy.

And when *both* candidates realized having half the population asleep pretty much guaranteed they'd meet their election promises—full employment, better standard of living, even reduced environmental impact—the Voter Hibernation Act was signed into law.

So now, it was no longer voluntary. Everyone on the losing

side who wasn't considered indispensable, wasn't a career politician, went into the tanks shortly after the election results were called. It took a couple of months before they were all frozen; same way it took a while to defrost them all. It was supposed to be done by ZIP Code lottery, but you could apply for an extension, if you were an employer rather than an employee, someone who had to wind up their business affairs.

There wasn't much to wind up for Charlie and me. Oh, there was my old station wagon, I supposed. No point in putting *that* into storage, though. Better to collect the bounty for scrapping a clunker. By the time we came out, most likely there'd be no gas stations left and cars like mine would sit silent in museums.

"I hear there are floaters who vote to lose," I mused, as much to fill the silence as anything else.

Charlie stared at me, eyes agog. "Why?"

I shrugged. "A form of immortality. They want to live forever, even if most of it is frozen. Like a time machine, lurching forwards four years at each hop."

"That's stupid. When do they get to live their lives?"

"In between."

She shook her head at the dumbness of it. She reached out a hand, entwined it in mine. "If we lose, you'll still be there, won't you, when we come out the other side?"

I looked down into those big, brown eyes. Tonight, we'd watch the results trickle in, a little drunk, a little fearful. If it was close it'd be early morning before we'd know for certain. But win or lose didn't matter half as much as the two of us watching them together.

"'Course. You and me, Charlie-babes, forever; frozen or not."

I leant over and kissed her hard and long; the taste of cherry cola lingering on her lips.

END

DUCK, DONALD: A TRUMP EXORCISM

Marleen S. Barr

When Trump, near the end of his second term, sat on his golden Trump Tower toilet, he was in for a big surprise. After eliminating—and still ignoring the fact that the majority of American citizens wished to eliminate him from office—he looked into the golden bowl. The toilet was filled with bright red liquid.

Feeling alarmed, Trump phoned Dr. Ben Carson to ask for a diagnosis. "Donald, I am a brain surgeon. I don't do rectums," Carson said. "And furthermore, I haven't practiced medicine in years. Since I am spending all of my time using my experience as someone who has lived in houses to serve as Housing and Urban Development head, my medical acumen has become a little rusty. Although you are not concerned with professional qualifications—everyone remembers how you hired a pollution lover to run the Environmental Protection Agency—I must say that I am not able to help you."

"What should I do?"

"Get a colonoscopy."

"Are there any ass doctors left?"

"I now regret to remind you that most of the ousted Obama administration H.U.D. employees got jobs as doctors. It was logical for them to pull this switcheroo. They figured that if a doctor with no government agency experience could run H.U.D., then H.U.D administrators could be employed as doctors. You may want to choose wisely as to whom you allow to probe you. These people have memories, and frankly, sir would you like to spend all day looking up assholes? Pussy groping is a lot more fun."

After Trump's symptoms continued and he was certain that he had colon cancer, he again sought Dr. Carson's advice. "You need to have surgery," Carson said.

"Are there any colon cancer surgeons left?"

"I am not sure. As you are aware, after you rescinded Obamacare, most people could not afford to see actual doctors. The whole medical system collapsed. Real doctors gave up their practices and were replaced by alternative doctors—such as the former H.U.D. folks. I will refer you to America's last qualified colon cancer surgeon.

Trump was wheeled into the operating room. The last of the Mohicans in relation to colon cancer surgery, Dr. Cochise Sitting Bull, slit open Trump's abdomen and peered inside. He saw, perched atop the President's bloated spleen, a bright red devil waving a trident. His feet were resting firmly on a cancerous colon. Afraid to remove the devil from inside Trump, he left the devil where it was, extracted the cancer, rerouted the colon to an Ivanka designed colostomy bag and sewed Trump up. Shocked by finding a devil within someone he considered to be a horror, Dr. Bull had a heart attack. Since cardiologists no longer existed, Dr. Bull died.

Trump did not enjoy life with an ostomy bag. Melania divorced him.

"I took all of your shit in order to have money beyond my wildest dreams. But that was alternative fact shit. I didn't sign up to deal with real shit," said Melania as she descended down the Trump Tower escalator for the last time.

Trump could not cope with the ostomy bag hanging from

his now flawed body. Alec Baldwin, using Trump's condition to comic effect--against a background tape of Trump mimicking the handicapped *New York Times* reporter--did a *Saturday Night Live* skit involving a plastic bag filled with chocolate ice cream. Chocolate ice cream sales plummeted. Unable to endure further public humiliation, Trump choose to have reconstructive surgery. After again facing the lack of a qualified surgeon and reasoning that a rusty brain surgeon was better than a former H.U.D. employee, Trump convinced Dr. Carson to perform the surgery.

Dr. Bull never told Carson about the devil. The latter doctor had a great surprise in the operating room. "Enough already," said the devil as he jumped out of Trump and landed feet first on the operating room floor. "I wasn't alone in there," he continued as a plethora of gremlins, trolls, witches, and fire breathing dragons followed in his wake. Carson looked as if he had seen a ghost. "Don't be so surprised. Trump is not thin. He has a big abdomen. There was a lot of room for all of us in there," said the devil. And with a great grin added, "but wait, there's more." He jabbed his trident into a particularly swollen portion of colon. It burst.

Flying feces joined the alternative personages parade. "Duck. Donald's shit is hitting the fan—again. Everyone take cover," Carson said to the operating room staff. Afterwards, when Carson supervised the sew up and cleanup, Trump opened his eyes in the recovery room. He saw a young attractive black nurse. (Unlike doctors, qualified nurses still existed.) "Since you're helping me, I can respond to you as a person," said Trump. "So even though you rate as a nine point two, I won't grope your pussy. Such a shame that you live in a crime ridden drug infested murder sodden ghetto."

The biopsy, done by secret agreement at a Canadian lab,

told the story. Trump never had colon cancer. The red liquid in the toilet bowl was merely devil urine—a red shower. Even Putin could not have contrived this alternative fact. The surgery, which exorcised the evil living inside Trump, had not been a waste. No longer a loud mouthed narcissistic barbarian, Trump reinstated Obamacare and stopped substituting alternative facts for facts. When Elizabeth Warren followed him as President, Trump made sure that a smooth power transition ensued. In memory of Dr. Cochise Sitting Bull, Trump never again called Warren Pocahontas.

During Warren's inauguration ceremony, Trump stood beaming next to the new Mrs. Trump. Mrs. Trump the fourth was seventy-five years old and she was not thin. Trump never found out that she was also not human. This spouse was a feminist separatist planet denizen sent to Earth to keep Trump in line—just in case he might have a relapse. To make Trump feel comfortable and to compensate for her lack of American popular culture knowledge, extraterrestrial Mrs. Trump presented herself in an eastern European guise as the long lost clone of one Angela Merkel. Donald and "Hildegard" Trump lived happily ever after. Donald never made his alien wife register as an illegal immigrant.

END

WALKS HOME ALONE AT NIGHT

Wondra Vanian

Everyone knows that it's dangerous for a woman to walk alone at night. What most people don't realize—or don't care to admit—is that safety is a privilege of the financially secure. It's easy to warn others against wandering the streets after dark when one knows they'll be tucked away safe behind locked doors in their gated communities long before evening falls. Everyone else? Well, everyone else takes their chances.

Meena scanned the darkness as she stepped off the bus. Her neighborhood had never been particularly safe but things had gotten steadily worse since Donald Trump rose to power. Harassment and hate crimes were so common that they no longer made the news. It was just expected that if you were dumb enough to visibly be anything other than Christian or unlucky enough to be just a little too brown, you were fair game.

Of course, Meena mused as she tucked the jersey hijab she wore under her chin, *plenty of people are both*.

She didn't like to think about that very long.

In normal circumstances, it would be wiser for a woman on her own to stick to the brightly lit streets where it was easier to maintain the illusion of safety. But nothing had been normal in America for some time. Meena clung to the shadows as she walked in the direction of her apartment building.

She heard the growl of the truck before its headlights fell on her. Her stomach tightened anxiously as the vehicle drew near. It was difficult to keep her step steady. The hem of her abaya seemed determined to wrap around her legs and trip her up.

Meena knew what would happen the moment the truck crawled to a idling stop beside her. She took a deep breath as she braced herself for what came next.

"Well, lookie what we got here," a man's voice called out. "It's one of them Allah girls."

Meena knew there was no point trying to pretend they weren't talking about her. She turned in time to see a pair of men climbing out of the truck's cab. Two more spilled off of the open flatbed. They all looked solid, brawny types. Probably from some building site or road crew, if the high visibility jackets they wore were anything to go by.

She held her tongue.

"Sure looks it," one of his companions agreed. "Reckon she's gotta bomb under there, TJ?"

"Maybe we oughtta check. Be damned un-American of us not to."

"Immigration status," the one called TJ demanded. He held out a hand.

Meena knew the drill. The ID card declaring her a third-generation Muslim American from India was affixed to the front of her gown, as federal law required, but she didn't want the man's meaty paws anywhere near her chest. She unclasped the card and handed it over.

"That can't be right," TJ said after a glance at the card. "This ID belongs to an American. But you don't look like no American to me. Whatcha think, Maxie Boy? She look like a patriot to you?"

The one who had suggested Meena be searched for a bomb spit on the ground near her feet. It took a considerable effort to keep herself from taking a step back. Instead, Meena flicked the hem of her abaya back and lowered her eyes so the thug couldn't see the anger building in them.

"Nope," Maxie said.

TJ tossed Meena's ID card to one of his companions. "You know what the penalty for an Illegal impersonating an American citizen is, curry pot?"

Meena gritted her teeth against the angry retort that wanted to be heard. The insult wasn't that bad; far worse had been flung in her direction. What really bothered Meena was that "Maxie Boy" grabbed his crotch and winked at her as TJ spoke.

"Man asked you a question, bitch," one of the others said. "Answer him before I knock your goddamn teeth out."

Did Meena know what happened to so-called Illegals who were accused of using ID cards that weren't their own?

Had she been in a cave the last eighteen months?

No. She knew.

The penalty was the same for just about any crime

perpetrated by a non-Christian or person of color: immediate relocation to a detainment camp where, if they were lucky, relatives in a country that wasn't too afraid of President Trump's power might arrange for their relocation. But the list of countries that refused to cow to Trump's unpredictable, weaponised fits of rage grew smaller every week.

India, in a bid to protect its burgeoning economy, had decided to toe Trump's line a long time ago. Meena had cousins in Great Britain who would take her in, if she asked, but the British had problems enough of their own. The post-Brexit race riots still raged.

Welcome or not, America was all Meena had.

"The ID is my own," she answered instead. "Feel free to call the Department of Nationalized—"

Wham.

The blow was not entirely unexpected but the shock of it rocked through Meena and left her dazed. That was the bit she'd been worried about.

She might have given up, like her brother had done. When the constant slurs had gotten too much for him, Mo had put a gun in his mouth and swallowed a bullet. She could have become reclusive, like her mother had done after Papa was killed by so-called freedom defenders. Now, Mama relied upon the generosity of friends and neighbors to keep from starving.

She could have chosen a dozen different paths, at any time. But, no, Meena had decided to stand up for what she believed in—which was pretty damn hard at moments like that.

The men laughed. TJ tossed a smile over his shoulder at

them. If he stuck out his chest and started flapping his arms, he couldn't act a bigger cock.

Meena's lip stung. She brushed the back of her hand against it and the hand came away bloody. Clearly, her usual defenses of being polite and keeping quiet weren't going to work.

"Listen," she said, "I don't want any trouble tonight. It's been a long day and I just want to get home."

"Shut your lying mouth," TJ barked. "This ain't your home."

"Yeah," one of the men called. "Where you *really* from, raghead?"

There were two answers to that question, the one that they wanted to hear, and the truth.

Meena had never been one for telling people what they wanted to hear.

"Richmond."

Wham.

The second time TJ hit her, it was with enough force to knock her sideways. One of the men caught her and shoved her forward. Meena barely had the time to put an arm between her face and the concrete.

Loud guffaws filled her ears and fueled the rage simmering in her blood. Before she could push herself up, a heavy workman's boot came down on her shoulders, grinding her face into the sidewalk. A jagged pebble bit into her cheek.

Gruff, masculine laughter filled the night air.

Her tormenters were obviously enjoying themselves immensely.

Rough hands grabbed her arms and hauled Meena to her feet. They didn't release her.

"I'll only ask you once more," TJ said. "Where. Are. You. From?"

Meena raised her head to meet his eyes. She held his gaze steady as she spoke.

"Richmond."

TJ shook his head. He threw his hands up in the air.

"Call the Agency, Kenny," he said. "Got us an Illegal for Detention."

"Now just hang on a minute."

One of the men paused, cell phone in hand.

Max stepped forward. "Maybe we could be persuaded to look the other way this time," he said, rubbing his crotch with the palm of his hand.

She'd expected something along those lines from him. Max hadn't taken his heavy-lidded eyes off Meena since he climbed out of the pickup. He was hulking and walked with his chin up, shoulders back.

Ex-military, Meena thought. They usually weren't difficult to spot; acted like they owned the world and only knew how to take what they wanted at gunpoint. She was willing to bet he was packing under his thick Caterpillar jacket.

Max glanced at TJ. The other man shrugged, "Whatever you want, man." He walked over to the truck and leaned against the side.

Looked like Max was in charge then.

Things were going to get messy.

"Gee, Max," one of the others said in a tone of mock confusion. "What *do* you mean?"

And the Oscar goes to... Meena only just stopped herself from rolling her eyes.

Max's grin was malicious when he answered. "Ya know... if we had the right... *motivation.*"

Meena turned her attention to the man with the cell phone. "Go ahead, Kenny," she said around Max's large frame. "Call them."

It would take some time for them to run her through the system; even longer if the man with her ID should "lose" it. Eventually, though, Meena's paperwork would prove valid and she would be released. A month in hell. Maybe two months, max.

She could live with that.

Kenny looked to Max for guidance. Max took a step closer to Meena. He smelled like stale sweat and coffee.

"Maybe you don't understand," he said in a low, threatening voice, "this is going to happen. But, if you try *really* hard to make us happy, we'll go easy on ya."

He grabbed the front of her abaya in one meaty fist and pulled Meena hard against him. When he spoke, his voice was full of violence and his hot breath fanned her face. "Well, *they* might. Me? I'm gonna fuck ya 'til you bleed. Then, I'mma wipe my dick on this."

Max caught her hijab in his other hand and pulled it off. Several strands of dark hair went with it. Meena winced.

The sound of a door slamming told her that at least one of Max's cronies, though happy to beat her around, drew the line at rape. TJ, if she had to guess. She was almost impressed.

"Uh... Wait a sec, Max," the one with Meena's ID said. "I think-"

"Shut yer cakehole, Geoff," Max snarled. "If ya don't wanna play with the big boys, go hide in the truck with TJ."

The fabric under his fist tore. Meena's gown fell open.

"Really, man," Geoff tried again. "You gotta-"

Anger made Max's face turn an unhealthy shade of purple. He turned on his friend.

"You some kinda faggot?" he snarled. "You got some kinda problem with an Immi getting what's coming to her?"

"No! It's just-"

"It's *nothing*. Shut the fuck up or fuck the fuck off."

Geoff told Max to go fuck himself, then turned his back on them.

Max laughed off the other man's insult. Meena's hijab fell to the ground as he wrapped this thick fingers around her neck. "Now," he said, "where were we?"

Then he shoved a hand between her legging-clad legs.

Max's eyes opened wide in surprise when his searching fingers found more than they had anticipated.

Because Meena *did* have a bomb, of sorts, under her abaya. The kind that pumped poison through her body and ticked down to the male pattern baldness that hit her older brother at twenty-six. If she followed in his footsteps, she had maybe four years before her hairline started receding.

What a sickening thought.

On the day that Donald Trump took office, Meena was eight months, two weeks, and three days into her year-long life trial. That was before the president signed an executive order that created a blanket ban on all gender reassignment surgery performed within the United States. Many hospitals in Canada were still happy to provide the surgery for American citizens but, even if Meena could have afforded it, there was always the possibility that she wouldn't be allowed back in the country afterward.

And it wasn't a good time to be a Muslim without a country.

Meena had plenty of time to ruminate as Max stared at her in confusion—though it was a little hard to do while the man had a tight grip on her penis.

"Find what you were looking for?" Geoff said unkindly. He sniggered then said, "Can't say I didn't try to warn ya."

The ID card was passed to Kenny, who laughed uproariously when he read, 'Sex: Male'. "You some kinda faggot?" he mocked. Geoff's laughter joined his own.

Max started to recoil. "What the-"

Quick as a flash, Meena caught his wrist and held tight. She spoke to the whole group, though her eyes didn't leave Max's.

"I didn't want any trouble," she said. "I just wanted to get home."

Meena raised one carefully shaped eyebrow when Max struggled against her surprisingly strong hold. With a flick of her wrist, she knocked his hand away and wrapped her long, slender fingers around his throat.

"I've been on my feet for the last ten hours. Do you want to know why? Because I have to work sixty hours a week, just to keep up with my rent and buy a few groceries. Why? Because a bunch of jackass, white men decided that a Muslim's work is somehow less valuable than other Americans'."

She glared at Max's friends. "Would any of *you* accept a job that paid half minimum wage, just to *have* a job?"

They floundered. "No," Meena said with a shake of her head, "I didn't think so."

Max grunted. She relaxed her grip enough to let him speak. "Get yer fucking hands off me, you fag-"

She tightened her grip. Max's eyes bulged as he struggled to breathe.

"Wrong answer," she said. Releasing his hand, Meena brought hers up. Her long sleeves muffled the *snickt* of a dagger being released. Silver flashed in the glare of the truck's headlights.

"What the hell, man?"

"Shit. Shit."

Meena slid the blade up, between the fourth and fifth ribs, then held tight as Max thrashed wildly against her. The seconds it took for his companions to process what had happened were seconds too long. She pulled the dagger free and released the man's body. Before it hit the ground, she let the blade fly.

Her aim was true; Geoff's jaw dropped as his fingers groped

uselessly for the handle protruding from his chest. He slowly sank to his knees. Blood gurgled up and out of his open mouth.

Kenny looked from one fallen man to the next, his eyes wide. Curiosity made Meena pause. She wondered whether he would run or beg for his life. Not that it mattered. Both options led down the same path. Surprising her, though, Kenny did neither. He fumbled with the cell phone he still held. Forgotten, her ID card fell to the ground at his feet.

Uh oh, Meena thought. She hadn't considered that option— a dangerous oversight on her part. Meena needed to be a long way away before anyone found the bodies. Though she had no fear of the Agency, people like her did *not* do well in the criminal justice system.

Launching herself at Kenny, she tackled him in a way that would have made her JV football coach proud. Kenny's head smacked against the pavement with a sickening crunch. Meena grabbed the would-be assailant by the hair and smashed his head down twice more, for good measure. Glassy eyes stared up at her, frozen forever in a look of fear.

Meena snatched her ID card and rose. Ignoring the destruction around her, she crossed to where the long strand of her hijab lay on the ground. She'd bent to retrieve it when she heard, "Jesus Christ. What have you done?" from behind.

TJ.

She'd completely forgotten about the fourth man. Stupid mistake. Potentially a costly one.

TJ stood beside the pickup's open door. Meena couldn't make out his features; against the headlights, he was just a dark shadow. A very dangerous dark shadow, if he made it back into the truck before Meena could reach him. While she weighed her options, she tried to distract TJ with, "You did this. You and your friends."

Meena judged the distance between them and the verdict wasn't good. She was fast, but TJ was close enough to the idling vehicle that he'd be inside and away before she could get to him. And, from there...

The night erupted in a shower of squealing tires and automatic gunfire. Instinct made Meena hit the ground and bring her arms up to cover her head. Heart racing, she didn't dare look up until she heard, "You okay, Meena?"

A second vehicle stood across the road. The first truck's lights lit up a nondescript, dark flatbed. It wasn't so different from the one her assailants had arrived in, but Meena recognized it instantly as one that belonged to the local chapter of the D.N.A.R. Relief made her laugh out loud.

Daughters of the New American Revolution, a subversive movement that had appropriated its name from a conservative organization with roots in a time when words like "American", "revolution", and even "daughters" had very different meanings. Meena had been fighting alongside the Lexington D.A.N.R. since her father's death.

She was glad to see them. But...

"How did you know?" she asked as Carlota, who had crossed the border in her mother's backpack when she was less than a year old, helped Meena to her feet.

"We got a ping from someone calling the Agency," called a young woman from the truck's passenger seat. Rasha, a Syrian refugee, leaned out the window to add, "Since we knew this is the route you'd take home, we figured-"

"You were in deep shit!" Annabelle finished, laughing, as she vaulted from the truck's bed to join Meena and Carlota. She was a slight girl, younger than the rest, with a bright smile and haunted blue eyes.

Annabelle had barely escaped a certain death sentence when her own parents, insisting it was their "Christian duty", turned her in after Annabelle returned, bleeding and aching, from an illegal abortion. She threw her arms around Meena. The two had been close as sisters since Meena had gutted a sheriff and two deputies to secure the girl's freedom.

"Wanna ride?" Annabelle asked when she pulled away.

Meena couldn't help but smile. "Please! My feet are *killing* me."

"I told you not to wear those godawful shoes!"

"Pick your battles," Meena said as they took up an old argument over whether or not employers should be allowed to force women to wear high heels in the workplace.

They climbed into the back of the truck. The small window that separated the cab from the bed slid open and Rasha thrust her hand through. "Wanna do the honors?" she asked.

Her grin grew. "Do I?" Meena took the grenades her friend offered and pulled the pins as the truck shifted into gear. As they drove away, TJ, Max, their friends, truck, and any sign of an attack disappeared in a burst of fire and twisted metal.

Meena was thoughtful as they made their way through the dark city. The morning newspapers would call it a terrorist attack, of course. In a way, Meena mused, they were right. There would be a backlash, she knew, just like always.

And, like always, Meena would weather it because she had to. Because it was the battle she had chosen.

END

THE HISTORY BOOK

Voss Foster

The sun shone bright, for once not tucked behind the endlessly gray clouds and smog. Bright and hot. Sweat beaded on the back of Jane's neck, soaked into the collar of her T-shirt, and dripped down her spine like a crawling insect. She'd taken advantage of the sunbreak, found a yard sale just down the block.

Now, the slender old woman smiled at her as she walked through the gate. "Lovely day, isn't it?"

"Absolutely." Jane offered her a cordial smile, then carried on through the folding tables set up in the old woman's lawn. Brown grass crunched underfoot where the lawn wasn't just dust.

Mismatched glassware for twenty-five cents apiece. A rack of clothes that must have been forty years out of style. Jane passed them all by and went straight for the little square table in the corner, loaded down with books. Spines taped together, permanent squares of dust where price stickers left their adhesive behind, covers replaced with cardstock and labeled with tidy letters. Jane sorted through them, looking for anything that caught her interest. Those old books were always so interesting.

She stopped at a history book. It was in decent shape, compared to everything else. Corners worn and fraying, colors faded, but otherwise fully intact. She flipped it open to the front page. A card taped to the inside had names in impossibly tight cursive, so small she couldn't make them out, and dates stamped next to them. All from the early two-thousands. Approaching a hundred years old. *Incredible.* She'd heard stories about this kind of stuff at yard sales. Apparently it was her turn.

She grabbed that along with a couple of old category romances—pirates—and carried her finds back to the front, to the old woman. "This'll do for me. Three books, that's three dollars, right?"

The old woman didn't smile. "Could I see that big one you have there?"

"Sure, of course." Jane handed over the textbook and dug into her purse. "I only have a five. Do you have change?"

"I told him to throw this stupid thing out." The woman fixated on the book, her lips pursed. "This really shouldn't have been out here for sale."

"If it's a problem, I don't have to buy it."

The old woman blinked, flicked her head up. "No. No, it's fine." A strained smile crossed her lips. "Just let me mark something out on here. My son of all people." She chuckled as she picked up the thick black marker that sat on her table. "Really, it's bad enough he didn't give it back to the school when the year was over, but to write such nasty things in here. Teenagers." She made several long strokes across the title page, blacking out some sort of writing, then handed it over. Her smile was still sterile, joyless.

"Are you sure it's all right?"

"Perfectly fine." She eyed the two romances in Jane's arms. "Let's call those fifty cents each. So two dollars."

Jane handed over the five and got her change, as well as an old cardboard shipping box to carry it all in. As she walked away, her mind stayed on the oddness of it all. Maybe the woman was senile. Maybe it had just been too long since Jane had gotten out and dealt with other people. Maybe that really was normal.

She was just climbing the stairs to her apartment when a finger of cloud dragged across the sun, obscuring it and darkening the world around her.

~oOo~

Jane sprawled out on her ratty sofa and popped the history book open. She tried in vain to read through the old woman's blackout, or to make out any of the names on the checkout card. She had guesses, but that was about it. Faded ink and an oddly messy scrawl turned them into nothing but ghosts of what once was.

She flipped to the table of contents, scanned across it. Familiar topics like the Revolutionary and Civil Wars, but no mention of The Great War that she could find.

But her eyes immediately dropped onto three letters: WWI. A few entries later was WWII. She flipped to the page for WWI and scanned across it, picking up pieces of information here and there. It sounded like The Great War. The assassination of Archduke Ferdinand, Sarajevo, trench warfare. But throughout the chapter, it was only ever called World War One.

Back to the table of contents, then onto WWII. She knew it

could only mean one thing, but she wanted to see. When mentions of World War Two greeted her, Jane closed the book. It wasn't even worth the dollar she'd paid for it. Fake history. Crap.

~o0o~

Days passed and the history book sat on Jane's coffee table. She worked two jobs, and only got one full day off a week. The clouds and smog were particularly thick, and dust flowed across the ground in waves. The world sat in a constant state of dim.

There was really only one thing to do with the book, if she could: sell it. It was still a "vintage artifact," and maybe the errors would make it worth more. How many could there really be floating around out there? Maybe it was a clever work of fiction.

Jane clacked out "world war 2 history book" into the search bar and waited for the results. A dozen different books on The Great War, some articles theorizing about what could have thrown them into another situation like that, but nothing else. No results. She added and removed search terms. Textbook. Type. Misprint. Vintage.

Nothing ever came up.

Her heart beat hard. Did she have something that was actually... valuable? Was that a possibility? She forced her head down out of the clouds, but couldn't completely squash that glimmer of hope. Maybe the book was rare enough the internet didn't have anything on it. Unlikely...but maybe.

She erased her search and looked for a local antique shop. There was one up town, and she *did* need to swing by the grocery store a block away, anyway...

~oOo~

The man who ran the antique shop was large and round and jovial. And very, very lonely. Jane was the only customer when the bell signaled her entry. The owner raised a pudgy hand high in the air and waved as though they were old friends. "Welcome, welcome! I'm Calvin!"

"Jane." She walked to the counter, looking at the artifacts filling the shelves. Jewelry boxes, silver mirrors that gleamed under the fluorescent lights, wooden sculptures full of detail, depicting figures she didn't even begin to recognize. She also looked at the price tags and made sure to stay well clear of touching *anything* she hadn't brought in with her.

When she got to the counter, Calvin leaned forward. He had no hair left, and brownish-red spots speckled his hands, but he grinned wide, showing eerily white dentures. "What can I do for you, young miss?"

"Well, I don't know." She slipped the book free from her tote bag and set it on the counter. "Do you deal in books?"

"Sweetie, I don't have room to be picky. If I think I can move it, I'll sell it." He pulled the book closer. "An old, beaten up US history book doesn't seem like the kind of thing I'm going to move."

"I just thought you might be able to take a look at it. Or know someone who could. It's... well, I think it's a misprint. A pretty big one."

"Why would you say that?"

She held out her hand and he gave her the book again. She flipped to the section about World War Two, then handed it back. "This whole chapter is about a war that never happened. I mean, that has to be pretty weird for a textbook, right?"

He stayed silent for a few moments before shaking his head. "Go flip that sign over to closed, would you sweetie? This needs some special attention."

"What's going on?"

"I think you have something special, is all, and I'm the only one working here. Can't watch for thieves or anything and deal with such *unique* merchandise as you brought in." He sighed. "Plus you're the first customer I've seen all day."

"Right." It didn't make any sense to her, but she wasn't going to question. If he thought she had something worthwhile, flipping a stupid sign was a small price to pay. She walked to the door and turned it to "CLOSED," then back. In spite of all her best efforts, she couldn't keep the slight smile off her face.

It fell when she went back, saw Calvin dousing the book with a glass of water.

"What the hell are you doing?"

"I'm saving you a shit ton of trouble, sweetie."

She grabbed his arm and tried to pull it down, but couldn't budge him in the least. "That—that was mine, damn it!"

Calvin sighed. "How old are you, huh?"

"What?" She couldn't even comprehend... how could he do that? Her book. The longer she stood there, the more sure she was that it had to be worth something. But now she'd never know.'

"How old are you? Twenty-two?"

"Twenty… twenty-five." The pages had turned translucent, the words all but unreadable, now.

"Then you don't know what you're getting into with this thing, and you really don't know what kind of favor I did for you just now."

"By destroying this book? If you didn't want it—"

"Sweetie, you and I are going to talk. I'll fill you in, but you don't want anything to do with this book." He squelched the book to the side, closing it, and dumped the rest of the water on it. Out of spite or something. Then he lifted up the little trapdoor in the counter and waved her through. "In the back."

"I'm not going anywhere with you."

"Listen good: you want to know about the book? You want to know about your *misprint*? Come with me."

"And if I don't care?"

He chuckled, smiling again. "Even if you don't, it's too late for you." His face darkened, smile faltering, and his voice sounded suddenly so tired, worn and rough at the edges. "You saw the book, sweetie."

Something about that voice dug into her. Jane didn't know him at all, but that was out of character as far as she'd seen. In that moment, he wasn't so jovial. He was… frightening, somehow. So she followed. Her eyes lingered on the book, dripping wet on the counter.

She followed him into the back room. Calvin pulled out a chair and popped it in front of her. "You drink?"

"Get to it."

"Fine." He pulled a bottle over from the corner and plonked it on the counter next to him, then sat in his own chair. "That book doesn't have any mistakes in it."

"There's a fake war." What was he playing at? "Did you even look at it?"

"World War Two is not a fake war, sweetie. It was real as all hell."

"Right." He was delusional. "I'm going to go. Forget about the book."'

"You think you're safe to just leave?" He shook his head. "I'm protected by logistics, sweetie. They can't go around and off everyone who remembers the war. Well, maybe they can now, but they couldn't when they decided it was going off the books."

A conspiracy theorist. Just what she needed. "If you keep me here, I'll scream."

He sighed and lifted the bottle to his lips, drained a measure of amber liquid out. "Let me guess: you went online first thing to see what the book was about? And you got nothing from it, so you brought it to me?"

"Umm... yeah." She wouldn't let herself believe that was profound, that it meant anything. What else would she have done?

"Government controls the internet. Used to think it was some crazy thing that only happened in other countries." He snorted. "Half the web's filtered out for us here in the land of the free.'" He sighed and took another drink. "They can make your life hell. Probably won't come kill you, but they're onto you. They know that you must know something, even if you don't believe it. And they don't like to take chances."

Jane's blood slowed to a creep through her veins. Everything tightened. She had to get away from Calvin. He wasn't just out to destroy her book. She didn't know if he was a danger to her or not, but she knew damn well she didn't want to find out the hard way.

"Please." She rose from the seat slowly, backed up as she spoke. "What do I have to do to just... just go?"

"If you go, I have no guarantee that you'll be safe. Like I said, they *probably* won't come kill you. Not just for this." He shook his head and looked down at the floor. "I'm to blame. Me and everyone else left who knows. When they put the bans in place, we should have ignored them. But it was... people were dying if they talked about any of it. It was a complete shutdown on anything they didn't want us discussing." He stood, reached out, and clasped Jane's hands.

She fought the urge to yank back. She couldn't break out of his grip, anyway, and who knew what would set him off. Best to play dead.

"I know you don't understand it now, but I hope you can forgive me. I regret it, sweetie. I regret all of it." He sighed, then took another swig from the bottle. "Go on."

She waited for more, expecting him to snatch her back. When he didn't, she moved through the door. Her eyes lingered on the book again. It was ruined, but maybe there was something in there worth holding onto...

No. It was a book of lies, and now it had no value in money, even. It was worthless, and Calvin could clean up the mess he'd made of it.

She was almost out when that rough-edged voice caught her around the spine again, held her in place. "*Arbeit macht*

Frei. World War Two, they liked that little *catchphrase.* Used to strike dread in the heart of every decent human being who heard it after that." He sighed. "Work will set you free. Nazi bastards thought it was work... never mind. Flip the sign back around when you leave."

Arbeit macht Frei. Work will set you free. It dragged at something in her memory, but nothing she could grasp properly. As Jane left the shop, she flipped the sign over.

~oOo~

Jane stood out in front of the county Detainee Center. It had been a boon to the town when the economy turned down, but now it was just another eyesore. Gray and stout, surrounded in a fence as tall as three men. The words stood above the entrance in clean, sans-serif font: Work Will Set You Free.

Of course, he was just translating to German. It took her two seconds to plug it into an online translator. It did speak to the level of Calvin's delusions, at least. He'd created some kind of fantasy, found or fabricated details that made sense to him, somehow.'

"Hey! You!" A guard in pseudo-military gear walked up to the gate, pistol clutched in his fist. "This isn't a zoo, y'know. No lookie-loos, if that's what you're waiting for."

"No. I'm sorry. I got in my own head." She hiked her empty tote bag higher. "Have a good day."

She hightailed it back to her rundown Chevy. The door didn't open. Her heart leapt into her throat. "Come on." It would choose now to act up again. She jiggled it back and forth, harder and harder until... *pop.* She slid inside and slammed the door behind her.

She forced herself to breathe, slow and deep until her heartbeat leveled out. "No one is after me." Was she really going to let Mr. Crazy Antique Guy get into her head? The guards at the Detainee Centers were there for *her* protection. The people they kept in there were dangers to the United States, and every single citizen. Radicals and Muslims. Black Panthers. Threats to what they still had.

But she still struggled against the urge to check over her shoulder.

~oOo~

A knock at the door interrupted Jane's yogurt. She was still in her bathrobe, makeup half-on, when she answered. It was a uniformed police officer. Square-jawed and swarthy. "Jane Fitch?"

"Yes? Is everything okay?" Evacuation? Escaped Detainee?

"I just wanted to ask you about someone." He pulled a notepad out of his pocket and squinted at it. "A Calvin Mitchell. He runs an antique shop in town."

She brushed a hand through her hair. "Never met him before."

"We got word that your car was at his shop yesterday afternoon." He flipped through the little notebook. "A... black Chevy Spark? '71?"

"That's mine." *Shit, shit.*

"Still driving a manual?"

Not everyone can afford a modern vehicle. And the lanes for manually drive cars were getting less and less crowded every day. Not to mention how cheap that damn car was in the first place. But she just nodded.

"Well, we definitely have it out in front of Mitchell's shop. And it's not exactly a common make and model, anymore."

No, it wasn't... *were* people watching her? "I was downtown yesterday. I might have parked over there. I wasn't paying attention."

"Well, it's probably just a misunderstanding. He tipped his cap to her. "Sorry for bothering you."

"What's the issue, anyway? Is he into something I should be worried about? Coming after me or something?" She wouldn't put it past him.

"He's dead." The cop shook his head. "Trying to figure out what happened, but between you and me, it's not working out so well." He rolled his eyes. "Sorry. Best if you don't mention I said that. Official statement is that we're working on it." He waved the idea off, as though homicide could be shooed like a gnat. "Don't let it bother you. It was a freak thing."

"He was murdered and I'm supposed to not worry?" *People were dying if they talked about any of it.* But that couldn't be it. She was just remembering the words because he died. Right after she saw him, brought him the book.

"It might not be murder at all, Ms. Fitch." He took the cap off his head and scratched across his scalp. "There are just some loose ends. Now you're no longer one of them, as far as I'm concerned." He put the cap back on. "But someone else might come talk to you, if they think you might have info. So fair warning about that."

"So... I'm safe." She wanted an answer, but she wanted to force herself to say it, too. Put it out there in the world in the hope that it would actually be true.

"If you want, I can try to get a black and white to drive by every now and then and check. No promises, but—"

"You don't need to waste the resources." She should have said yes, but she couldn't make it come out. Too much to be coincidence, wasn't it? Of course not. Not mathematically. Not logically...but he died right after warning her about everything. If she could have just listened, maybe she would know something more. Maybe she could piece it together.

"I'll still try. It's not a waste." Another tip of the cap. "I'll let you get on with your morning."

Jane just nodded and saw him out the door. And then she locked it. A cop driving past. Were they part of this? Was this whole conspiracy *really* a thing? Why would anyone— why would the *government*—hide an entire war from everyone? Control the internet? What purpose could any of that possibly serve?

Jane sank onto the sofa, no longer interested in what remained of her yogurt. It was ridiculous to put any stock in what Calvin had told her, but she felt that same slowing of the blood, the tightness and the worry. She knew she couldn't afford to call in sick, but... damn it all.

~oOo~

The convenience store was dead. It was almost always dead in the middle of the week. People stopped in on paydays, for the most part, or during those all-too-rare sun breaks. Neither was true of that day, and it left Jane alone with her thoughts. Her worries. She couldn't shake what happened. Calvin dead. Cops showing up at her door. And now she knew *something* about it. Whatever insanity he was trying to tell her about. Did that make her a target? Was anyone a target?

Did she actually *believe* this?

She wanted to say no, to throw it all out like she did before, but it wouldn't budge. This World War Two, *Arbeit macht Frei*, government cover-up thing lodged in her chest and stuck there.

The bells blessedly drew her attention away from her own head. It was an old woman, cane-bound and hobbling from the door straight to the counter. Jane unlocked the register in anticipation.

The woman stopped and stared straight into Jane's eyes. "You were there when Calvin died?"

Shit. "I... who are you?"

"Were you there or not?"

"I didn't do anything... you should leave if you're not going to buy anything."

She leaned her cane against the counter. "If you were there and you weren't a part of it, you are in danger."

Jane said nothing. It made no sense. Should she be worried about them? How could... somehow... "You're here to kill me, too."

The old woman shook her head. "Do you think I could do anything to you in my state?" She picked up her cane again, moved closer. "You have a choice to make. You can either go back to your normal, safe life, or you can learn about this." She shuffled and clunked closer, right up to Jane behind the counter. "I don't care what you do, but it's too late for you not to do *something*." She reached into her pocket and pulled out a small disposable drive, the kind they used to pass nudes around on in high school. "Take it, destroy it, I don't care... but this is my duty. To make up for... everything." Her eyes glazed over. "It's not enough. Can't fix it. But at least you have an option."

Slowly, Jane extended her hand and grabbed the drive. She stuck it into her pocket and surreptitiously glanced to the black dome of the security camera.

Apparently the question of belief was done: she believed. Somewhere in herself, Jane was buying into it. *But what* was she buying into?

The old woman nodded. "Good luck... whatever you do. If you want to be a really good citizen, you'll turn that drive into the authorities." She sighed, offered, a sad smile, then hobbled her way back out the door.

~oOo~

Jane went to the library after work. They had access stations. If this drive really was dangerous, it wasn't as easy to track. Hopefully. Theoretically. Maybe. It was the best she had.

She sat at the station for a solid minute, playing with the drive, considering her options. The old woman told her nothing about the contents, but Jane had ideas. It was a safe bet it had to do with Calvin and the book and World War Two.

If nothing else, it might quell her stomach. It could stop the consistent indecision, and maybe that would make her feel better. She didn't know for sure, but she could be damn well sure that turning it in, that destroying it, that ridding herself of the information... those wouldn't solve anything. Those would leave the indecision, the unknown. They would leave her in that state of constant fear and tightness.

She didn't allow herself to hesitate any longer, pressed that drive against the reader. After a few seconds, the window appeared on the screen. Jane opened the folder. It was full of numbered photos and documents. No clues to what they might be.

Jane opened one. It was an image of a gate, just like the one outside the Detainee Center. And there was the phrase: *Arbeit macht Frei.* She flipped to the next one. Dozens of bodies stacked up. Just bodies. No life. Thin and ravaged and naked. Jane shuddered and clicked off. But it was just more bodies. Different angles, different piles, none of them alive.

She closed the pictures, opened a PDF. It was a newspaper from the nineteen forties. "Adolf Hitler Dead." She scanned across the article, and it didn't cure any of her unease. Leader of Germany. Crimes against humanity. Holocaust. That word kept coming up, and she didn't recognize it. She didn't dare search for it, if this all was as dangerous as everyone said. As dangerous as she was starting to believe it must be.

More articles, more newspapers and essays from across decades, all the way up into 2023, 2024. Those grew more and more hopeless, more and more terrifying. Comparing the president and the US government to Adolf Hitler. Muslim registration. But it talked about the registration of the Jews. She'd never heard anything about it. Six million of them dead during...World War Two.

Six million dead? Jane couldn't even *conceive* of it.

Later articles talked about people being offed for speaking out against the administration. Federal judges removed from their positions, moving out of the country all the sudden right afterward. All hearsay, but it didn't paint a lovely picture.

She closed the folder...or tried to. It wouldn't go away. The entire screen froze. She pulled the drive, crumpled it in her palm, but that window remained. Her whole body tensed. Would that be enough to tip someone off? Enough to get someone coming after her?'

After her. It was ridiculous, of course. She'd let herself get pulled into this idiocy, but there was not going to be anyone coming *after* her. She couldn't explain how the old woman found her, figured out where she worked. She couldn't explain why so many people were in on this. But it wasn't something to get so worked up about.

No part of Jane actually believed that. When she stood up to leave, she held the power button on the station until the whole thing shut down.

~oOo~

Jane couldn't shake it. The horrors she'd seen clung to her like thick mud. It filled her throat and blocked her breath, pressed in on her, heavy from all sides. It kept her from sleep, kept her from any semblance of comfort until she finally got up. She sat at the computer. Her webcam was on, the red light a beacon of terror. She hadn't used it in months.

It turned off as if commanded by her thoughts, but her hackles still raised. She unplugged it and turned it away from her. She'd heard of people spying through cameras...would they do that? To a US citizen? That couldn't be legal, could it? They abolished the Patriot Act for good when Jane was just a child, outlawed it and anything else like it.

There had to be a way to find out if this was all real.

Rapidly, a thought formed, grew in her sleepless brain until it filled her. There was no reason she couldn't or shouldn't do it. As long as she could afford it. She searched for tickets to Germany. If this *was* a conspiracy from the government, it wouldn't stretch across national borders. Nobody else liked or respected the US. Not anymore. They certainly wouldn't take part in protecting their citizens from the truth.

The tickets weren't cheap, but not bad enough they were impossible. Payday loans, dipping into her savings, her couple of paid vacation days saved up... she could swing it.

It was all completely insane, wasting money that way. It sounded unreasonable, even on no sleep. Unreasonable, but not entirely out of the question.

If she still felt it was right decision in the morning, or in a few days...

Jane's computer screen flashed blue, displaying white text.

Not a coincidence.

~oOo~

It took some doing. Jane sold things. She lied to the payday loan clerk about her sick, dying mother in Germany. She sublet her apartment for far less than she should have. But she was there, at the Jewish Museum Berlin...and they had it. They not only knew about the Jews and the Holocaust, they remembered it clearly. Tears welled in her eyes at the thought of it, the unbelievable loss. Inconceivable. Too much to wrap her brain around. It was all documented.

Jane's knees shook as she saw real, physical copies of the images from that drive. The bodies. The emaciated forms, skin pressed to bone. The children. So many children...

"Are you an American?" A woman in heels clacked up to

her. Her hair was pulled back in a tight bun and her eyes gleamed with light and warmth. Even through the heavy accent, Jane could hear the pity in her voice. The sadness.

"I... I am."

The woman nodded. "I've learned the look." She sighed. "You won't go back. No point lying about it."

"What are you talking about?"

"Your passport, will be denied when you try to go back. If you push it...don't push it." She sighed. "They don't let people back in after they come here." She draped an arm around Jane's shoulders. "I'm sorry, for what it's worth."

Jane couldn't even bring herself to doubt it anymore. She would try, of course. She would go to the airport, but any hope of getting on the plane drained out of her when the woman told her as much. Jane was getting used to strangers knowing more about her life than she did.

"Why?" She looked into the woman's eyes. "Why did this happen?"

"I don't know. Just theories."

"Then give me a theory." Anything. *Anything* that could be some sort of answer, some sort of explanation.

"It was when my mother was a child. She told me about it. But I know the US government built the Detainee Centers. They put supposedly temporary travel bans on Muslim countries. Then they started registration, to keep track of Muslims in the country. They tried to convince the rest of the world to do it, too." She pointed to the image of the gates. *Arbeit macht Frei.* "Everyone said it was the same, that it was a repetition of the concentration camps. Auschwitz. Buchenwald. Dachau." She sighed. "Muslims instead of Jews, but the same. Except they had a playbook of what worked and what didn't work."

"How could they do it so fast?" It couldn't be real, couldn't be true... but it was.

The woman closed her eyes tight. "It started long before any of this actually happened. All the historians say it started almost a hundred years ago."

As old as the book, and the articles on that old woman's drive. "Did... was it six million people who died? In the... Holocaust?"

The woman nodded. "It was. It was a tragedy." She pulled her arm away. "I know some others like you. They can help you find a place to stay. Unless you really want to try and get home."

"It won't work." It was numbing to say it herself. Numbing because it was true, and she knew it. She was stuck here. "I shouldn't have come."

"You're not there, anymore." The woman walked and Jane trudged along after her. "That's the best I can give you. It's not a good situation."

"They did this... I still don't understand."

They were out in the sun. There was *sun* here, and it had been out since she landed.

"If people knew what happened, people could protest. People could demand that nothing like this happen again. If nobody knows the risks and people are afraid, then it plays the way they want it." She walked a few steps in front of Jane, then turned around. "I'm Simone."

"Jane." She suppressed a shiver. "I...can I trust you?" She

didn't have the energy left to avoid bluntness.

"I understand. You've been fucked, Jane. But I want to help you." She nodded, as though that was that. "I know you don't have any reason to trust me, but I hope you'll give me a chance. Just a small one." She smiled slightly. "There's an American who lives a few blocks away. Let me take you that far."

Jane hesitated, but only a moment. She had nothing else.

So she followed Simone.

END

WE'RE STILL HERE

Rebecca McFarland Kyle

"The citizens of America can ill-afford another tragedy like Armadillo, Oklahoma." The White House spokesperson waved a hand at the images of devastation. "The rioting and wanton destruction by these illegal Mexican thugs is yet another attack on the property and lives of the American people." She looked past the interviewer and into the camera. "How can our president protect us if the borders are still open?"

"We're still here!" I shouted at the television. On the screen, a panning camera shot displayed a scene of wreckage with felled trees, black mud, and overturned cars. "What is this picture, Northern Ireland?"

Anyone who'd ever been to Western Oklahoma knew the dirt was red and it was a semi-arid desert biome getting dryer every year. If you were lucky you might see the wind-shaped bush that looked like someone took a weed whacker to it.

I reached behind the counter of Armadillo's only convenience store and grabbed the dusty remote control. It was so old the numbers were worn off. I switched the channel only to find that same spokesperson yakking about the Armadillo, Oklahoma Massacre on yet another talking head show. I hit the mute button. It was the next best thing to duct tape.

"That's a pack of lies."

"What's that?" John McKay, the good-natured septuagenarian owner, called as he moved from the back to stock the beer coolers. Like my family, the McKays descended from the original settlers who occupied the land in the Land Run of 1892. In just a few weeks, Armadillo would celebrate the anniversary of the Run with a church social, same old lecture from the blue hairs, and a mock Land Run for the kids.

"According to our President's spokesperson, Mexican immigrants just torched our town," I replied.

John shook his head. "Hannah Wagoner, it's not patriotic to criticize our President."

"Patriotism means to stand by the country. It does not mean to stand by the president or any other public official, save exactly to the degree in which he himself stands by the country. It is unpatriotic not to tell the truth, whether about the president or anyone else," I said.

"Don't lecture me, Hannah," John frowned.

"I'm not," I said. "That was President Theodore Roosevelt. We're still here."

"I'm sure it was a mistake," John said in that tone adults used for small children and agitated animals. He averted his gaze. "Now what did you come in here for besides trouble?"

"Air conditioning," I did my best to lighten up. "Place's so hot, we've lost our mascot. All the armadillos moved back East."

"So've the fiddlebacks. Saving me a bundle on bug—" John abruptly grabbed for the counter as the ground shook and stock tumbled off the shelves. I sank to my hands and knees on the scarred-up green linoleum floor, hoping the quake would pass quickly and nothing would fall on my head. My whole body felt like a giant picked me up and shook me as the quick-pickup items stocked by the register tumbled around me.

"You okay, Hannah?"

"Yeah." I was more concerned about him. We were thirty miles from the nearest hospital. John had open-heart surgery twice. His voice sounded like he'd done helium. His cheeks were pale, but he was breathing. I brushed red dust off my blue jeans and quickly moved around the store putting items back where they belonged as best I could, keeping one eye on John.

He was lucky this time. Both his heart and the store withstood the shock. Then again, he'd finally stopped smoking and started leaving the glass items in their cardboard boxes instead of shelving them where they could break.

We all knew it was fracking that caused the quakes, but enough folks still got checks from the oil leases that nobody dared complain.

"Thanks," he said. "But you might want to get on home and check on your folks." John suggested kindly.

I nodded. Despite the earthquakes, Mom still had tall bookshelves in nearly every room. I grabbed windshield wiper fluid, which was what my Dad actually sent me to get, a coke, which in my case, was the generic Okie term for every soft drink (actually a Cherry Pepsi), and a Snickers bar, and laid them down on the counter.

John quickly rang my purchases up. I loaded into Dad's dust-covered F-150 and headed for home. I stopped along the way going live on Facebook, commenting about the "massacree" while shooting photos of the main street, my high school, and the Baptist Church.

We lived just outside of town on a red dirt single-track road in a turn-of-the-past-century frame home with a white picket fence. I parked and headed into the house to deposit my goodies in the icebox and then went out to the detached garage with the jug of wiper fluid.

The garage was actually the most modern building on our property. Dad rebuilt it eighteen years ago when a tornado swept the old one away on their wedding day. He joked that was a harbinger for the rest of his marriage.

"Hey," Dad said as I entered. He'd found a vintage Ford Galaxie 500 to restore and was working to get it as close to spec as he could to sell it at auction. "Good to see you survived the quake. Nothing major here. Just a few books fell off the shelves."

"Yeah," I smirked, handing over the jug and his change. "And we all survived the Armadillo, Oklahoma Massacree."

Dad raised a dark brow. He was a tall man with a trim figure who still kept his dark hair cut "high and tight" Marine style.

"The news said illegal Mexicans rioted and destroyed Armadillo."

"Really," he said. "Good thing they put it back when they were done." Then he gave me the look. "Got homework?" He asked, seeing as I was still hanging out.

"Algebra, History, English," I muttered and headed back to the house. I'd be up until midnight as it was and with midterms including Algebra and History tomorrow. Coach Perkins, my "history" teacher loved the essay question, and you better agree with his politics if you wanted an A.

I stopped at the icebox to grab my snack and then headed into my room to boot up my MacBook.

As always, I checked Facebook on the way to homeworkville. My live session had 2,317 shares! I stared stunned and hit refresh just for fun only to see the number double.

I was about to click off when Amanda from my History class PMd me to tell me that #werestillhere was trending on Twitter with my live video of the town attached.

My heart skipped when Josh, who played on the football team and only noticed me as a study buddy, PMd next:

Going to sell t-shirts. Want to help

design them?

I glanced at my pile of books and back at the PM. How many times in a lifetime did the POTUS' spokesperson "accidentally" say my home was destroyed? I typed almost faster than the thud of my heart:

Sure, come on over. But I have to

study.

If I'd held my breath any longer, I might have fainted. As it was, my shriek brought Mom, my little brother, and our three Coonhounds running into the room.

"Josh Johnson is coming over to study," I announced triumphantly to my assembled family.

"You like him. You wanna kiss him...." my little brother, Ethan, sing-songed from the doorway.

"Mom, can I duct tape his mouth shut just long enough to have a social life?"

Mom laughed, her cheeks going a tinge pink. Both Ethan and I favored her ashy colored hair and brown eyes. "I still caught your Dad and you know about Uncle Matt."

"Tell you what," I said to Ethan, holding up the Snickers bar. "You stay away, I'll give you this."

I didn't hear his answer over the roar of Josh's red Mustang GT. His family were one of the lucky ones with oil rights and the town's Ford dealership. His Dad was the mayor and had served on the town council for most of my life.

I swore under my breath realizing I didn't have a chance to do anything to my face or windblown hair.

Of course, the brat opened the door just in time for Josh to see me racing for the door. There I was, an A student failing at cool. On the other hand, Josh's brown hair looked perfect as always, his polo shirt spotless, his jeans fitting and faded in just the right places, and his eyes sparkled with mischief.

I dislodged Ethan and got Josh to my room just in time for Dad to make sure the door was open.

"It's cool," Josh said. "My sister, Jessica, has to keep her door open."

My stomach knotted at the name. Jessica was the popular girl in our small high school. I was nowhere on her level and she reminded me of that every chance she got. Those of us on the bottom of the totem pole referred to Josh as "The Good Twin."

"So what did you have in mind for the shirts?" I asked, pulling up the design program on my MacBook.

"How about an armadillo on the front with the slogan I survived the 2017 Armadillo, Oklahoma Massacree?"

Josh quickly sketched out an armadillo wearing a battered Oklahoma baseball hat standing by a beat-up prickly-pear cactus. We set to work and created a cool t-shirt available on a popular sale site.

"So we split profits 50/50?" Josh asked.

I nodded, numb. I never thought about profits or that Josh would split anything with me. Yeah we were friends, but that was the best I hoped for. We both shared the design on our Facebook and Twitter. Instead of ordering one ourselves, I used my printer and a t-shirt iron-on and made us shirts.

"Did you get any studying done?" Mom asked as she passed around the mashed potatoes after Josh went home.

I swallowed and shook my head. "We designed a t-shirt commemorating the massacre."

"I'm quizzing you on that study guide after supper. You better know it." Dad glowered. Then he grinned. "Let's see the shirt."

~oOo~

I woke exhausted and bumbled through my chores and drank black coffee for breakfast. As sleepy as I was, I opted to ride into school with Dad and Ethan so I didn't wreck anyone.

My history class greeted me with a mixture of applause and cold stares.

"You put us back on the map," Coach Perkins said quietly as he handed out the essay test questions. I noted a few of my fellow students wore various armadillo t-shirts in support. Even our teacher wore a pair of armadillo cufflinks.

"Do I get extra credit?" I rubbed my bleary eyes and asked.

"Looking at how you've occupied yourself instead of studying, you appear to be attempting to make history rather than study it," Coach Perkins replied.

I was the last to finish the test.

I finally had time to check Facebook only to see a pink banner saying my account was disabled. Twitter said my account was locked for security purposes.

"Dad," I was near in tears when he drove up. Then, I looked into the back seat and saw my kid brother sporting a black eye and my own troubles were forgotten.

I opened my mouth and Dad shook his head. I didn't need to ask what Ethan had gotten in a fight about. He wore the armadillo t-shirt to school this morning and had on a plain one now.

"Both Facebook and Twitter suspended my accounts."

He nodded. "Suspecting it's about the massacre film?"

"But it's the truth."

"That's not always enough."

"But why do people defend a lie?"

"It fits what they want to believe," Dad said. "There are people in this town who will excuse the Armadillo massacre and claim the Holocaust is a lie."

I shook my head.

"I'm cut off from the world," I stared disconsolately down at my phone. "I can't communicate with any of my friends."

"What?" Dad shook his head. "You forgot how to punch in a number?"

"We—" I started to protest and I realized he was right. I laughed. I did have phone numbers for most of my classmates. I just never used them.

Unfortunately, I had more homework and chores piled up. By the time I did that, it was bedtime. I didn't argue with Mom. I was too tired.

~oOo~

I drove the next day since I had choir practice for the Spring concert after school. I stopped in at John's after practice to grab a Coke.

The normally well-stocked shelves were barren and John looked like he'd aged about ten years in the two days since I'd seen him.

"What happened?" I asked as I contemplated my choices in the cooler and settled for an orange soda. It was my least favorite, but I had the feeling John could use the business.

"When my suppliers heard the town was destroyed, they took me off the route," John said tiredly. "I've spent all day trying to get someone to bring me merchandise. It's the same with the grocery."

I shook my head and noted for the first time I could recall the television was off.

"You know there's a storm alert?" I told him, noting the skies were turning an ominous black. I added a package of cookies to my purchases pretty certain we would be spending part of the evening in the storm cellar. John didn't have my favorites in stock, but I figured Dad and Ethan would eat anything.

I drove back home quickly and pulled into the garage to keep the truck from getting bent out of shape from the hail I was pretty sure would be here soon from the green in the clouds. Dad was back working on the Galaxie.

"How's it coming?" I called when I got out of the pickup.

"Not good," Dad said. "Tried to order a starter and the website wouldn't accept our address. Seems we're no longer on the map."

"We were barely there to start with," I shook my head.

Dad nodded, his lips pressed in a firm line. "Place in Oklahoma City has the part. We'll go this weekend."

"Yay! May I go to the mall? Please?"

Dad made his long-suffering face, which I knew meant he was planning on a trip to the mall already so Mom and I could shop and my kid brother could buy LEGOS®.

"We probably should take the ice chest and buy groceries, too." I suggested. "John says his suppliers and the grocer's have both dried up."

Dad said words which would have gotten my mouth washed

out with soap. I wisely knew not to mention that, but I stored the verbiage away because a girl never knew when she needed to inventively cuss someone out and ex-Marines were good sources of material.

Mom was on the phone when I went inside. She didn't look much happier than Dad.

"What do you mean, we can't participate in College Bowl, we put our entry in on time," Mom said. "Look, the town's still here and my students are still ready to participate. So please-."

She slammed the old fashioned phone down so hard, it sounded like it was ringing.

"I brought cookies in case we have a storm tonight," I held up the package, hoping to put her in a better mood.

A faint smile crossed her lips. "Yeah, we need to stock the cellar again before the season starts...though I guess it already has and earlier too."

I nodded. Being from Oklahoma, we looked at what the weather did rather than what the politicians told us because our lives and our crops depended on it. Folks were planting earlier and dealing with even more irrigation costs due to climate change though a lot of them just called it a "hot year" instead of admitting our planet was getting warmer.

We were Okies, but we also lived in the State of Denial.

"I'm going to get started on my–"

The storm siren finished my sentence for me. I picked up the cookies and some bottled drinks, yelled at my brother, and followed Mom outside to the cellar.

~oOo~

We survived the storm, with just wind damage. The little town of Eustis, just twenty miles from us got blown away, literally. Three tornadoes had taken turns. There wasn't much left.

The next day was Saturday. Knowing the news about Eustis, Mom woke us up early so we could clean out our closets of stuff we'd outgrown to take to our church where some of the folks who'd lost their homes had taken shelter.

"Hey come in here," Ethan yelled. "You've got to see this."

His tone of voice had me racing to the living room. The national news was on and film rolled, showing the Eustis tornado, only the reporter claimed it was from the Armadillo Massacre. At least the dirt was red this time.

"You have got to be kidding!" I shouted at the set. I could see the name Eustis on several buildings.

"What—do they think those illegal aliens are super beings from Mars that they can throw old cast iron tubs up into the trees?" I shook my head at the footage.

My shout brought Dad out of the bathroom, half his face coated in shaving cream and the other half hairless.

"They're serious." He shook the razor at the set spattering shaving cream on the hardwood floor. "They're doubling down."

My stomach clenched at that. I could see from Dad's face, he was worried, too. I smiled at my kid brother, who simply giggled about illegal aliens from Mars and found a cartoon. I finished boxing up the clothing and we drove to the church on the way to Oklahoma City.

It was still raining so Mom and Ethan stayed in the van while Dad and I brought out the stuff we'd gathered to the refugees. Everybody was in the small fellowship hall where we had Wednesday night dinners, wedding and funeral receptions. Instead of the rows of tables I was used to, cots were set up with people either sitting up or snoozing. My stomach growled from the delicious smells. Church members had already been there with crock pots and casserole pans full of food. Whether someone wed, died, or any other event in between, these people knew how to feed you.

I blinked away tears, seeing whole families huddled together in corners of the hall sectioned off by sheets and shower curtains. Some talked animatedly, while others stared hollow-eyed and hopeless at us as we passed.

"This is your fault," a woman with uncombed white hair wearing a pink chenille bathrobe pointed at me with a shaking finger, her voice shrill as chalk on a blackboard. "If you people hadn't told everyone your town was okay, they wouldn't have to destroy our homes."

I backed away, my stomach lurching, unable to think of a response.

"It's okay, honey." Work worn hands caught my shoulders and stopped me from tripping backwards. "Grandma's in shock. You didn't make the tornadoes."

I turned and faced a smiling older woman, who offered me a hug and thanked me for coming. I nodded and skedaddled out of there. It was reassuring to know that some people did believe in science, but I saw several people's heads nodding when the old woman accosted me and I knew they agreed with her.

"I'm moving soon as I graduate," I told Dad in a quiet voice once we left the church. Cold rain practically steamed on my upturned face. I just stood there for a moment to calm down. They really thought this was my fault.

"Let's get there," he said and we jogged through the downpour to the car. "The mall awaits. You need a dress. Show off those pretty legs for your young man."

Josh isn't my young man, I wanted to correct him, but I was too busy blushing in front of my dorky little brother and wishing Josh would notice me as more than just the girl to share homework with. I caught Mom's smile in the rearview mirror as I buckled up. Maybe we would actually change the town ordinances and be able to have a dance by the time I graduated in two more years.

We stopped to check on John. He stood beneath the awning in front of his store holding up his cell phone. "Can one of you tell me how this camera works?"

"Sure," I said. "What do you want to take pictures of?"

"The town," John replied. "I want to tell folks everywhere that we're still here."

Dad coughed and I knew precisely what that meant. John initially referred to the massacre story as a mistake. I was pretty sure he wanted to believe that. While John's business was never political, he'd proudly contributed to POTUS's campaign and sported a sign in his front yard. I got out and showed him how to take pictures and even helped him attach the video to an email he was sending to his social media savvy kindred in Oklahoma City, Wichita, and Dallas. This time, they'd spread the word for us. I hoped it would do some good.

We continued down the street toward the Johnson's Ford dealership. Josh was also out beside the road doing a video using a high-end camera that his father used to video used cars. Dad stopped and pulled into the dealership lot when he waved us over and gave me a minute to talk with him.

"My Dad's going to whip my butt for this," he said in undertones to me. "I'm the only one in the family who's mad. Dad says POTUS is good for business."

I swallowed hard and impulsively gave Josh a hug. His strong arms tightened around me reassuringly.

"You like him, you love him, you want to marry him," Ethan taunted when I got back in the car. I ducked my head and tried to hide my blush, but it wasn't much use. Mom just grinned at me in the rearview mirror and gave me a thumbs up. She poked my Dad in the ribs.

"Why don't you invite your friend to join us?" Dad suggested.

Ethan started to tease and my Mom gave him a look that shut him up.

We pulled up alongside Josh. I rolled down the window and asked him to come with us to Oklahoma City. When he accepted, I slid over to the middle of the back seat and he sat down next to me. My parents spent the time quizzing Josh on his schoolwork and what he planned to do this coming summer.

My spirits lifted the minute we hit the mall. We followed Ethan, who ran to the LEGO® store and watched as he raced from one kit to the other, trying to choose between Star Wars and Batman.

"Get them both," Dad relented. It wasn't Christmas or his birthday, but I knew Dad wanted to cheer us up. We all sat around the table in the evening helping the kid put his kits together. I didn't know what I was going to be when I grew up, but I was certain Ethan would be an engineer.

"I'm sorry," the clerk said. "Your credit card's declined."

Dad stared at the woman. "Any idea why?"

She shook her head.

"Will you take a check?" Dad asked.

She nodded. He wrote the check and she stared at it.

"Does this place even exist anymore?"

"I can assure you, it does." Dad said. "We just came from there."

We ate at Braums instead of the cool Mexican restaurant we'd planned. Luckily, we had enough cash to pay for that and our groceries.

"Hey, you're that girl on TV," an old man in the booth across from us said. "You made that fake video about that stupid town still exist—"

Dad stood to his full height. My accuser's mouth snapped shut and he backed away.

I plugged myself into my phone and listened to my music as I stared out the window going home, watching the raindrops trace down the pane, wondering if anything would be right again. Josh patted my arm in comfort. The red clay had turned to the color of old blood beneath the leaden sky.

We drove back through the rain in silence. Even my little brother didn't try to play with his new LEGO® sets like he usually did. Mom would occasionally touch my Dad's thigh and I wished I could do the same with Josh.

"Stop!" Josh yelled as we got close. It was near midnight and I was paying attention to the rain slick road and not to the skies. I stared up to see dozens of lights above Armadillo. Flashes like lightning rained down on the town. Dad hit the brakes and cut the lights and we coasted along the side of the road until we found the shelter of an abandoned truck stop just a couple of miles on.

"Video camera's in the floorboard," Josh said in a tight voice.

I fumbled with the zippered case and managed to get the expensive camera out without dropping it. My body shook so hard I could barely stand or see, but I held onto the camera and steadied enough to capture Armadillo going up in flames. A dozen Apache helicopters flew in low and fast, blanketing the town with cannon fire. The attack happened so quickly we couldn't have called anyone and gotten them out. I climbed back into the car, startled when I realized my Dad had disabled the cabin lights. We stayed there until the skies were dark once again.

We'd told the truth and they'd turned the lie into a reality. Likely all of our fellow townsfolk, along with the refugees from the Eustis storm perished.

"What are we going to do?" Josh asked, sitting beside me in the dark.

"We're going to survive and we're going to tell the truth and fight," I said quietly holding onto the video camera like my life depended on it. "We're still here."

END?

ABOUT THE AUTHORS

K.G. Anderson's work as a journalist and technology writer gives her a front-row seat for the whole dystopian circus and a special pass to the sideshows. Her short fiction appears in anthologies including *Second Contacts, Story Emporium, Triangulation: Beneath the Surface*, and *The Mammoth Book of Jack the Ripper Stories*, as well as online at *Metaphorosis* and *Every Day Fiction*. She lives in Seattle with her life partner, bookseller Tom Whitmore, and enough cats. Find out more at *writerway.com/fiction*

Marleen S. Barr is known for her pioneering work in feminist science fiction and teaches English at the City University of New York. She has won the Science Fiction Research Association Pilgrim Award for lifetime achievement in science fiction criticism. Barr is the author of *Alien to Femininity: Speculative Fiction and Feminist Theory, Lost in Space: Probing Feminist Science Fiction and Beyond, Feminist Fabulation: Space/Postmodern Fiction,* and *Genre Fission: A New Discourse Practice for Cultural Studies*. Barr has edited many anthologies and co-edited the science fiction issue of *PMLA*. She is the author of the novels *Oy Pioneer!* and *Oy Feminist Planets: A Fake Memoir*.

Adam-Troy Castro made his first non-fiction sale to SPY magazine in 1987. Among his books to date include four Spider-Man novels, 3 novels about his profoundly damaged far-future murder investigator Andrea Cort, and 6 middle-grade novels about the dimension-spanning adventures of that very strange but very heroic young boy Gustav Gloom. Adam's darker short fiction for grownups is highlighted by his collection, *Her Husband's Hands And Other Stories* (Prime Books). Adam's works have won the Philip K. Dick Award and the Seiun (Japan), and have been nominated for eight Nebulas, three Stokers, two Hugos, and, internationally, the Ignotus (Spain), the Grand Prix de l'Imaginaire (France), and the Kurd-Laßwitz Preis (Germany). He lives in Florida with his wife Judi and either three or four cats, depending on what day you're counting and whether Gilbert's escaped this week.

Gregg Chamberlain has been a community newspaper reporter for more than 40 years, and after four-plus decades in the trade his general opinion of politicians is that they get in the way of progress. But they make such wonderful targets for satire that he was more than happy to provide his own potshot at POTUS45 for the inaugural *Alternate Truths* anthology. Gregg lives with his missus, Anne, in the rural part of Ontario. The couple shares their home with a clowder of cats who all have agreed to let the humans think they are in charge. Gregg amuses himself with writing genre fiction and has compiled a list of almost four dozen short fiction credits in *Daily Science Fiction*, *Apex*, *Weirdbook*, *Pulp Literature*, and other magazines and various original anthologies.

Sara Codair lives in a world of words, writing fiction in every free moment, teaching writing at a community college, and binge-reading fantasy novels. When not lost in words, Sara can often be found hiking, swimming, or gardening. Find Sara's words in Helios Quarterly, *Secrets of the Goat People*, *The Centropic Oracle*, and at https://saracodair.com/ and @shatteredsmooth.

Joel Ewy is self-employed and lives in South Central Kansas with his wife and two kids. He went to Bethel College in North Newton, KS where he took the liberal arts concept way more seriously than it was intended, taking more history, writing, painting, and computer science classes than they thought he needed in order to complete a B.A. in Philosophy, which he reluctantly did after seven years. He's interested in post-industrial desktop manufacturing tools and antique computers from the 1980s.

Bobby Lee Featherston is a southern refugee who has settled onto 32 acres of farmland in Prosser, Washington and contentedly grows Ukrainian sweet peppers and crook neck squash with the able help of his loyal dogs Jules and Verne. He enjoys his early mornings watching the sun kiss the world hello and the company of his friends over a good rye whiskey.

Voss Foster lives in the middle of the Eastern Washington desert, where he writes science fiction and fantasy from inside a single-wide trailer. He is the author of several novels, including the *Evenstad Media Presents* series, and his short work has been featured by a variety of publications, including *Andromeda Spaceways Magazine* and Vox.com. When he can be pried away from his keyboard, he can be found singing, cooking, and playing trombone, though rarely all at the same time. More information can be found at http://vossfoster.blogspot.com

Paula Hammond has been in love with stories since she was old enough to read them for herself. When not hunkered over a keyboard, she can be found prowling London's crusty underbelly in search of random weirdness.

Diana Hauer is a writer of words, both technical and fantastical, who lives in Beaverton, Oregon, with a dog and a fiancé. When she is not writing, she also enjoys gardening, hiking, and studying martial arts.

Janka Hobbs lives in the Puget Sound lowlands, where she studies Aikido and Botany when she's not playing with words. Visit her blog at http://jankahobbs.com

Larry Hodges is an active member of SFWA with 81 short

story sales, including 17 "pro" sales—nine to *Galaxy's Edge* and eight others. His third novel, *Campaign 2100: Game of Scorpions,* came out in March, 2016, from World Weaver Press. He also co-wrote a novel with Mike Resnick and Lezli Robyn, *When Parallel Lines Meet*, which comes out in spring, 2017. He's a graduate of the six-week 2006 Odyssey Writers Workshop, the 2007 Orson Scott Card Literary Boot Camp, and the two-week 2008 Taos Toolbox Writers Workshop. In the world of non-fiction, he's a full-time writer with twelve books and over 1700 published articles in over 150 different publications.

Liam Hogan is a London based writer. Winner of Quantum Shorts 2015 and Sci-Fest LA's Roswell Award 2016, his dark fantasy collection, *Happy Ending Not Guaranteed*, is out now from Arachne Press.

Find out more at http://happyendingnotguaranteed.blogspot.co.uk/, or tweet at @LiamJHogan

Daniel M. Kimmel was nominated for a Hugo Award for *Jar Jar Binks Must Die...* and other observations about science fiction movies. His *Shh! It's a Secret: a novel about Aliens, Hollywood, and the Bartender's Guide* was a finalist for the Compton Crook Award for best first novel. His latest is *Time on My Hands: My Misadventures in Time Travel*.

Born on Friday 13, **Rebecca McFarland Kyle** developed an early love for the unusual. Dragons, vampires and all manner of magical beings haunt her thoughts and stir her to the keyboard. She currently lives between the Smoky and Cumberland mountains with her husband and three cats. Her first YA novel, *Fanny & Dice*, was released on Halloween 2015. In 2017, she will be editing a charity anthology and releasing works in young adult, urban fantasy and dark fantasy. She's working on both short and long fiction on her own and with co-conspirators.

Bruno Lombardi is a Canadian author of speculative and weird fiction, with a number of writing credits including a novel *Snake Oil*, and stories in *Weirdbook* and other anthologies.

Susan Murrie Macdonald was a fifth-generation Republican until November 9, 2016, after which she could no longer support the GOP with a clear conscience. She is the author of a children's book, *R Is For Renaissance Faire*, as well as several short stories. She has also won the Arkansas Scottish Festival annual poetry contest twice, in 2014 and 2017. She currently lives in Tennessee with her husband and two teenagers. Mrs. Macdonald enjoys Highland Games, Native American pow-wows, science fiction conventions, and Renaissance Faires.

Louise Marley, a former concert and opera singer, has published nineteen novels in various genres. Feminist, activist, mom, wife, yogini, and dog lover, wanderer of the beaches of the beautiful Olympic Peninsula where she now lives and writes and worries about the future.

Victor Phillips, recently retired after four decades' career in natural resources management and education, shares time between Wisconsin's Fresh Coast and Costa Rica's Pacific Coast. His interest in writing short stories fulfills a lifelong passion in creative fiction. Through both non-fiction and fiction, Phillips strives to lighten the load of contemporary society through humor and to suggest a different, more durable path forward. His former professional writings—technical scientific works—are approved to cure insomnia.

Irene Radford is the bestselling author of the beloved *Dragon Nimbus* Series and the masterwork *Merlin's Descendants* series. In other dimensions she writes urban fantasy as P.R. Frost or Phyllis Ames, and space opera as C.F. Bentley. Lately she ventured into Steampunk as Julia Verne St. John.

She is also the editor of numerous anthologies including the popular, *How Beer Saved the World*.

She is the proud servant of her cat and has been known to chase the occasional bear off the deck of her rural property in the shadow of Mount Hood.

If you wish information on the latest releases from Ms Radford, under any of her pen names, you can subscribe to her newsletter: www.ireneradford.net

Ken Staley lives and works in the lower Yakima Valley in Eastern Washington. When not at his keyboard, Ken can be found working in stained glass or visiting one of the many area vineyards and sampling their offerings.

Wondra Vanian is an American national who moved to Wales, in the United Kingdom, to marry the love of her life and raise an army of four-legged furbabies. She left her job working for The Man in 2014, after earning a BA in English Language and Literature, and is currently focusing on writing.

Blaze Ward writes epic science fiction in the Jessica Keller Chronicles and the Science Officer series. He also writes other Alexandria Station stories, including *Doyle Iwakuma*, and *Henri Baudin*, as well as Modern Gods superhero myths and exotic things like *The Collective and Fairchild*. You can find out more at his website www.blazeward.com, and on Facebook, Goodreads, and other places.

Blaze's works are available as ebooks, paper, and audio, and can be found at a variety of online vendors (Kobo, Amazon, and others). His newsletter comes out quarterly, and you can also follow his blog on his website. He really enjoys interacting with fans, and looks forward to any and all questions—even ones about his books! *The Last Ranger* is the first in the *Alt National Park Service* series.

Jim Wright is a retired US Navy Chief Warrant Officer and freelance writer. He lives in Florida where he watches American politics in a perpetual state of amused disgust. He's been called the Tool of Satan, but he prefers the title: Satan's Designated Driver. He is the mind behind *Stonekettle Station*. You can email him at jim@stonekettle.com. You can follow him on Twitter @stonekettle, or you can join the boisterous bunch he hosts on Facebook at Facebook/Stonekettle. Remember to bring brownies and mind the white cat, he bites. Hard

Made in the USA
Lexington, KY
29 April 2017